WHEREIN LIES JUSTICE?

WHEREIN LIES JUSTICE?

Barry Johnson

Book Guild Publishing
Sussex, England

First published in Great Britain in 2013 by
The Book Guild Ltd
Pavilion View
19 New Road
Brighton, BN1 1UF

Typesetting in Baskerville by
YHT Ltd, London

Printed and bound in Great Britain by
CPI Group (UK) Ltd, Croydon, CR0 4YY

A catalogue record for this book is available from
The British Library.

ISBN 978 1 84624 819 1

1

Josey Billinghurst and I stood in the wrecked police station. The windows were gone; the walls showed evidence of the fire and damage by shells and bullets. The smell of wood smoke and explosives filled our nostrils. The debris had been cleared away and the dust from sweeping still hung in the hot, dry air.

'You really bring me to such delightful places, Captain,' said Josey.

'Behave yourself, Sergeant, or I'll send you home.'

'Promises, promises.' She smiled.

Josey felt the table. It rocked. Somebody had repaired it by nailing a rough piece of wood across a break in a leg. She hunted around and found something to put under the leg to reduce the rock. She put two reasonably stable chairs on one side of the table and one on the other.

There was a knock on the door and a military policeman came in. He was formal and smart. He and his squad had come through three days of battle and two days to get some sort of order back into this apology for a police station, yet his trousers had knife-sharp creases and his boots gleamed. My men continually amazed me.

'I've Sergeant Jason Phillips CGC for you, sir.'

'Corporal Michael Munro?'

'Will be here in half an hour, sir, brought under guard by Sergeant Peterson, sir.'

'Thank you, Corporal. I'll see Sergeant Phillips, informal, please.'

'Yes, sir.'

He turned smartly and left. A minute later, Sergeant Phillips appeared, accompanied by the Red Cap.

'Sit down, please, Sergeant.'

He sat and moved so that his back was upright and firmly against the chair back. His feet were resolutely planted on the floor, his feet and knees were shoulder-width apart and his hands were clasped lightly in his lap. I recognized the firm, balanced confidence of his seated position. Jason Phillips seemed relaxed and attentive. The smell of his Brut competed with Josey's Exclamation and the background of the battle after-smell. Of the three, I thought I preferred the smell of battle: a sharp, acrid, sulphurous smell coupled with the smell of burnt wood and smoke. We had all smelt it, never talked about it, but it was the thing that brought back memories so clearly. My sister sent me Kouros every birthday and Christmas; I didn't really notice that body spray anymore.

The line from *Apocalypse Now*, 'I love the smell of napalm in the morning' echoed round in my head. I could hear the buzz and rumbling swish of a helicopter passing overhead, and that made me feel good. No, not *good*: safe. Perhaps I'd been in Iraq too long. Pay attention, Jake, you've a job to do.

'The reason...' I got no further.

'I shot the bastard, sir.'

There was a sting in the word 'bastard'. Clearly, the shot man was not liked.

'Hang about a bit, Sergeant. If you're going to make statements like that, I'd like you to have a lawyer and I want you to be cautioned and fully understand your rights.'

'Sir, I don't want a lawyer.'

He had maintained eye contact when he spoke. He knew what he had done, he knew what he had said and the chances were that he had a good idea of the consequences.

I turned to Josey. 'Sergeant, caution Sergeant Phillips. Make sure he understands his rights.'

I looked at the corporal and said, 'Can you find me a tape recorder that works? Better still, two tape recorders.'

'Yes, sir.' He left. I was quite certain that Corporal MacLeish could do anything I asked of him and that his total vocabulary consisted of 'Yes, sir,' delivered with the strong, rolling 'r' of a Highland accent.

As the corporal left, Josey Billinghurst cautioned Sergeant Phillips and ensured that he understood his rights. I observed Jason Phillips: he listened attentively. This was an intelligent man. By the time she had finished, Corporal MacLeish had returned with two tape recorders. He made sure the recorders worked.

'Thank you, Corporal.'

'Sir.' He left.

Josey started the tape recorders and we did the identification bit.

I started again. 'You're Sergeant Jason Phillips.'

'Sir,' the word snapped out.

'Is that a "yes", Sergeant?'

He smiled, nodded, relaxed a little, and said, 'Yes, sir.'

He had been tense, but as a professional soldier he wasn't going to show it. Now the tension was easing.

'Who's the bastard you referred to?'

He paused, thought and then said calmly and clearly, 'I shot and killed Major Michael Carmichael, sir.'

'Then, Sergeant, you're going to have to explain to me the hows and whys. I suggest you start at the beginning.'

So he did. He told his story smoothly and logically, maintaining eye contact, breaking it only occasionally when he had to think of a reply to one of my many questions. I rapidly gained a clear picture of a desperate situation, the other people present and the shooting of the officer. Jason Phillips may or may not be a murderer, but he was a well-balanced, confident, honest man. I liked him, even if I didn't like his Brut.

3

2

Josey and I worked through every step of what happened. The platoon had been suckered into the position they ended up in, but it could have been worse. It was Lieutenant Mortlake's smart thinking that had prevented a catastrophe. He attacked when most commanders would have retreated. If he had retreated, a second insurgent group would have cut his platoon to shreds. His advance enabled him to set up a defensive position that was very easy to defend if his troops had enough ammunition, and that was a key issue. The second key issue was that once the defensive position was established, there was no way back without facing the initial problem of the overwhelming force against him. Thirdly, there was a radio problem. Lastly, he had casualties, some serious.

The mystery was where Major Carmichael had come from with the two privates. Logically, there was no reason for them to be there. More worrying was the fact that the two privates seemed to have disappeared since the battle to rescue the platoon.

The stories from the soldiers in the platoon tallied. Jase and Mike did indeed shoot Major Carmichael. The reasoning seemed solid. In the opinion of the soldiers, they owed their lives to Mike and Jase.

So, we had rock-solid eyewitness evidence that both the sergeant and the corporal shot the major. The sergeant and the corporal made confessions that they had shot the major. The killing of the major by the sergeant and the corporal was fully supported by forensic evidence and a post-mortem. They did it, but was it justified? Can any killing be justified?

3

Six weeks later, the VC10 was circling in a holding pattern over RAF Lyneham. The Wiltshire countryside spread out below: beautiful green fields of different shades. There was comfort in the peaceful view. I could see the M4 as a dark grey to black ribbon running east-west, and a network of narrow roads joined the villages and small towns. I liked Wiltshire with its quaint place names, such as Wootton Bassett, Goatacre and Clyffe Pypard, all of which I could see as we circled and waited to be cleared for landing. When I get old and grey, perhaps I'd live in a tranquil, country village. It was a definite contrast to the harsh browns, and more browns, occasionally divided by strips of green, that marked out the watercourses we had left in Iraq.

I was in pain and all I wanted was to land. My knee was throbbing, the splint prevented me bending my leg and the strapping of my shoulder restricted my movements. At least the stiches on my cheek had been removed and it seemed it had healed, but I had been told I would have a scar.

This must have been the oldest and crankiest VC10 in the RAF fleet. Mind you, the VC10 had gone out of service with British Airways some twenty years before.

There was a dark, unidentified patch on the seat next to me. I didn't investigate. I could smell stuffiness and engine oil and the mouldering fabric. Perhaps it was an indication of the age of this aircraft or perhaps it was just my state of health. I shifted in a vain attempt to get comfortable. I needed a bed rather than an uncomfortable seat.

An RAF stewardess came down the aisle: young, slim and attractive. Now that was a nice turn of phrase, 'came down the aisle.' I bet a few have wanted to take her down the aisle. Not me, though. I had enough problems just bloody walking. I was reaching the point that if this bloody knee didn't stop throbbing; I was going to ask some butcher to hack my bloody leg off. I hunted around for my painkillers. The Yank doc said, 'Keep ahead of the pain.' Funny things, doctors say. I found the pills and my bottle of water: two Tramadol and one Diazepam. I knew I shouldn't take the Diazepam, but sod it, so I did. Then I took another one. I hoped it would relax me.

I enjoyed watching her move gracefully with the gentle sway of the aircraft. It was one of the best memories of that flight. Some people stagger as if drunk, but this girl had it taped. She was more relaxing to watch than the effect of the Diazepam. Perhaps it *was* the effect of the Diazepam. She seemed to be the most senior of the stewards. Mind you, I would have called her a stewardess, but the corruption of the English language seemed to be endemic. Have you noticed that actresses are called actors and heroines are heroes? Why was it always detraction from the feminine to the masculine and never the other way round? Women moved to wearing trousers, but men were thought strange if they wore skirts, apart from Scotsmen and David Beckham. It seemed a shame that women were being so debased by being classed as second-class men instead of the superior beings. I thought I would call my Aunt Claire, 'Uncle'. I then imagined, with some amusement, the abuse I would get. I was miserable, bored and in pain.

I tried to shift my leg to a more comfortable position and failed. Anyway, it was nice to see an attractive girl, slim with short hair, an easy smile and an ability to make a standard-issue working uniform look like it fitted. The stewardess stopped by my seat.

'We'll be landing shortly, sir.'

I nodded. Her smile was warm.

'The captain suggests the prisoners are secured.'

I liked that: *'the captain suggests.'* Politeness always made me want to do things for people.

'Thank you, Laura.'

I knew her name was Laura. It said so on her badge. She smiled again and returned toward the front of the aircraft. I watched her. Nice bum as well. It shifted laterally with a slight rotation as she walked. The pain had reduced to a steady throb. It must have been the effect of watching her bum or even the Tramadol.

I looked up the aisle toward the rear of the aircraft at the two military policemen. They were professionals; they didn't have to be told anything. They probably guessed the stewardess' message. One slight nod from me and they uncoupled the handcuffs securing the prisoners to the seats and put them onto the prisoners' wrists. At least they would be able to get out if there was an accident on landing. The Red Caps checked that the seats were in the upright position and the seat belts secured. I wasn't happy about the handcuffs, but when dealing with highly trained, experienced soldiers who had killed people in the line of duty and were now accused of murder, it seemed the best policy to use handcuffs all the time. The military policemen settled themselves into the aisle seats opposite each other, with the prisoners to the window side of them. All secured. I checked my seat and buckled my seat belt.

I thought about the prisoners who I would shortly hand over. Sergeant Jason Phillips CGC and Corporal Michael Munro were two brave infantrymen. Nobody got a Conspicuous Gallantry Cross who wasn't brave. Both on second tours in Iraq after having served in Afghanistan, these were men who volunteered for the sharp end of soldiering. I admired such men. I'd seen them up close in action and they were the sorts of men I'd had occasion to rely on. They had been accused of killing Major Michael Carmichael DSC:

7

an officer noted for his gung-ho bravery. Actually, they had just plain shot him; justifiably in my view.

Dashing, handsome, Major Michael Carmichael DSC was a man tipped to one day reach the highest level in the army, but the DSC was an odd medal for a soldier, awarded for exemplary gallantry during active operations against the enemy at sea. Not a lot of soldiers got one of those. Royal Marine and naval personnel were the usual recipients. Rumour had it that his elevation to lieutenant colonel had already been approved and he was due to return from Iraq to take up a prestigious appointment in Washington. The rumour was that it was jobs for the boys, but I was not up with who was on the inside track and had connections. It seemed the major either had a death wish or he badly wanted a gong for bravery. It must have rankled that the sergeant had a Conspicuous Gallantry Cross, an award second only to the Victoria Cross.

I was coming back to the UK to get my leg sorted. Well, I hoped it would be sorted. I also had the job of overseeing the passage of the two prisoners – lucky me. I would have had to come back for the court martial anyway, but the buggered knee and the shoulder wound ensured I came back early. I felt, however, it was inappropriate that the major's body was on the same transport as the guys who killed him. I don't know why I thought that; I must have been catching the dreaded disease of political correctness.

My ears popped as we descended. I wondered how the pressure change affected corpses. I could imagine the major swelling up as we ascended and deflating as we descended. I'd always had an odd mind that posed odd questions. Well, that's what I was told at school, as the teachers used to look at me and shake their heads, probably because they didn't know the answers; either that, or they thought I was strange, but asking the off-the-wall questions had definitely helped me as a policeman.

An old song from the 1960s was playing in my head: 'They're Coming to Take Me Away, Ha-Haaa!' Then came the rattle and whir of the flaps that, through the porthole-type, sealed windows, I could see trailing out. I felt the final shudder of the aircraft as they stopped with a jolt, accompanied by the pain in my knee and the whistle and grumble of the undercarriage coming down. Oh, I was tense, waiting, thump, crunch, pain. We were hanging in the air. It was coming; I waited for the pain. We hit the tarmac: thump, bump, lurch and rumble, followed by the scream of the engines' reverse thrust. I felt like screaming with them and then I heard the steady noise as we ran forward. We rumbled off the runway and around the perimeter track. I was now more relaxed; I could cope with the gentle bumps of the aircraft taxiing. We smoothly came to a stop in the disembarking area. I was sweating but relaxed. Relaxed? It must have been the Diazepam. The seat belt signs went off.

I moved and looked through the window. There were three different groups of people. The first were awaiting the major, although from then on I was sure he would be considered a colonel. They were standing in a cluster, not really talking, but supporting each other by their closeness. They were dressed in dark clothes, formal. I could also see the RAF Honour Guard marching onto the hard standing.

Next to what I assumed to be the reception building was an RAF police van and a couple of RAF police. They'd be waiting for my two prisoners. There was also the normal complement of passenger and aircraft handlers. Each of the three separate groups had different reasons to be there and very different emotions: sadness, duty and what appeared to be boredom. Perhaps, for this last group, it was just the monotony of routine.

9

4

I limped, one stiff leg held nearly straight in a brace, back to the Royal Military Policemen and their charges. I eased myself down in a seat a couple of rows in front of them, my stiffened leg again protruding past the seat in front of me into the aisle. We would be the last to leave.

The forward doors opened. Fresh, freezing air poured in, complete with the smell of kerosene. The stale air that we were used to poured out. Before anybody disembarked, a couple of men came on board. They were dressed in suits: dark, navy blue, formal with ties and dark, woollen over-coats. One spoke to Laura Tansy and showed her some-thing. She pointed at me. He then squeezed past the departing passengers toward me, not rushing, but not tak-ing his time either. He had an air of authority. He smiled, held out his hand and spoke to me.

'Captain Robinson? Jake Robinson?'

His hand was firm and cool: a handshake that imparted confidence, as the owner was confident.

'Yes.' I didn't get up. He noted my leg stuck out in front of me.

'Good. I'm Chief Inspector Wilkes SCD attached to the Serious and Organized Crime Agency.'

He handed me a warrant card. I must admit I was sur-prised. Why would the Serious Crime Division be involved in what was destined to be a military court martial, parti-cularly when all the police work had been done?

'You need to read these documents.'

He handed me two four-ring binders. Together they were quite weighty.

10

'When you've read them, I suggest you make a decision.'

'What are they?'

'They are copies of the official outcomes of the investigation that you held into the murder of Major Carmichael and there's also a copy of the report you wrote and other information you submitted. There are summaries of the military records of your prisoners, and there are notes and a report made by the Army Prosecuting Authority. You may note differences between your report and the information as used by the APA.'

Now that should be interesting. I wondered how the chief inspector obtained them. It was unusual for the APA to make a decision to prosecute a serious crime without talking to the investigating officer and it was very unusual for the APA to change an investigating officer's report. In fact, it was also very unusual to rush into a prosecution as fast as they had with this one. The accused were only now returning to the UK and the court martial was to be held in a couple of weeks. That didn't bode well for the defence. This court martial was not following the routines I'd come to expect.

The chief inspector continued, 'I don't know what you can do because the powers that be are trying to get you shipped out so that you don't present the investigative evidence and your findings. Those two men are heading for life and you know they shouldn't be.'

He looked past me at the prisoners. There was something in the way he looked at them, but I couldn't place what it was. Did he know them?

I was stunned, what on earth was this man talking about? The evidence was crystal clear. Sergeant Phillips and Corporal Munro did kill Major Carmichael. All the court had to decide was whether it was justifiable. If it was not justifiable, they would get a prison sentence, and if it was justifiable, then I was sure some lesser penalty would be dreamed up.

11

The army, being the army and infested with politically correct civilians, was bound to give them some penalty. I was sure the hierarchy and the civilians would be saying that you couldn't kill your officer no matter how justified. I shook my head.

'One last thing, Captain.' He handed me a business card. 'That's the defending counsel.'

I now had the impression that this police officer was unsure. It was almost as if he did not want to be here; for some reason, his confidence had ebbed away. Maybe it was the way he spoke or the way he hovered from one leg to the other. I was totally confused. The only solicitor they had seen was in Iraq and they didn't have one in the UK, so how the hell could they have a barrister? He saw my confusion.

'Wheels within wheels, Captain. This is a case the APA have no intention of losing.'

This was an odd thing to say. The APA wouldn't go ahead unless they felt sure of a verdict. To some extent, I was surprised that they had. I supposed they had felt pressure from the press. I read the card: *Peter Bartholomew*, with loads of letters after his name, only some of which meant anything to me.

'And?'

'And Bartholomew's a political animal. Those guys will look like they are getting a great defence, but they will be sold down the river. They need a proper defence.'

I was uncomfortable, out of my depth; this was all wrong. This was totally outside of my experience.

'So what do you expect me to do?' I'd never been asked, nor should I be asked, to advise on who the defence counsel should be for people I was attempting to bring to justice.

The chief inspector noted my confusion. He smiled knowingly. 'Nothing, except persuade them to take this guy.'

He handed me another card. It said *Roland Parsley* with all the letters and other stuff.

'What's in it for you?'

'Great! A typical, cynical policeman.' The look on his face indicated that he believed what he was saying. 'Jase Phillips is my brother-in-law, sort of. He married my sister.'

So that was the look; he did know them.

'Sort of?'

'They've split up. He's too busy volunteering to save the world. And one other titbit that may convince you that all is not kosher: Major Michael Carmichael was the cousin of Antony Bray.'

'Is that supposed to mean something?' I'd never heard of Antony Bray, yet the name was said as if I should be personally acquainted with him.

'Antony Bray is the personal private secretary to James Bradshaw, our current, illustrious home secretary. He's moving fast and is tipped to be a member of the justice committee. He's expected to be the chairman shortly and then a junior minister.'

'So?' Things were getting only marginally clearer.

'Bray and Carmichael were at school together – Ampleforth – and university – Oxford, Jesus College; they both did politics, philosophy and economics. They're more like twins than cousins. Bray's the older by only three months. He won't let anything tarnish his cousin's name. Bray's the brains – he got a first – and Carmichael was the brawn, rugby blue and boxing – he got a lower second.

'Look, I have to fly. Oh, this guy's a great solicitor.' He handed me another card. 'If he's no good for your boys, he might come in handy for you. If you decide to help them you'll be digging a hole for yourself. You may need a very good solicitor, but they will try to isolate you so you can't testify.' He stopped and shook his head. 'They *will* stop you.'

The *they* registered with me: the ubiquitous, all-powerful *they*: the *they* that was emphasized as the enemy.

'You're these guys' only hope.'

'Who are "they"?'

'Look, this is very dodgy ground.' This wasn't discomfort; this was fear I was seeing in his body language and hearing in his voice. 'There are some very powerful people in high places. Bray and Carmichael are related to these people. Just watch your back, Captain.' It was clear this man didn't want to say any more.

'What are you going to do?'

'Me? Nothing. I think I've been rumbled. I'm now on a survival course that consists of keeping my head well below the parapet.' The chief inspector smiled: a short, humourless, good-luck smile. He shook my hand and joined the exiting passengers.

This guy Wilkes was good. He talked for only a few minutes and I had the picture; help these two and you're in deep doo-doo; don't help them and perhaps it will keep you awake at night. Another fine mess you've got yourself into, Jake Robinson, but there was no time to dwell. It was decision time and there really was no decision to make; I would help these two.

I limped back to where my two charges were sitting. Purpose had reduced my pain, or perhaps it was Tramadol. I waved the MPs away, one toward the back of the plane and the other to the cross aisle where the over-wing emergency doors were. That would seem natural to them.

I sat next to Jase Phillips and spoke quietly. 'Sergeant, you are in deep trouble and you shouldn't be. I think you will definitely be charged with murder and the court martial will go for life. I reckon you should have a slapped wrist, but I'm just a copper. When you see your solicitor I want you to ask for this guy to be your barrister.' I gave him the card. 'Under no circumstances accept a guy named Bartholomew as your barrister. If the solicitor puts up resistance, change your solicitor to this guy.' I gave him the second card. It said *Keith Todd*.

'Why, sir?' I could hear the uncertainty in his voice.

'Politics have entered the situation, and you're the sacrificial lamb to preserve the reputation of Major Carmichael. He has a relation in a high position, who, apparently, wields a lot of power. I'll do what I can, but I'm buggered if you have Bartholomew as your barrister.'

Jase looked at me. He now had a decision to make and it all hinged around trusting the man who arrested and charged him.

'How do I...?' his voice petered out.

Here was a man who could lead men in a battle, but in this different environment he was totally out of his depth: simple fodder to be chewed up.

'Jase, you don't know shit. You've a choice: trust me or trust the politicians. If you trust me and it turns to shit, blame me. If you do what the politicians want you to do, you won't know who screwed you.'

I watched him struggle with indecision. Then he looked me straight in the eyes.

'Okay, Captain, I'll trust you.'

He smiled the relaxed smile of somebody who has made a decision and thinks it's the right one. All men need a leader when lost and I had just accepted that role. I didn't feel I was as confused as a few moments before.

'You know the man I just spoke to?'

'Yes, Captain. He's my-brother-in-law, but relationships are a bit strained at the moment.'

'With him?' I needed to take a step back.

'No, he just got caught in the cross fire.'

'I see, no I don't see.'

'Well,' he paused. "Well when I told her I was going back

15

to Iraq she blew a fuse and the next thing I knew she had taken the kids to the states.'

'And how did that affect Wilkes?'

'Well Rod had tried to smooth it over and ended up with a battle with both his sister and his mum. He's a good guy though.'

'You trust him.'

'Totally.'

'Good, get yourself the new barrister.'

I walked forward to the front doorway. From the top of the steps, I looked out onto the hard standing. The passengers had gone. Six soldiers from the Royal Lancaster Regiment carried the coffin at a slow march to the beat of a bass drum. A sergeant, complete with red sash across his body and pace stick under his left arm, followed it. They were certainly putting on a show. I was surprised. I would have thought it would be kept quiet as the deceased was supposed to have been murdered by his own men, but there were television cameras and flash photographers. The guard was called to the present as the coffin passed. Then, with dignity, the coffin was slipped into a hearse and the guard came to the slope; the hearse pulled away and the guard turned right and marched away in the same direction.

The group of mourners walked slowly in the same direction: an older woman and older man, two younger women and a man of the same age as the major, probably Antony Bray and his wife, the wife or sister of Major Carmichael, and his parents. There were some others, but they didn't seem part of this core group. A tall man, who was accompanying a nun, linked the two groups and a broad man seemed to be guarding them. How strange. When the group reached the building and the media had dispersed, we left the aircraft.

The two prisoners stood and I shook hands with them the

best I could with them handcuffed. I then waved my MPs to take them away.

The RAF police had a secure vehicle and we headed toward it. An RAF police officer, a flight lieutenant, approached me and we exchanged salutes. I handed over the transport and custody documentation and he signed my paperwork and joined his dutiful pair of military policemen. Bureaucratic formalities complete, the handcuffs were removed and given to one of the RMPs. At the back of the van, Jase turned and saluted, as did Corporal Munro. I returned their salute. This clearly came as a surprise to the RAF contingent and it did to me.

The van drove away: one officer, two RAF police, two RMP and two prisoners. I was left alone in the chill, late January wind, which was blowing across the airfield.

I knew this was going to be a tough assignment and I knew I would do all I could for the brave sergeant and the corporal. I liked them. They were honest soldiers, tough and straightforward. The other men who had served with them liked them; more than that, they admired them. Just watching Jase, you could see why. He was a little shorter than me, perhaps 5ft 11in, but outweighed me. He must have been 15 stone of solid muscle and he moved with the grace of a cat. You could see he was tough, with wide-set, direct-gazing eyes, a square jaw, cleft chin, and a scar on his lower lip. Perhaps, more than that, it was his hands: large, strong, powerful hands with stubby fingers on the end of muscular forearms. They fitted in with his broad shoulders to give him a look of power. Yet, he was quietly spoken. It wasn't that he had a soft voice; he just used it softly but clearly, with enough projection that you wouldn't miss a thing he was saying. In an odd sort of way, he was hand-some, carved out to be a hero. Yes, you could see why his platoon followed him, and his closest follower was Mike Munro: the ideal Robin to Jase as Batman.

17

5

I walked toward the building: a flat-roofed, square affair that seemed to be made of green, concrete panels ('walked' was a relative term). It was marked *Reception*, so I assumed it was the correct place. My word, Jake, perhaps you were a detective. The RAF handling staff must have been pretty quick because my gear was stacked against the wall and all the other passengers had gone. That sort of thing always surprised me. Have you ever watched football on television? While the pundits summarize the match, 30,000 to 60,000 people leave the ground. Ten minutes after the end of the match, the stands are empty except for the ground staff and cleaners clearing away the detritus.

A lieutenant colonel in civilian clothes was waiting for me with another man. The colonel stepped toward me and held out his hand. I didn't know he was a lieutenant colonel until he said, 'I'm Lieutenant Colonel Willaby-Alexander; Captain Robinson, I presume.'

Oh no! What I needed was a doctor, not a brass hat. He was tall and gaunt, probably in his early fifties, with an accent that you could only catch like a disease if you were a senior officer in the army. He was in what they called mufti: the ordinary clothes worn by senior officers who usually wear a uniform. I'm not sure 'ordinary' clothes were the correct description; the Harris Tweed jacket that didn't quite fit and the brown, corduroy trousers were the most usual manifestation, and that was exactly what we got. He was complete with a light-cream shirt with a wide check, a green, knitted tie and a pair of very smart, heavy, highly polished, brown brogue shoes. This was a uniform to

18

indicate that normally he wore the military uniform of a senior officer.

'Yes, sir.'

'This is Mr Barrow Jones.'

Mr Barrow Jones was very different, apart from being of an age shared by the colonel. He was much smaller, about 5ft 8in, a bit overweight with a slight paunch that was disguised by an extremely well-cut, dark blue, tailor-made suit with a white shirt and black and grey, diagonally striped tie. He had dark eyes and swept-back black hair going grey at the temples.

We shook hands. His grip was firm, dry and positive.

'Barrow?' I queried.

He smiled. 'Yes, I know. I think I'm the only person alive with the first name Barrow.' His voice was light and he spoke with an educated pronunciation and just a trace of Welsh accent.

'Was your dad having a laugh?'

He laughed; it was a pleasant, likeable laugh.

'No. My grandfather was called Barrow; why, nobody seems to know. My father says it has something to do with ancient burial mounds, but that is only a rationalization.'

The colonel interrupted, 'Shall we go to an office?' He led the way.

The office was a superior waiting room with comfortable armchairs and two-seater settees around low tables. We drew up armchairs on three sides of a low table. I eased myself down into a chair, my gammy leg stuck out in front of me, and the two greeters watched my manoeuvring. I waited. Was this the start of getting me shipped out?

The colonel started, 'I'm stationed in the MOD. My role is military liaison with the security services. That includes MI5, MI6 and SO15. There are one or two other units and links with whom I liaise.'

So what? This was the question in my mind. First a special

branch officer – was he SO15? – and now I meet a military liaison officer.

'With all this terrorist activity,' he continued, 'the security services are stretched. There is a need for some specialist officers to join some of the teams. Barrow here has such a need. It seems you fit the bill and you are, at the same time, due to your injuries,' he looked at my leg, 'available.'

'Can I be clear, sir? I've become available when there is a shortage of police officers in Iraq to train the Iraqi police. We have the armed forces stretched to breaking point around the globe and that is creating understandable disciplinary problems, and I'm about to be involved in a murder trial as the senior investigating officer. I don't wish to appear bolshie, sir, but I'm sure you recognize my surprise and concern.'

The colonel looked at me. He did not seem in the least surprised at my response. He almost seemed to expect it. I'd never been so blunt with an officer of his rank before, but, on the other hand, I'd never felt the need to.

He smiled. He almost seemed pleased at my outburst. 'Your record indicates that in the face of bureaucratic nonsense or a manifest lack of reasonable logic, you can be a bit, yes, a bit spiky. I apologize for my lack of clarity.'

I thought he was going to do the 'you will do as you're told' bit, but he didn't.

'This is not an order; it's a request. You're at liberty to turn it down and we will offer it to the second choice. In that event, nobody will know the offer was made and, when fit, you can return to where you would normally be serving.'

'Thank you, sir.'

Barrow Jones spoke. 'Captain, we – no, I – want you. I need someone who has your background. I don't particularly want somebody from the army, but I think that you would be an asset. The response you've just given about this opportunity demonstrates something I want, but did not know you had until you spoke.'

I was mystified. Did he want a bolshie bastard?

'What do you want, then?' I almost sounded petulant. It was the *then* that did it. No, I *was* being petulant. God, I could have done without this until I could get this bloody leg fixed.

'Spot on, Captain. That's exactly the right question: open and to the point.' He nodded, it seemed, in appreciation. I was surprised. This guy Barrow was reading me like a book. He smiled his encouraging smile. 'I want somebody who's been an investigator, who has demonstrated courage, who can make decisions under pressure and has training and some practice in interrogation: not just the usual police interviewing-type interrogation, but hard-nosed stuff. In you, there appears to be a bonus. When disagreeing with your selection, it was not personal, but – how can I put this – more general. You used the broader picture. I meet too many people who think too narrowly. I'd like you to join a special section in my unit.'

He was looking at me encouragingly. I was being won over. No, I *was* won over.

'Tell me about your unit.'

'I'm the head of a unit that has been given the title Investigations and Execution, I and E; it's a new, specialist unit: separate, free-ranging. Our prime area will vary over time, but currently we are concerned with organized crime that sits within the financial and political arenas. What used to be Special Branch, now Counter Terrorism Command and SO15, are our allies in this, but our focus is different. We have other support. For example, SO6 looks at fraud and such like and their specialist skills can be of great value to us. SO15 and SO6 are primarily anti-terrorism and crime-based as opposed to politically-based. Political threat can be much longer term. Boundaries are difficult. We start from what it is that politicians are doing, what the influences and pressures on them are and how that might impact the social and economic welfare of the UK. It follows that most of the people in I and E are nerds of one form or another and we need some people to be at the strike force end, the muscle in an intellectual environment. What do you think?'

'I think I'm just bloody confused.' It seemed to me that he was being deliberately confusing. No, he was being deliberately unclear. The colonel also looked confused at all this gobbledygook.

'I understand that. Let me see if I can paint a picture,' said Barrow. 'Political criminals aren't necessarily interested in the same things as normal criminals and, in general, terrorists used to be ideologically based. Now they're more religiously based. Normal criminals want – to put it crudely – money. All politicians seek power; some to do good, whatever that is; some because they believe in a particular philosophy; some because it's their career choice and some it just happens to. Political criminals are also interested in power but power in the exercise of their own ends. Some, of course, are just criminals and some are mentally ill. Often, when politicians do things in the business arena, it's difficult to see any personal gain. Different sectors of people may gain or lose, but it's sometimes an almost philosophical thing. They manipulate the truth and bend the rules, and sometimes that crosses the boundaries, but it's all grey and murky. It's more than fiddling expenses or taking a back-hander to push something though. We have real criminals and spies with networks in the civil service as well as among MPs. We have a new situation: organized crime in league with a political base.'

'Supposing a politician was set on manipulating a criminal court case; would that sit within your remit?'

'That's exactly what the Krays did. Let's be concrete. You will have heard of the East End criminals, the Kray Twins.'

I nodded.

'Well, they corrupted, or rather used, two corrupt politicians, a labour guy named Tom Driberg and a conservative guy named Lord Boothby. With their protection, the Krays built a criminal empire in London in the 1950s and 1960s. I and E are more interested in longer term criminal and political implications, but as a wise man once said, "If somebody is breaking the law in one area, they are likely to be breaking it in another area".'

'So you've criminals using politicians.'

'No, it's more sophisticated than that. The world has moved on. We have people with political power in league with people controlling financial institutions, and organized crime syndicates working in concert with them. So, where one ends and the others begin is difficult to determine.'

I was beginning to feel frustrated. 'Barrow, what aren't you telling me?'

Barrow turned to the colonel. 'Could you give us a couple of minutes, please, Colonel?'

The colonel nodded. 'I think I just need to stretch my legs. Please excuse me, gentlemen.'

He stood and strolled out of the room. There was no embarrassment; not even an uncomfortable feeling. Barrow and the colonel were in sync. I was amazed.

Barrow looked at me and said, 'Beautiful, you're just beautiful, Jake. You're up to your ears in a murder inquiry, you know the case for the defence has already been compromised and you may or may not know the opportunity for the defence to call witnesses has also been compromised. One reason I want you is that you're in the middle of a fix put in by, shall we call them, The Family. I want you in a very special unit fighting The Family.'

It was clear now.

'Let me just check, Barrow. We have politicians who are

part of organized crime. You call them The Family. I've tumbled into this through the Carmichael case and you want to use me?'

Barrow looked at me, smiled a thin smile and nodded. 'I spoke briefly to Rob Wilkes; he thought you would be up for it. And your record indicates you'll be up for it. Think for a few minutes, Jake, while I fetch the colonel.'

What was there to think about? It was different and it had elements of fighting on the right side.

Five minutes later, Barrow and the colonel returned.

'What do you say, Jake?' asked Barrow.

'Okay, I'll join you with one proviso. I'll be free to participate in the court martial of Sergeant Phillips and Corporal Munro.'

Colonel Willaby-Alexander came into the conversation. 'They're the two that murdered Major Michael Carmichael?'

'Yes, sir.'

'Weren't you part of the prosecution?'

What an odd thing to say: past tense.

'I was the investigating officer. I'm therefore a witness for the prosecution.'

'Yes, Robinson, I think some things have changed. Somebody else will present the investigation for the prosecution. We need you, or rather Barrow here needs you and you need to get that leg fixed.'

So the chief inspector was spot on. I'd been side-lined.

'I was the investigating officer, so I should be a witness, sir.'

'Yes, I understand that, Captain, but you have been replaced.'

Well, that was kind of final.

'Okay, sir, I've decided I'll find a way to participate and give my findings as a witness. Given what I have to say, I've a feeling I might be a witness for the defence.' I hadn't worked this out; I just knew that this was what I was going to do.

'Is that wise?'

'I'm sorry, sir. I don't understand.'

'Well, they murdered an officer: a very courageous officer and an example to the country.'

'Sir, with due respect, it's for the court to decide their guilt and the major's record as an officer and role model has little bearing on the guilt or lack of guilt of the two accused men.'

'Captain, I was looking at this from a different perspective. It could be that to appear on behalf of these, these,' the colonel controlled what he was going to say, 'her-hum, men, um, could damage your career.'

'Very true, sir. It's just that I consider the impartial conduct of the process leading to justice to be more important than my career.' I couldn't believe I just said that. I sounded like some twee, middle-class, lefty ideologue. 'Let's just give the court martial the facts and let the jury decide. I have the facts from the investigation. What the jury decides to do with them is up to them.' That's better: more me, less twee.

Barrow coughed gently. 'It would seem the captain has bravely taken a broader perspective than you, Colonel.'

'By God, I do believe he has. I like it, Captain. Yes, you're right. Justice is the most important actor here. I'll have to make some arrangements, but first you're off to hospital to get that knee looked at.' He paused, seeming to remember something. 'Oh, I hadn't told you. If you accepted the job, and I had every expectation that you would, you were programmed to go on a short interrogation refresher course in the USA. Now I'll have to change that.'

'That's interesting, sir. Who arranged that for me?'

'I don't really know. Somebody in the Home Office fixed it and I thought it was a good idea. I'll have a word with them and get the dates changed.'

My word, they were confident I would take this job. Was it a fix?

'The Home Office, sir?'

'Yes, I know, but you'll be doing a lot of work with them.'

'So they knew I was to be offered this job?'

'I wouldn't have thought so. I've no real idea what the job is. Barrow here is a bit of an anomaly. Anyway, I'll get it changed.'

This confirmed that the chief inspector was right; somebody wanted me safely out of the way.

'It would be unwise for me to go to the States until I get this knee fixed anyway.'

'Yes, you're right. How's the shoulder?'

'Healing nicely, sir. Thank you.'

'What happened to your knee and shoulder?' asked Barrow Jones.

'Oh, the silly, brave bugger waded into the middle of a riot and got himself stabbed and hit on the knee with a brick. Should've got a bloody medal, but the MOD are really stingy about these things now. Have to be rescuing somebody under fire to get a gong these days. It's these bloody politicians and civilians, you know.' The colonel smiled at me. 'Bloody well done, anyway.'

'Thank you, sir.' I was constantly amazed by the Colonel Blimp persona adopted by these highly intelligent, highly experienced senior officers. I suppose it was a way of making the unacceptable and horrific acceptable. He also seemed totally unaware that Barrow Jones was, in the colonel's terms, a civilian.

Barrow cut in. 'I'm supposed to give you these things: an open train ticket to Newhaven, another one from Newhaven to London and an appointment time to see a specialist. When that's sorted out, give me a ring.'

'Thank you, sir.'

'Forget the "sir" with me; stick to Barrow. I'm looking

forward to having you in the team. I'll give you a lift to the station if you want one.'

'Thank you, Barrow.'

The colonel stood. 'I'll be monitoring what's happening, Captain. From the army's point of view, you report to me. So if you need anything, just holler.'

'Thank you, sir.'

The colonel held out his hand and we shook. I had the feeling that he did not expect a call from me unless I was in trouble. He turned and left.

Barrow said, 'Hang on here and I'll bring my car round.'

6

From the main gate, we turned left and, at the roundabout, turned right onto the A3102. I was on my way to my sister's home. I thumbed through the papers. The plan was clear. I was to go into hospital four days before the start of the court martial. As I may not be available to present the findings of the inquiry, Lieutenant Cannon would do it. What an interesting choice: 'Doggie' Cannon: Law degree, Sandhurst, in the same class as me, RMP training, office jobs and should have been a captain, but for some reason he had been passed over. He was a bit wet. Had the face and build of a bloodhound, droopy cheeks and a skinny body, all angles and bits sticking out. If I were unkind, I would say that was due to his blue-blood inbreeding. His elder brother was a duke or earl or some such thing, but he regarded himself as part of the impoverished nobility (well, impoverished apart from a job in the city that earned him millions each year in bonuses). To someone like him, having to work was the indication of being poor. No, he was totally different from Doggie: big and round, about 6ft 2in tall and built like Humpty Dumpty. You would never have believed they were brothers.

So, it seemed that Doggie Cannon would be the man who gave the evidence at the murder inquiry. All he had seen was the paperwork, not my paperwork but the APA's paperwork. Still, he would do a painstakingly detailed and competent job. I wondered why my sergeant, Josey Billinghurst, wasn't doing it. After all, she trudged the miles and did all the interviews with me. Doggie didn't really know what happened and Sergeant Billinghurst did. Doggie

28

wasn't going to probe or challenge. Perhaps that was the point of his selection.

As we trundled along (Barrow was not a boy racer; that was for certain) we chatted.

'Tell me about how you selected me.'

'It was serendipity really. I did a trawl of the people who were in the brackets.'

'In the brackets?'

'Yes, we needed somebody who had investigative experience, so the CID-type background. Also, we were looking for interrogation and the armed services has that. I must admit I expected to find somebody from the security service. Three people popped up and you were one of the three. The investigation into Major Carmichael's murder was the thing that brought you to my notice. There were a couple of others, but you seemed the most likely.'

'Why?'

'The major had Family connections. The connections were of interest to us. It was a bit vague and then it became evident that they wanted you off the case. As that was the situation, you were likely to be what I wanted, so I gave your record to the people in the department: Frances, Nikki and Howard. I caught nothing from Nikki or Howard.'

'Only three?'

'Well, only three in the section you'll join and it's important that what they do is kept hush-hush. Anyway, Frances – she will be your boss, by the way – had seen you somewhere: in the States, I think. So we checked it out and found one of the MI6 guys who had been on the interrogator's course with you. He thought you were just right for what we told him, which wasn't exactly the truth, but anyway he approved. We then pulled your detailed records, or rather the colonel did, and they checked out. Your boss didn't want to lose you, but you solved that problem by getting your knee banged up. There was also a good report

29

from a Major Forsythe, a Royal Marine. He had said you deserved another medal. Every button we pressed came up positive. However, your co-workers will personally check you out before we finally accept you.'

'So it's not done and dusted.'

'Um, no, the colonel knows that. We had to have your assurance before we went to the next stage.'

'And if my knee's truly buggered?'

'Yes, that may be a problem, but let's cross that bridge if we get to it.'

'But you knew about my knee and how it happened; I don't understand.'

'Not quite. I knew about the riot thing and the knee thing, but I had assumed that they were not the same thing, as different people wrote up the information. Anyway, I hate paper, so my secretary gives me a set of oral summaries and sometimes things get disjointed.'

This didn't really fill me with confidence, but I'd see how things went. 'Tell me about my co-workers.'

'You'll meet them soon enough and you can make up your own mind.'

'They've a preview of me, Barrow.'

'Yes, well, I suppose. Frances – what can I say about her?'

'How I would recognize her? Background? What's she good at? What she might improve? Standard stuff.'

'Yes, right, um, how would you recognize her? I suppose she's mid- to late thirties, but looks younger than she is. Very attractive: slim with cropped, brown hair and blue eyes. Normally dresses for the occasion.'

'Dresses for the occasion?'

'Yes, she never looks out of place. At formal or business meetings, she will be in a suit; at a summer event, she will be in an appropriate dress. What I mean is that she blends in so she's not noticed, or rather she's noticed as one of the people who belong. Background? Yes, let me see – very ordinary family background. Her father was a bricklayer and her mother worked in Tesco. She did well, though, all considered. Went to Cambridge and did... I think it was a four-year magna-cum-laude honours master's degree that included forensic psychology, criminology and law. Um, I'd better tell you about her career. She joined the Met. Why, I don't know, but as you might expect, she shone from the first day. When she ended her probationary period we, rather MI5, "tapped her up", as I believe they say in football circles, and she decided to join us. It created a brouhaha at the time and some bureaucratic obstructionism, but she joined us and went straight back to basics with the induction at the academy, joined a team and then did a couple of appropriate courses and some really good work. She was good and was put on an exchange scheme with the FBI. Once again, she went back to basics: sixteen weeks of instruction at the FBI Academy in Quantico, Virginia – interrogation, shooting, driving, self-defence, handling situations, typical gung-ho American stuff. She flew through it and went to New York. I don't know what she did there except that she was again a star, but she met a policeman working in narcotics and fell in love. It was a whirlwind affair. They got married and went on honeymoon. In the month they got back, he was shot and killed. She was pregnant, lost the baby, fell apart and was shipped back to us. And that's when I got her. I ran a unit called Special Projects. It was for people who for some reason couldn't operate as they should operate. My job was to get them up and running or kick them out. As you can imagine, it wasn't a high-morale unit. She made it and was back on track, but mud sticks, so her assessments were always a bit guarded or ambiguous. If she was successful, it was put down to her taking risks and if she wasn't a blinding success, it was because she was too cautious. I picked up this job and she was the first one I recruited for the special section of I and E.'

'Special section?'

'Yes, we'll talk about that in detail only after selection is complete.'

'Okay, why did you recruit Frances?'

'Because she's bloody good, I can trust her totally and she's loyal.'

'Sounds good to me. How many teams do you have?'

'Five.'

'Are they all led by people who have at some stage come off the rails?'

'I suppose they are. I want people who know what it's like to fail or, as you said, have come off the rails in some way and climbed back on. The resilience to recover is an important element. I only have one unit that you might call "covert", though, and it's totally staffed by misfits. I intend to have two such units. You'll join the present one.'

'Thank you.' I must admit that made me feel a little inadequate.

'Don't misunderstand me. One of your attributes is that you're a non-conformer and eventually you may be a misfit. I've just got you early.' Barrow smiled in the slow way he had. I just knew I was going to enjoy working in his outfit whatever it was. I wasn't feeling as inadequate now. He just generated confidence.

'So, the other two are also misfits?'

'Yes, fortunately they are.'

I loved the balance he had: an unconventional ability to accept that if you want something done you pick people who can do it, not some theoretical ideal.

'Nikki, let me see,' he continued, 'the delectable Nikki.'

I could see him imagining her.

'Five-foot-eight or nine of gorgeous womanhood, or that's what she looks like. She has what I think the modern term is "big boobs", a very slim waist and an exotically round bum. Atop of that body is a face that I'm certain makeup advertisers would pay a fortune for. I'm sure she just waltzed through selection because all the men had their tongues hanging out.' Barrow sighed. 'What a shame.'

'She has no legs?'

Barrow laughed. 'She has legs: the greatest pair of pins I've ever clapped eyes on.'

'How did this beauty end up among the misfits then?'

'Well, she was leading an MI5 team, handling a particularly tricky operation. She had the whole thing sussed. She's a great investigator, but she has some more valuable skills, as I was to find out.'

'Sounds good, but I'm not very clear.' Barrow seemed to be avoiding an issue.

'She broke a man's back.'

'Are you talking sex or violence?'

Barrow chuckled. 'Violence, I'm afraid. A chief superintendent with an eye for the ladies attempted a dalliance in his office and it was goodbye Vienna. She just threw him across his office and he hit something hard. Um, I mean a piece of furniture.'

I had to smile at his clarification.

'That was a bit over the top, wasn't it?'

'Well, she's a, um, well, we didn't know and–'

'She's gay?'

'Oh no, she could not be described as gay. She's a lesbian.'

'Is there a difference?' I was confused by his reply.

'Oh, in this case, yes. Gay means brightly coloured, carefree, sexually uninhibited with an orientation for the same sex. But when it comes to the realm of sex, this is one serious lady. She will tolerate sexual language and jokes, and it's as if she were normal; by that, I mean a heterosexual, broad-minded person. But don't take liberties. She has a companion who keeps house for her like a perfect stay-at-home wife.'

'What happened with the chief superintendent?'

'Nikki is a black belt in every damn martial art you can name. I'm sure she could punch holes through a challenger tank. Anyway, she went for a meeting in his office and her version was that he laid hands upon her. His version was that it was accidental and she attacked him. Other women in the offices said that they tread carefully around him and he had made advances on most of them. In the end it was all brushed under the carpet and he was put out to grass on a disability pension. She ended up in special projects and met up with Howard.'

'Why did she end up in special projects?'

'Yes, that was interesting. She was traumatized by the fact that she was not in the least concerned at the damage she had inflicted on the chief superintendent. This is the opposite of what she thought she should have felt. She was suffering a cognitive dissonance.'

'How did you resolve it?'

'I didn't; Howard did. She saw that he doesn't appear to give a damn about people, but he does relate to some people. She accepted that she had to be caring about a limited number of people, such as Howard and her partner, and she was entitled to feel nothing for others. At that point, she became very valuable to us. They were both sent on some unusual training that equipped them to come and work in my special unit. I think it was them that actually created the idea.'

I was getting a feeling as to what she did for this special section, but I thought it best to bite my tongue.

'Are there other special sections like your one?'

'Officially, there are none. Unofficially, here in the UK, there are two. The other's in MI6, but it operates differently, as individuals, not as a team.'

He went quiet. I got the message to ask no more. He then continued talking about Nikki and Howard as if there had been no interruption.

34

'They just helped each other into equilibrium. Lucky they were there at the same time. They are a great team: brains and brawn.'

'He's the brains and she's the brawn then?'

'Yes. He says little, but when he speaks it's worth listening to. He has a mind that can absorb apparently unrelated bits of information and draw connections. He can picture the outcomes of something and plan for all the contingencies that are likely to occur. He minimizes collateral damage, but accepts it without a qualm.'

Now I was sure I knew what this team did. I was just unsure what my role would be.

'They are a sub-team then?'

'Yes, but she's the leader. He outlines the options and she makes the decisions.' Barrow was thoughtful. I could see he was now imagining the pair of them. 'Yes, a delightful matching combination.'

There was something about the way he said that. 'Howard is also a homosexual?' I asked.

'Yes and no. He's also definitely not gay.'

'He has a boyfriend?'

'Um, no. He's celibate. I'd better explain. He realized he was homosexual when quite young. Like young people, he experimented. He didn't like what he found, so he tried girls. He just hated that, so he made a decision. If a Catholic priest could be celibate, he could too.'

'He's a Roman Catholic?'

'Not really; he was brought up in that faith, which probably gave him the superego and consequential guilt about his sexual orientation. I would say he's agnostic, unlike your atheism.'

I was going to ask how he knew I was an atheist, but he had read my documents and it said that in them. 'You know a hell of a lot about them,' I said instead.

'Yes, um, I suppose I do.' He did not expand.

'So, he was a special projects nutter?'

Barrow knew I wanted to know how Howard ended up in special projects.

'Sort of! As you may know, we move people around every eighteen months or so. Nobody wanted him. He's a bit of a loner, not a team player and some people found him uncomfortable to work with. Too dammed efficient, plans everything and able to outthink them and outguess them. When he explains things, he's terse giving the minimum of information, totally to the point, assuming you know things because he knows them. It sometimes sounds as if he thinks you're an idiot. He doesn't really; it's the impression that he gives. He lacks social graces. No, that's wrong; he just doesn't think about the way that what he says will be heard. Mind you, he's not academic. He has an upper second in economics. It was that that brought him to my notice.'

'The economics?'

'No; his efficiency, his planning skills and his breadth of vision were my interests in him. His intelligence is off-putting or it would be if he talked more, but he seems quite normal with Nikki and Frances. Well, with Nikki, lots of people think they are – you know – at it; they are so normal together. I think he's the only person who can touch her with what appears as affection and live. It's a sort of close brother and sister relationship, the way I see it.'

'He sounds autistic the way you talk about him.'

'That was a concern I had when I first got him in special projects and he does have some elements of that in his social interaction, but his value as a planner and organizer far outweigh his social limitations.'

'Is he a savant then?'

'He perhaps has savant syndrome abilities in the way he can forward visualize. He seems to sense all the things that can go wrong and pick a path through them to achieve a goal and a recovery if one of them happens.'

I didn't know if I was happy or disturbed. I seemed to be joining a bunch of misfits.

'Are you normal?' I asked Barrow.

'Good God, no! How can a psychiatrist be normal?'

'You're pulling my pisser, aren't you?'

'Perish the thought. I was in medical services then seconded into interrogation and advising active units before making the change into real intelligence work. From there, I was setting up special projects and now this job.'

I was not comforted. Had I been selected to join the nut squad because I was considered a nut? Barrow let the silence continue. I was beginning to understand how he knew so much about his squad of nutcases.

'Don't worry, Jake; you'll fit in famously,' he reassured me.

'That's what bothers me.'

The station appeared ahead. Barrow turned in and stopped the car at the entrance.

'Give me a call when you're ready to come to work,' he told me. 'I'll get Frances to visit you in hospital.'

'She won't come dressed as a nurse or my mother, will she?'

He smiled. 'I think you're just the man I need.'

That didn't make me feel better either.

I sat on the platform in the station waiting for my train. The past hour or so was circulating in my head. I'd been selected to join a special section that did something that I hadn't actually been told about. My fault: I should have asked. An apparently very intelligent, well-educated woman, who has had some sort of emotional breakdown, led this section. A female and a male, both homosexual, also staffed it. The female, who had a description that would fit a glamour model, had some unspecified special skills, but I did know that she was a martial arts expert and was prepared to use her training. The male was a social misfit, but had some characteristics that fit an autistic savant. And the man this bunch reported to was a psychiatrist who thought I'd fit in well with this gang of misfits. A saying popped into my head: 'A man is known by the company he keeps.'

7

I spent a few days at my sister's and went through the documents given to me by Rod Wilkes. There were changes and bits missing. I checked my hand written notes and compiled the answers to the questions I was likely to get at the court martial. Somebody was definitely out to get the two soldiers. I phoned a contact in the APA. Her advice was swift and clear, 'stay the hell out of it, Jake'.

With that warning clear in my head I went to hospital.

Hospital was a non-event. I arrived and the specialist and his sidekick took some more X-rays, prodded, pulled and twisted my knee, and said, 'Okay, Captain, a little nick and a load of antibiotics, and we will have you as right as rain in no time.'

I would have been happier if the antibiotics were not injected into my backside by the bucketful, via a very large hypodermic syringe, using a needle the thickness of a pencil. It seemed to me they were using my bum as a dartboard.

The following morning, after another series of rapier thrusts into my buttocks, I was carted off to the operating theatre. A very small cut was made in the side of my knee and, after some fiddling about, I was sewn up. I couldn't believe the pain had stopped, but I couldn't bend my knee because they had re-strapped the support thingy behind my leg to prevent me from doing just that.

The surgeon came back to see me. 'How does it feel now?'

'Absolutely great. No pain. You're a genius.'

'Not really. Whoever did your knee did a fantastic job.

Whoever it was, is much more skilled than me. He deliberately tacked some ligaments and tendons with ligatures. If we'd had some notes, we would have fixed it ages ago. His action enabled the healing to occur and will enable the knee to be free moving rather than stiff. It was more by luck that my houseman recognized what had been done. It was something pioneered in American sports surgery. We did some snipping, took out the foreign objects and will continue to pump you full of antibiotics to kill off any bugs. I reckon you can hobble out of here tomorrow. Come back in a couple of weeks and we will give you the all clear and some exercises to do.'

I bet some bureaucrat neatly filed my notes with no thought that a surgeon or I might need them.

After a lunch that I was sure must have been nutritious but left me hungry, I wandered out into the grounds. 'Wandered' might be a bit exotic; I hobbled onto the grounds. It was not warm, but it couldn't be after Iraq. In fact, it was damned cold. I sat in the small, green area, well wrapped up, and observed the bronze statue and the cast-iron railings that separated the grounds from the busy street beyond. The railings looked very old – a Victorian design, I supposed – but could not have been older than the late 1940s, as iron railings had been used as raw materials for the Second World War. Strange, the things I knew that were of no use to anybody.

A nurse was walking across the grounds toward me.

'Captain Robinson.'

'You're being formal today, Sister. What have I done wrong?'

'You've a visitor: a *Ms* Portello.' She emphasized the *Ms*.

'Ms Portello? I don't know a Ms Portello. Is she Spanish?'

'I wouldn't think so from her accent.'

'Is she beautiful?'

'Why do you ask?'

'I just wanted to make you jealous.'

She laughed. 'Actually, she's attractive and well dressed. Very smart: smart casual, perfectly matched, I would say.'

'That's probably Frances.' I now knew her surname – Portello – or was that a pseudonym?

'She's in the visitors' lounge.'

That's what I liked about private hospitals; they treated patients with dignity. In the NHS, the hospitals were the domain of the doctors and patients entered to be practised on. In the private arena, the doctors used their skills in the service of the patients. Was it a positive attitude thing or was it a commercial incentive? Oh, cynical me.

Sister Atkinson took me to the visitors' room. 'There's your visitor, Jake.'

I saw an attractive woman. She matched Barrow's description: very attractive, slim with cropped, brown hair and blue eyes. She looked like she belonged there. How extraordinary.

She stood up as we came in.

'Thank you, Grace,' I said.

Sister Atkinson smiled.

I crossed the room and we shook hands. She had a firm handshake with cool hands and a light grip. She was looking into my eyes.

'So you're the Captain Jake Robinson whom I've heard so much about.'

I was surprised. She was supposed to have seen me somewhere.

'So, what have you heard, Frances? I assume I can call you Frances.'

She nodded. 'Yes, please do. I was told you would be direct. Shall we sit?'

I eased down sideways onto one of the armchairs so that I could keep my leg straight. Frances showed some concern. 'Oh, I forgot about your leg.'

41

'So did I last night and it caused a little embarrassment.'

She put her head to one side. 'Do tell,' she said as if she expected some salacious gossip.

'Three of us went to the cinema. We had booked the left-hand end of the row so that I could park my leg along the aisle. When I sat down, I was too far back in the seat. My weight going down on my splint caused my leg to shoot up. I lost my balance and my foot landed on the shoulder of a small man in front of me. He was not a happy bunny, particularly as I started to giggle. I couldn't move.'

Frances laughed. 'Yes, I was under the impression you could get yourself into trouble.'

'I thought that was a requirement of the job.'

'You're probably right. Do you mind if I ask you some questions?'

'I thought that's why you were here. Fire away.'

'I see you were expelled from your school. It says *behaviour unbecoming of a student of Cranford College.*'

'Good Lord, you're going back a bit. Yes, we were caught under the stage in the hall.'

'Doing what?'

'If I remember correctly, the headmaster referred to it as inappropriately indulging in sexual intercourse. I rather liked the description. I suppose the inappropriate part was that the young lady in question was employed by the school.'

'Well, it doesn't seem to have affected your career. You took a degree in psychology and then joined the army. Why?'

'Psychology, because I found it fascinating; joining the army was more complicated. My father died. My mother became ill: E.O.A. I had to earn a living and the army looked a good option.'

'What is E.O.A.?'

'Early Onset Alzheimer's.'

'I see. That created a problem for you?'

'Not really. My sister took her in and looked after her.'

'Is she still alive?'

'My sister? Yes. My mother died.'

'I see I'll have to be careful about the way I ask you questions. You went to Sandhurst and then opted for the RMP. Why did you want to be a policeman?'

'I've absolutely no idea. It just seemed like a sound option.'

She was looking at me intensely. It seemed she was trying to make up her mind about something.

'Let me try you with a tough one. Have you ever killed anybody?'

'I suppose so. I'm in the army and I've fired at people shooting at me.'

'Avoidance, hey, Jake? I had assumed that. Let me rephrase; have you taken aim and deliberately shot somebody?'

This woman did not beat about the bush. Why had I ducked the question? She picked it up... smart.

'Yes.'

'Tell me about it.'

This was a line of questioning I didn't expect.

'First time, a soldier, one of our soldiers, was threatening a couple of my MPs with a semiautomatic weapon. I told him to drop it or I would shoot. I killed him, but he got off two rounds. One hit an MP and the second hit a wall.'

'How did you feel?'

'Hot, like I had been topped up with a vindaloo and hot water was being poured over me.'

'And your emotions?'

'Angry with myself, sorry that one of my men was shot and totally depressed that I'd killed someone.'

'Did the MP die?'

'No, he recovered and is still in the army.'

43

'How long were you – I think you said – "depressed" for?'

'Not long. Too much was happening, but I occasionally think about it.'

'When you think about it, what do you feel?'

I had been through this during compulsory counselling and I really had a problem with answering these questions.

'I feel a heavy weight at the back of my eyes and my neck is stiff so that I can't look up.'

Frances looked at me for a long time. She was nodding a slow nod. 'I asked what you were feeling and you answered. Tell me the emotion you experience when you feel the way you described.'

'Sadness.'

'Sadness about what?'

'Sadness that I had to kill a man.'

'You accept that you had to kill him.'

'Definitely.'

'If faced with that situation again, what will you do?'

'Fire sooner.'

She raised her eyebrows. 'Why?'

'So my man wouldn't get shot.'

'Okay, what about the second man you deliberately killed?' She didn't miss much; she had picked up 'the first time', so she was a listener.

'I'm okay about that. He deserved it.'

'A man deserved to die?' She sounded surprised.

'Yes.'

'Tell me about it.'

'I had a patrol guarding some children at a school. They were Iraqi children: boys and girls.'

'The man was a bomber. He wanted to blow the children up and he was running toward the school. I shot him. The odd thing was he knew I was going to kill him before he got to the children.'

'How did you know that?'

44

'He had to run past me; he was looking at me. I knew he knew I would kill him.'

'What was your emotion about that?'

'My emotion? My emotion was exhilaration that I had stopped the bastard.'

'Do you think about it?'

'Occasionally.'

'And your emotions now when you think about it?'

'Pleasure.'

'Pleasure.' She sounded surprised. 'Pleasure at what?'

'Saving children's lives.'

'But you killed a man.'

'True, but he was less than a real man. He wanted to be a killer of children and he set out to be a killer of children. I stopped him.'

'What do you see as the difference in these situations?'

'The second was a premeditated, deliberate, thought-out, callous murder of innocents in the name of some ideological nonsense. The first was a poor bastard who was lost and couldn't see a way out – a victim of circumstance – and I had no way to help him. A second factor that applied to both situations was that I killed to save lives.'

'If you were ordered to kill someone, would you do it?'

I felt I wanted to joke to reduce the pressure on me, but I didn't. 'It depends on the circumstances.'

'So it's conceivable that you would refuse?'

'Yes.'

'Would you kill, say, a woman or children to save your own life?'

'Yes.'

'You have no doubt?'

'None.'

'Why would you kill to save your own life?'

'Because I'm no use dead and I like being alive.'

'You're a soldier and you're required to kill to order, but you said it would depend on the circumstances?'

'Yes, one of the circumstances is the situation and the other is who has given the order.'

'As a soldier, if your commanding officer says, "Shoot those soldiers firing at us," would you shoot?'

'Yes.'

'So you obey orders to kill someone.'

'I agree, but that's not my decision. That's on the conscience of the person who sent me to war. Let him or her have the sleepless nights, but it's more than likely that my life is on the line, so from that point of view it's self-defence. It's possible to rationalize these things and that's necessary to stay sane.'

'You think the person who sent soldiers to war should feel the responsibility of the deaths inflicted by the soldiers.'

'Yes.'

'Do you think that they do?'

'Good Lord, no. They're politicians and by definition they have no ethics.'

'Do you really believe that?'

'I only have my observations of them lying or at best evading the truth.'

'Are you this cynical about everything?'

'I don't think so. I think I'm more sceptical than cynical.'

'Would you kill to save my life?'

That was out of left field. 'Probably, but it depends on the circumstances.'

'So, let me see if I have this right. In general terms, you're prepared to kill and take responsibility for that killing when killing is the lesser of two evils. If you're ordered to kill in the line of duty, you will because you do not see that as your responsibility but your duty?'

'I suppose that's right.'

'It seems to me that you don't have a conscience about

46

killing or a value about it; you're logical. Tell me your view about you killing people.'

This was very strange. Was I being assessed as a hit man? I wondered what my view really was.

'I'll try. It's not something I've sat and thought about.' I was trying to get my beans in a row. 'I value life. Random and senseless killing is wasteful and as such is unproductive. I believe in the death penalty for deliberate murder. I have reasons for that belief. I believe in euthanasia, as I believe that it's a human right, but I also believe that there must be safeguards in both those situations. But you asked me about me killing somebody. I'll not lose sleep about killing somebody if they are intent on killing me. I'll kill to save the lives of people, though I won't be able to rationalize that outside of a particular event. If I kill somebody by accident... um, well, I think I can live with that. It would do no good not to. What is done is done.'

She was looking at me and assessing me. I'm not sure what her assessment parameters were. No, that wasn't right; I had absolutely no idea what her assessment parameters were.

'Let me backtrack. You spoke of ideological nonsense and politicians by definition having no ethics. Those sorts of statements do sound cynical.'

'Your question is?'

'Explain.'

'Ideologies are about belief systems and that is fine; everybody has some beliefs. But if they are based, as that murderer's beliefs were based, not on some social norms but on some unproven, un-provable and unshakeable dogma then there is no rationale. To me, that believer is an extremist, insane or defective.'

'What about the ethics of politicians.'

'Politicians are seekers of power. Ask them a question and many couch their answer in a form that will gain votes or not lose votes, not in the form of truth.'

She had reached a decision. I could see it in the little nod and the clarity of her gaze at me. 'I think we can work together, Jake. Do you think you can work with me?'

'Definitely.'

'You're very positive. Why?'

'Easy. You *asked* me whether I could. If you had just assumed I could then I'm not sure that I would.'

'Good. I'll see you tomorrow. Here's an address. That will be where you can live until we decide differently.'

'How did you make the decision that we can work together?'

'I asked you straightforward questions. You just answered the questions I asked. You did not evade; you did not justify; you just answered. When I asked you the difference between two situations, you demonstrated discrimination. When I asked you about your view, you related it to your values and beliefs at a logical and not a theoretical or theological level. But you didn't bother to give the reasons behind your statements, so there was no clouding of your views. Now, is there anything you need?'

'You said about the living arrangement "until we decide differently". Who are "we"?'

'You and me, Jake. That's my flat and, for a while, you'll be my flatmate. Oh, here's a key.' With that, she smiled, put her hands on my shoulders, kissed my cheek and walked out.

I'd never really considered the killing of other people before. On the face of it, there was all this morality stuff, but when it was them or me, I was going to pick me. I hadn't thought about the duty aspect overtly, but I suppose it had been there all the time. I really couldn't cope with the holier-than-thou people who condemned soldiers when they had never been on the wrong end of a rifle, when they had never had to cope with a cold-blooded murderer who didn't give a shit about killing an innocent person. I suppose, from one point of view, I was a cold-blooded, practical bastard, but I thought I was the one with valid principles. I suppose everyone thought that about themselves.

I wondered why she chose that line of questioning. I suppose she knew everything else about me and just wanted to confirm that I was as potty as the rest of Barrow's nut squad. The business of sharing a flat was okay but surprising.

8

With Frances gone and me on the mend with somewhere to live, I could get onto important matters. I rang Keith Todd and a secretary answered the phone. Have you ever dealt with a gatekeeper secretary? They have one aim in life: protect their principle from all contact with the outside world. I told her who I was and the case. She assumed I was a journalist. When I told her I was the investigating officer, she virtually called me a liar because a Lieutenant Cannon was presenting the prosecution evidence from the police inquiry. In the end, I made it quite clear.

'Give Mr Todd the message that I called and the hospital I'm in. If I don't get a call and his clients go to prison, I will arrange they sue you personally.'

Her response was, 'Well, really, what an unreasonable man.'

I waited – silence – and then Keith Todd came on the line.

'Good afternoon. Keith Todd.'

'Good afternoon, Keith. My name is Jake Robinson and I was the investigating officer in the Carmichael murder. I think you may want to hear my version of events as I think Jason Phillips and Mike Munro are about to be railroaded.'

'Where the hell have you been? We have been trying to get hold of you.'

'I'm in St Mary's Hospital and you can visit me any time.'

'I'm on my way and Roland Parsley will be with me.'

Within the hour, they arrived, complete with a bunch of grapes. Three hours later, they left with big smiles. I was exhausted and they had paid a large photocopying bill.

9

Frances was a surprise. She arrived the next day to take me home. I use the word 'home' with some trepidation, as it was Frances' home and I was but a lodger.

We weaved our way into Chelsea and pulled up in an underground garage below a very expensive-looking block of flats. There was no way I could afford to live there. It seemed palatial to me. The entrance lobby on the ground floor even had a porter.

As we entered, he said, 'Good afternoon, Ms Portello.'

'Good afternoon, George,' said Frances.

He would have to be a George or James; nothing else would have suited really.

'This is Captain Robinson. He will be staying with me until he finds a place of his own.'

'Good afternoon, sir.'

'Good afternoon, George.'

He turned back to Frances. 'Yes, ma'am.' George had clocked me, but I couldn't read whether he approved or not. 'Your laundry has arrived and is in your reception closet.'

'Thank you, George.'

'My pleasure, ma'am.'

I was not comfortable. It was a ritual exchange of the sort you might see in films of the 1950s. I couldn't believe Frances earned enough to have a place like this and the security service certainly wasn't going to provide it. On my pay, I probably couldn't pay the monthly service charges.

The lift was smooth and fast. We stepped out onto the third floor. We were in a large reception area with two passageways going off to the left and right, each with a set of doors and on each door was a number. 'This is the reception closet,' said Frances. 'We are number thirty-six, as that is the flat number.'

'So there are six flats on this floor,' I said, sussing that there were six cupboards.

'Yes, the next floor up has four flats and the top floor has two flats. On the ground floor are some offices and a small spa: really a cardio room, some weights and a small swimming pool. As you saw, the basement is a garage. There is some parking out back and I've arranged a space for you. The spaces out front are for deliveries and visitors, etc. If you've somebody to visit you, tell George or James. At the weekends, we often also have Barbara and she sometimes does weekday cover.'

There you are. I just knew it; both a George and a James.

'Is there a night shift?'

Frances looked at me in silence for a minute at least. 'I'm going to have to get used to your sense of humour. Yes, a guard from a security company comes on about six in the evening and there is one here until about eight in the morning when our own staff come on.'

'Are there millionaires living here? No, I shouldn't ask.'

'Actually, yes.'

She was waiting for the obvious question from me, but I was not going to ask it and I didn't care how she got this flat. Well, it might be interesting, but I wouldn't ask.

'That's good. I'll feel very safe.'

She laughed. 'Let me walk you through the flat. Here in the hall is the burglar alarm. The number is 0708.'

This seemed totally superfluous to me, but I wasn't rich. The hall was polished wood block with a large, round, Chinese rug sitting in it. There were three bedrooms and a study complete with two computers, a twenty-one-point-five-inch iMac and a twenty-seven-inch iMac, two printers, one fax machine, two telephones and a radio bank with winking lights and a couple of alphanumeric keyboards. It was designed for two people.

The lounge was large with thee armchairs, one of which was a rocker, and a four-seat settee, a TV (more of a plasma screen cinema really), some super paintings, all originals (and some I knew would have cost a few bob, well, a lot really) and a nest of occasional tables. Through the lounge was a kitchen diner with all the exotic gadgets you might expect.

'Frances.'

She looked at me.

'I can't afford to live here.'

'I know,' she said. 'If I didn't own it, I wouldn't be able to live here either.'

'So, what are you going to charge me?'

'Seven thousand a year, paid quarterly in advance. But don't sweat it; this unit pays eight thousand a year in special housing allowance, so you make a thousand a year. It will help pay for your laundry and incidentals.' She laughed, probably at the amazement on my face. It hadn't crossed my mind to question what I would be paid in Barrow's unit. I had just assumed that the army would still pay me my standard captain's pittance.

'You'll be much better off now than when you were wholly owned by the army. The pay, allowances and expenses are totally different.'

I was feeling a lot better.

'Which is my room?'

'That one.'

She pointed to a closed door. I went in. The room was large with a built-in wardrobe with mirror doors and a matching chest of drawers. Then I noticed all the wood was the same – a light beech – even the skirting boards and windowsill. I had never seen that before and the ceiling was a very light green, reflecting the green carpet. There was a door and I went through into the large en-suite bathroom. This was luxury.

We sat in the kitchen and discussed financial matters and work-sharing responsibilities. It sounded good to me, particularly as Frances had a cleaning woman who came in regularly and did things like the laundry and shopping, as well as keeping the flat spick and span, but she did point out that I was on duty twenty-four-seven – no change there then – but I wasn't going to be staying long; I had a trial to attend.

Frances rustled up a cauliflower cheese, with bacon bits in the cheese sauce, and we sat looking at each other across the table.

'Go on. What is it?' she asked.

'I've about three thousand questions to ask.'

'Well, the answer to the first one is my father-in-law gave it to me.'

'Aha!' It wasn't one of my most pressing questions, but it was nice to know. 'He was rich then?'

'Not really. He changed his will, leaving everything to me when Jack died. A month after the funeral, he just upped and died. Jack was his whole life. There was nobody else, so I inherited. The will had only one condition; all the estate had to be invested in a property, so here it is.'

I said nothing. She was looking at me. She was in pain.

'Thank you for confiding in me.' What else could I have said?

'That wasn't what you were going to ask, was it?'

'Well, no, that would have been a bit presumptuous.'

'So, what is it you want to know?'

'What is the job I've taken on?'

She laughed. 'Yes, you really do need to know that. I'm not going to give you the full SP until you're fully at work, but as an overview, it's like this. There is a major organized crime syndicate. It's entrenched in society, politics, finance, gambling, drugs and some other peripheral bits and bobs. Currently, we know sweet FA, but we did know our entry was likely to be through a certain Major Michael Carmichael. Then he was shot, so we will have to find another weak spot. The problem is we don't know who to trust, so there are only the five of us until we can find the boundaries. We have a few people, um, at arm's length in positions to feed us information and of course we have the other teams that are monitoring, researching and finding things we can feed to other bodies to take action on.'

'Such as?'

'The revenue, the police, the social services, but they are just pinpricks in the scheme of things.'

'You must know the main players.'

'Oh, yes, but they are totally untouchable.'

'You're not going to tell me?'

'Not yet. Not until we're absolutely sure about you.'

I wondered how I was going to be tested to see if I was kosher.

'Let me suggest one thing. It has already leaked that you'll be a witness for the defence at the Major Michael Carmichael court martial. That will make some people very unhappy. All the soldiers who you interviewed have requested that they should not be called.'

'How do you know this?'

'Keith Todd told us. They could be called anyway, but Keith thinks it would be unwise.'

'Right, what about Sergeant Josey Billinghurst?'

'Interesting; she was all ready to give evidence and suddenly backed off. We chased it for Keith. It's messy: amounts to intimidation. Then you turned up, so we let it go.'

'Right.' I really wanted to know what they had on Josey and who the 'they' were. I had some names from Rob Wilkes. I suppose he was one of the arm's length people.

'I know what you're thinking, Jake. I'm not going to tell you what the blackmail was, but the "they" are The Family. We think they will try to get at you. We know you're clean when it comes to blackmail or you wouldn't be sitting there. You could be bribed, but we don't think so. So, we are left with direct intimidation.'

'Am I to be in some form of protective custody?'

'Good Lord, no. We want you out there as bait and that could be your best protection.'

'You knew where I was. Why didn't you tell Keith?'

'Yes, it was a test. We wanted to see what you would do, but you did leave it late.'

We spent the rest of the evening just chatting, finding out about each other. It seemed that when I started proper we would be a team, like Nikki and Howard, but with an investigative role. I was still unclear about their role, but I could guess.

10

The next morning, as we chomped our way through corn-
flakes, Frances said, 'I've arranged for you to meet the
others.'

'The others?'

'Yes, Nikki and Howard.'

'Am I ready for this?'

She laughed. 'Not really, but they want a sight of you –
well Nikki does – and you need to pick up your car.'

'My car?'

'Yes, you know, like a big metal box with wheels and
windows that takes you places. It's not a new one but it will
do you until we can get you a new one. I assume you have a
driving licence. Oh, and you're off to Essex for the court
martial.'

'Well, yes.'

'Good. Come on, then.'

'You're a bully.'

'Yes, I know. Good isn't it?'

I couldn't believe how well we were getting on. It was
almost as if we had known each other for years.

We drove through the town, to the offices and Frances
signed me in. I felt strangely shy. Odd really. It was all so, so
clean and civilized.

Frances took me to see a very large woman in her fifties,
who it seemed was some sort of administrator and had some
sort of staff responsibility. She then left me, saying that she
would come and collect me when Myrtle had finished with
me. It was almost as if I was being sold as a sex slave.

Myrtle took my photo and within ten minutes, I had

57

signed umpteen bits of paper that I was supposed to have read, had a new identity card that gave me access to the building, a number of booklets to read and forms to claim expenses and deal with other things. All the time I was being told that it was all straight forward and I would soon get used to it. This reassurance I had grave doubts about. I also had a new mobile phone, programmed with a range of numbers of people I had never heard of, which seemed to do things that other phones I had seen did not do. I was also taken to see a small dark man in the basement who measured me; quite what for I wasn't sure, but later I was to find out that it was for a shoulder holster and some suits and jackets that would be made for me. The whole thing was such a whirlwind that I was dizzy and immensely pleased when Frances rescued me.

'I do like your new boy,' said Myrtle as Frances came in. 'He's quite sexy and amazingly shy. You will let me have him when you've finished with him, won't you?'

'Now, you keep those claws of yours off him.'

'Oh dear. You get all the sexy ones. I'm quite jealous.'

I thanked Myrtle and as we left she said, 'Any time, Captain – I'm all yours,'

When clear, I said to Frances, 'What was that all about?'

'Just our Myrtle; she's desperate for a man and about as subtle as a Sherman Tank.'

'Sherman Tank? That's a bit out of date.'

'Spot on, Jake. Spot on.'

We negotiated a series of passageways and eventually passed through a guarded security door into a very different atmosphere. I didn't know how to describe it, but it was just friendly.

Frances opened a door and I was faced with four people. One I knew; it was Barrow. Two of the others had to be Nikki and Howard and the other one I was introduced to was Pauline, Barrow's secretary.

Nikki was everything Barrow had said. She took my breath away, but for me it was her eyes: blue as a summer sky with huge black pupils.

She took my right hand, firmly and gently in her two hands, held it between her breasts, looked deeply into my eyes and kissed me gently on the cheek.

'Oh, you do smell nice,' she said. 'I'd never thought of soldiers as smelling nice.' She then laughed. 'Yes, you will do.'

'Ignore her. It's always best to ignore her. She plays games until you know her. I'm Howard.' He held out his hand and I was able to shake it when Nikki finally released me.

The phone rang and Pauline picked it up. She looked at me and said, 'We'll have to become acquainted some other time. Your car is on the forecourt and it seems you have to go to Essex.'

11

The courtroom was cold. I've always found Essex a cold county and that day the military court centre at Colchester was far too cold to hold a case of murder. Apparently, there was something wrong with the heating. I bet all summer it worked fine, because you didn't need it. But in February, it packed up. Not only was it cold, but also the rain was beating on the high-set windows. This was not a good omen; well, not a good omen if you believe in such things. I, of course, claimed that I did not... believe, that is. In fact, I found that from the day I decided that there was no God, all sorts of other irrationalities disappeared; ever since I was a child, I had had this unsettled feeling going upstairs in the dark to a dark bedroom. Then I became an atheist and – Boom! – overnight, gone. Although I had decided there was no God, I still recognized the valuable things said by people such as Jesus of Nazareth and disciples, and the great Christians, who were, in reality, great philosophers. It was just the miracles and the threat of hell that turned me off. I dumped the fear of the vengeful God with the recognition that there was no God. I didn't have to be threatened with hell and damnation anymore to be good – whatever good is. I could choose to behave myself on my terms.

Anyway, it was damned cold; so cold that it had delayed the start of the court martial by a few days. I looked around. Some soldiers were plugging in electric heaters. I was just there to familiarize myself, but it was all already quite familiar as I had been there before; the judge advocate's bench stretched across the front of the courtroom with the Royal Coat of Arms behind the central position, where the judge advocate sat; the jury benches, where five lay members sat, ran out on the right-hand side with the president in the centre. He was a senior officer, a colonel. The rules were that he was only the foreman and must not influence the verdict. Some hope! Oh, cynical me. In a case like this, there was bound to be some bias. In a civilian court, peers judged the accused. In a court martial, the rules prevented this; the four lay members and the president had to be senior to the accused. In this case, the five who would decide on the guilt of Jase and Mike were commissioned officers.

The witness stand, where I would give evidence, was opposite the desks for the prosecutor and his assistant at the left-hand side of the court, and defence was across on the right. Jase and Mike would sit behind the defence counsel.

I had phoned Keith Todd and, after a half-hour chat, I was fixed up to see Roland Parsley. We went over my evidence and findings and from having nothing, Roland thought he had a winning case. Nothing had changed since our last meeting and they wanted assurance that I was still willing to appear. But Roland knew, as I knew, that pressure was being exerted on anybody who might disrupt the prosecution case.

I could already feel the tension in the court; not in the court really, but in my head. Court cases are battles fought using arguments containing facts and ideas expressed in the spoken word. They have tension, elation, despondency and a whole range of other emotions. I had felt them all in a court such as this, but this case was different. I had always been on the prosecution side before. Now I was on the defence side and for the first time. I felt the court was loaded against me. Perhaps the whole case was going to hinge on what I said. How odd. Same setting, same process and, for me, the same sort of relevant information, but I had always felt a winner before. In this case, I didn't. Was it because I was on the other side or was it because I knew the dice had been loaded against us? Us? I was no longer neutral. As an investigating officer, I had always thought of myself as neutral, just the facts. Now I had identified with Jase and Mike and I had never identified with a defendant when I was on the prosecution side. I knew there had to be a court martial, but my additional concern was that even if they were found not guilty of the primary crime of killing an officer, they would end up in prison for some lesser offence. Military justice was like that. Having a whole bunch of civilians involved, as there was, just made life tougher for the servicemen and added to their disbelief in justice. How could anybody who had not been in among the muck and bullets – who had not spent days or weeks living in a hole in the ground, or been patrolling streets where some religious nutter wanted to kill you – possibly know what it was like? And if you didn't know what it was like, how could you make informed judgments on what these real men and women, in life-threatening situations, felt like and the way they were likely to react to a situation? Yes, sometimes they behaved irrationally and sometimes they behaved disgustingly; sometimes their reactions seemed perverse and illogical, but if you'd never been there how could you judge? Yes, I had become too involved. I needed to create some space between this case and me.

I went out. In the stone-flagged court reception and passage areas, more soldiers were putting in paraffin and electric heaters and radiators. I had to get my head around that I was to be called as a defence witness. I had been the senior investigating officer and I had found that Sergeant Jason William Phillips CGC and Corporal Michael James Munro *had* killed Major Michael Phillip Carmichael, but my investigation showed me that they had no choice. The army was the army, though. You just couldn't go around killing your officers. I understood the army's point of view, but evidence was evidence. Well, it was less the evidence and more the motive. Anyway, it was for the lay members to sort it out.

I had participated in trials of various descriptions and never really thought about justice. Odd that. Now that I was on the defendants' side it made me think about what was really going on. It was obvious that in a case such as this that a jury of officers had to be biased. They may not want to be and they may not even think they are, but – let's face it – two men on trial had shot one of their own, one of my own. In these circumstances, even a weak case became a strong one.

The mystery to me was why Jase and Mike had not just pleaded guilty and explained why they did it in mitigation. Despite my experience as a military policeman, the behaviour of defenders and prosecutors was a total mystery to me. I had brought stone-cold guilty people to trial to have them found not guilty, and then seen extremely weak, circumstantial cases forwarded for trial and a conviction go through on the nod. I have had guilty people bang to rights with cast-iron evidence for the APA to turn it aside, and also presented cases that were so weak that I was embarrassed about them and seen them taken to court martial. The whole thing was a mystery to me.

Once a trial started, what witnesses said could be very different from what they said only a short few weeks before. All this added to the uncertainty, but the jury was the decisive factor. With commissioned officers trying the case of two non-commissioned officers shooting a high-profile, commissioned officer, it seemed to me that the verdict was a forgone conclusion. People may spout about integrity and stuff, but these jury members would have to go back to their regiments. Regiments were like families. The social pressure to find Jase and Mike guilty would be enormous, irrespective of the facts. It would not just be fellow officers who would pressurize the jury members through their attitudes;

the other ranks, deep down, wanted their officers to be whiter than white, the best, so they would also put pressure on their regimental offices to convict Jase and Mike. This made it even stranger that somebody was loading the evidence. Why had somebody cooked the books by changing the evidence? It wasn't needed. The manipulators clearly did not understand the army; they must have been politicians. I'd just have to stick to being a simple policeman. Jase and Mike were dead ducks, so to speak, despite the evidence I'd give, no matter how clever Roland Parsley may be.

A further problem came with the giving of evidence. For some reason, none of the soldiers were giving evidence for the defence. The defence needed them to corroborate the statements they had given, but they'd requested to be excused. This was extraordinary. It made no sense. The only conclusion I could reach was that they were under pressure not to participate. Must be the regimental family sticking together. It was what made the British Army the best army for its size in the world. In reality, perhaps it did not matter. Roland Parsley, barrister, and Keith Todd, solicitor, were smart cookies and had persuaded the soldiers to make statements in the presence of a notary and they had signed them. This was an extraordinary move, but we would have to wait to find out how it played out in reality. I was concerned, though. Who would or could persuade twenty men not to give evidence? I was just a copper and the legal niceties were just not my provinces, but Sergeant Jason Phillips was a hero; he was their leader; in battle they would die for him as some had done, but now when he needed them and they were not in any danger they had deserted him. It made no sense.

12

It was the opening day. All listed participants in the case were required to be there. I had not known this to happen before. The only non-listed people were the press and they had been screened. Those associated with the prosecution were on one side and those for the defence were on the other. The media was between them. All we knew was that the judge advocate general was going to make a statement.

The court officer came in and stood before the judge advocate's bench. 'Silence in the court.'

He waited. There was silence.

'All stand.'

We stood. The judge advocate general came in and sat at his bench.

'His Honour, Judge Advocate General Sir Nicolas Ross will make a statement. Be seated.'

We sat and there was a slight buzz of conversation. The judge advocate general rapped his gavel. There was silence; the only sound was the flick of notebook pages as the reporters settled to capture what Sir Nicolas Ross said.

'Ladies and gentlemen.' He had a deep resonant voice: the voice of judicial authority. He looked around the court and captured with eye contact all seated there. There was now an expectation: of what, I had no idea. 'There has been much controversy in the media about this court martial. The media coverage has focused on three main areas. Firstly, there has been speculation as to the nature of the evidence that may be presented. Secondly, there has been speculation as to whether there is a prima facie case and, thirdly, there is doubt as to whether the accused could receive a fair trial at a court martial. This third element has two threads. The first is the nature of the court martial structure and process and the second is about the nature of the deceased. I will make one personal comment on this final item. There seems to be a concerted effort to show the deceased in the light of a national hero. I will not comment on that aspect, but the effort in coverage across all media channels indicates a plan to influence the general public and perhaps the justice system itself. I must say I deplore such tactics.'

There we had it. He had laid out the three areas with no detail, neat. For the expression of distaste in the praising of Major Carmichael, he might get his knuckles rapped or he would if he wasn't a judge.

'Let me deal with each of these items very briefly. There has been much speculation as to the likely evidence that may be presented. I placed before the Adjutant General, Lieutenant General Sir Peter Mackenzie CMG MBE my opinion that the speculation has not been of a nature to render the likelihood of creating a bias within the jury.'

There was a muttering and murmuring among some members of the press. The judge advocate general looked sternly at the section of the courtroom. There was again silence.

'The second point I will deal with in a few words. The Army Prosecuting Authority decided this is a prima facie case. This court martial will hear that case.'

No messing about there then.

'Elements of the press have argued that trial by court martial comprising exclusively of officers violates the impartiality guarantee of Article 6 of the Convention, where the supposed victim of an alleged crime was an officer and the accused are soldiers from the ranks. This issue has been raised before. I intend to give you the findings of a review into a more controversial case, a case of rape.'

I could feel the rise in interest in the ranks of the press.

'A leading seaman was found guilty of raping a female, acting sub-lieutenant. On 22 June 2003, the leading seaman was convicted by a general court martial of the offence of rape of a junior, female naval officer. The accused was sentenced to seven years' imprisonment and dismissed with disgrace from the service. The GCM comprised four officers; none were below the rank of lieutenant, a permanent president, and a judge advocate. The reviewing authority did not alter the GCM's findings or sentence.

'The leading seaman appealed to the Courts Martial Appeal Court. The applicant had argued that trial by court martial comprised exclusively of officers violated the impartiality guarantee of Article 6 of the Convention, where the complainant was an officer. The accused was not commissioned and the issues in the case turned on the credibility of the evidence and the impartiality of the jury. The appeal was dismissed on 28 September 2004. I rely on that review that upheld the credibility of the court martial process and structure.

'In view of the media coverage, in particular the press, I make the following statement before the media and all those associated with this case.'

He turned and looked at the jury. I thought what he was doing may be considered risky in law, as I'd never heard of it being done before.

'President and members of the jury, you've been sworn in to do your duty. I remind you again of the oath you took at the outset of this case, to try this case without partiality, favour or affection. The reputation of the deceased officer is not part of your consideration nor can it be in the determination of any criminal charge against the persons on trial here. I remind you that everyone is entitled to a fair hearing by you as independent and impartial members of a tribunal. Rank, status or reputation has no place in the determination of guilt or innocence of those charged or of the victim related to the charges. It's up to the prosecution to prove beyond reasonable doubt that Sergeant Jason Phillips CGC and Corporal Michael Munro murdered Major Michael Carmichael DSC. What is required of you is a cold, clinical dissection of the evidence. Having looked at all the evidence impartially, you will reach a fair and just verdict.'

He turned and looked at the section in which the media sat.

'What I require from you, the members of various aspects of the media, is honest, unbiased reporting of the evidence.'

We knew where the judge advocate general stood. He wanted a fair trial and he believed the makeup and process of the court would deliver justice.

13

I wasn't required for a few days, so I went home. It was Wednesday morning and I was still in bed. Most people disliked Monday for obvious reasons. I, for no reason I can imagine, disliked Wednesdays. No, that was not strictly true; the worse things in my life had happened on Wednesdays. I liked Thursday, though, because the week was all uphill after the descent to Wednesday. I decided that I really must get up.

I forced myself out of bed and then took myself on a run. In retrospect, I had noticed the car parked opposite the flats, but I could not remember anyone in it. I thought it registered because it was on double-yellow lines.

I'd gone about half a mile and I was jogging toward the park. I heard the sound of an accelerating engine, the squeal of tyres and the rumble of a speeding vehicle. I jumped sideways – instinct, I suppose – and the rear, nearside wing just brushed my hip, sending me crashing into and over a low hedge into a previously well-kept garden. The flowers and other plants were mangled where I landed and rolled. I then heard the car crunch into something and speed away. I tentatively felt my shoulder – it seemed okay – and gingerly got to my feet. My left thumb was in agony and my left hip hurt. Apart from that, I was fine, if a bit shaky, but it was now clear to me that somebody didn't want me to testify. Before I could consider the full implications of this, a man came bursting through the front door of the house.

'I'm going to call the police.' His voice was raised.

'Call an ambulance while you're at it; my thumb's disjointed and it hurts like hell.'

He just stared at me as if I was some sort of apparition.

'Or you could drive me to A and E.'

He was still staring at me, then at his hedge, then back to me.

'Your leg is bleeding.'

I felt the trickle of blood running down my left leg.

'Yes.'

'What happened?'

'A car hit me. It mounted the kerb. It would have killed me, but swerved to avoid the tree and just clipped me.'

'Christ, I'll ring the police. No, I'll ring for an ambulance. I… Oh dear.' He looked lost and went inside then came out again. 'Come in.'

I went in. He dialled 999 and asked for an ambulance and the police. I went out and sat on the doorstep, as blood was dripping on his hall carpet.

As was usual, the ambulance arrived first. By the time Mr and Mrs Plod arrived, I had a dressing on my leg and my hand was strapped so that it couldn't move.

I told my story to the police; they looked sceptical, but made some notes.

'I see, sir. You were jogging to the park. A car mounted the pavement and tried to run you down. You jumped over the hedge and the car drove away.'

'Not quite; it hit me and knocked me over the hedge. It then clipped a tree as it drove away.'

'I see, sir.'

The female police officer went out of the garden, looked at the tree and returned.

'The car hit the tree,' she confirmed. 'There are chunks of bark missing and some paint on it.'

'Right,' said the male officer. 'Why would anybody try to run you down?'

'Perhaps they don't like joggers.'

'I see, sir.'

'They may have just lost control or were drunk.'

'I see, sir.'

After a brief discussion, the two police officers left and I was taken to the hospital. For some reason, I was not impressed. I wondered why that might be.

The hospital cleaned and dressed my various scraps, gave me a painkilling injection, jerked my thumb back into position, immobilized my hand with an elasticized bandage, gave me some painkillers to take with me and told me to see my GP in a couple of days. They then sent me on my way. I hated Wednesdays. Not only that, I didn't have a GP.

Who had tried to kill me? The answer was obvious really – The Family. But why had they tried to kill me? To stop me testifying? Bit over the top. Perhaps I was paranoid. No. Just because I was *paranoid* did not mean they were not out to get me. No, I was just going to have to be more careful.

14

The case had been running for nine days and two days had passed since I was required to be present. I was just waiting to be called, not really knowing what was going on. The heating had been restored and the weather had improved, but the waiting area was still cold. Or was it just me who was cold? I was toying with the idea that whether you feel hot or cold was more in the mind than in the body. I'd read the best part of a book called *Balance of Power* about gun laws in the USA and I had a flat bum. I exercised my leg and, apart from it being understandably weak, it was progressing nicely. My hip was healing well and my hand had a fresh dressing, but I was cold and it was Wednesday. I still hated Wednesdays.

The prosecution had presented their case and the vibes I picked up were that the defendants were dead meat or would be if there was still hanging. I was not filled with joy as I entered the witness box. In fact, I had a chill in my soul.

The court officer asked me to affirm. I did and the defence barrister, Roland Parsley, stood and approached me.

'Are you Captain Jake Robinson MC of the Royal Military Police?'

'Yes, sir.'

'Were you the senior investigating officer in this case?'

'Yes, sir.'

'I'm therefore confused as to why you're a witness for the defence. Please explain.'

'The evidence upon which the prosecution is based is incomplete and in my view biased.' I was warming up.

The prosecution barrister was on his feet objecting. The defence barrister returned to his desk and the judge advocate general looked at me sternly.

'Are you suggesting that evidence was falsified?'

'No, Your Honour, just that elements were omitted from my reports.'

'That is a very serious allegation, Captain.'

He looked at the two barristers and said, 'Please approach.'

I didn't know what they were saying, but the judge advocate general was clearly very, I think the appropriate word is, 'concerned'. I was told to hold myself available and the legal eagles disappeared into the offices.

I sat in the cold waiting area, wondering what they would do. It was odd that the waiting room seemed cold. Apparently, the heating was back on, but I didn't think it had reached this room set aside for witnesses who had not completed their testimony. I eventually warmed up when I was called back into the courtroom.

The judge advocate general started first. 'You're aware of the evidence that Lieutenant Cannon gave yesterday?'

'No, Your Honour, I was in the waiting area.'

'I see. You're aware of the information in the military police report rendered to this court?'

'Your Honour, I wrote the report that went to the APA.' I was picking my words carefully.

A shadow passed across Judge Advocate General Sir Nicolas Ross' face. He had recognized that the way I answered was slightly oblique to his question.

'Is there anything in that given report with which you now disagree?'

'At the factual level, in the report I wrote and sent to the APA, no, Your Honour.' I could not openly say that the two reports were different; it would pose too many questions.

The judge's bright, intelligent eyes focused on me

through his rimless glasses. He again recognized my reluctance to directly compare the two reports.

'So, in your opinion, the evidence given by Lieutenant Cannon is valid.'

'I can only assume it is, Your Honour.'

'I don't want assumptions, Captain. Was it or was it not valid?'

'I don't know, Your Honour. I never heard the questions that he was asked or the answers that he gave.'

The judge advocate general stared at me, but he was not seeing me. He was thinking and I was feeling uncomfortable. I was getting cold again.

'That seems fair.' He turned to the barristers. 'Do you have the original report as presented by Captain Robinson?'

They both agreed that they did. I knew that the prosecution thought they did and the defence knew they did, but they also had the later version. I was very pleased that nobody asked me. They then set off to the offices again. I sat again in the waiting area and then was sent away to come back tomorrow at 10.30 a.m.

Rita McGee, Roland's number two, met me at about 10.15 a.m., when I arrived. She was one smart cookie and even if she had never served, she had a feel for the army culture.

'Jake,' she began then paused and looked at me. I waited. 'Roland is going to hit you with some tough questions. Just run with them as he will get to where he wants to be.'

'Okay, but how will he know what I'll say?'

'Oh, he has read your report and has noticed that it's substantially different from the report that precipitated the case.'

'Did he tell them in the judge's meeting?'

'No, he just agreed that everything in the prosecution report was in his report. We hope the evidence you give will demonstrate the differences. It could be that the judge advocate general may change the charges or, when it comes to the direction of the lay members, prescribe what they cannot find. We are in a dodgy area here and if it weren't for your very welcome bloody-mindedness, those two soldiers would have got life. Now at least they stand some chance, but, in my view, not a lot.'

Again, I took the stand and went through the bit that I was still required to tell the truth, etc. Then Sir Nicolas spoke to me.

'Captain, there is some lack of clarity about the report that you compiled as the senior investigating officer in this case. The questions you'll be asked must be answered with reference only to the report that you wrote and the information you elicited during your investigation. The court recognizes that you did not have first-hand experience of what occurred at Al-Zilfi. Do you understand?'

'Yes, Your Honour.'

Roland Parsley stood and approached. 'Did Sergeant Phillips CGC and Corporal Munro shoot and kill Major Michael Carmichael?'

'No.'

A buzz went round the room. Roland looked surprised. I think he was surprised. The prosecution objected. The barristers and the judge advocate general had a confab and then the judge advocate general said, 'Captain Robinson, I'm going to allow the testimony that you elicited in your investigation. I want you to ensure that you give only such information that you have received directly from witnesses to the event in the course of your investigations. Do you understand me?'

'Yes, Your Honour.' I found questions such as that a little ridiculous. I thought I understood, so I said yes, but he may have meant something different, so I couldn't say no because I didn't know what that difference was. No wonder the teachers at school shook their heads. Barrow was perhaps right; I was a nutcase waiting to happen.

Roland Parsley started again. 'Who killed Major Carmichael then?'

'Sergeant Phillips.'

'But bullets from both these soldiers' weapons were found in Major Carmichael's body; is that not true?'

'It's true, but the two bullets from Sergeant Phillips were the ones that caused the death. The single bullet from Corporal Munro's weapon would have caused serious wounding, but only if left untreated could it have caused death.'

'How do you know that?'

'Because the autopsy report says so.'

The prosecution was hunting through the documents that they had.

'I'm somewhat confused, Captain. I have the post-mortem report and it does not say that Sergeant Phillips' bullets killed Major Carmichael.'

'That is true, but the American autopsy report does.'

'So the report you wrote is incorrect.'

'No.'

'Explain.'

'The post-mortem makes reference to the autopsy, but the autopsy does not seem to have been included with my report.'

The prosecutor went to rise, but the judge advocate general waved him down.

Roland continued, 'Shouldn't your report clearly state who killed Major Carmichael?'

'It does.'

'Where?'

'The end of the summary on page two and on page twelve in detail, and that is cross-referenced to the autopsy report that was in the appendices.'

'I seem to have a problem, Captain. I do not see the references you refer to.' He was not holding my original report but the replacement report. He was playing a very dodgy game. The prosecutor and his assistant, the defender and his assistant, and the judge advocate general were all looking at the documents. There was a hiatus. The judge advocate general told Roland Parsley to continue. Roland seemed a bit lost.

'The fact is that both soldiers shot Major Carmichael.'

'Yes.'

'Which one fired first?'

'Corporal Munro.'

'How do you know?'

'It came out in my questioning of them.'

'Do you have evidence of this?'

'I wrote it in my report. It's on page thirty-two. It's also on page eight of the original interview under caution of Corporal Munro and on page six of the report of the interview of Sergeant Phillips, again under caution, and the interviews were taped. The army has a copy of each tape and the accused also have copies.'

I could feel the ripple in the attendees in the court. There was some confusion, but there was also a view that could be interpreted in the word 'skulduggery'.

'Captain, you've stated certain facts. You've given references from a report that you claim to have written. I can find no such references in the documents given to me that you purportedly wrote. Can you explain that?'

'No, sir.'

The court was very tense. The prosecution was clearly in a dilemma. Roland Parsley was asking questions that they, the prosecution, would want to ask. Either I was lying or there was a falsification of my report.

Roland looked relaxed. 'I notice you're giving me that information from notes.'

'Yes, sir.'

'Are they contemporaneous notes?'

'No, sir. I wrote them for this trial.'

'Did you know what questions you would be asked?'

Well done; he was guarding his arse against being accused of coaching me.

'No, sir. I've been a witness before as an investigating officer, so I've experience of the key points I'm likely to be asked.'

'What was the source of the notes you're using?'

'A copy of the report sent to the Army Prosecuting Authority.'

The prosecution objected. I had no idea why there should be an objection. The barristers and judge advocate general went into a discussion and then the judge advocate general addressed the court.

'It's not unusual for there to be a discrepancy of information between the defence and the prosecution. What is unusual is the nature of the difference in this particular case. It's the duty of this court to accept the integrity of witnesses who have sworn or affirmed. I intend to proceed. Mr Parsley, please continue.'

'I'd like to ask you about other sources of information. If I were to tell you that the tapes given to the accused were taken from them with all their other belongings and the tapes were lost in transit to the UK, what would you say?'

The prosecution barrister was objecting. I was stunned. Someone was out to get these two guys.

Roland apologized. 'I'll rephrase my question. Captain, I must admit to some ignorance and I would like your confirmation. Am I correct in saying that the copy of evidence tapes given to soldiers are treated in no different way from any other items belonging to a soldier?'

'You're correct, sir.'

'There is, therefore, no reason that an evidence tape should be removed from a soldier's belongings.'

'No reason that I know of, sir.'

'If such a thing was to happen and that event was reported, how would that event be treated within the army?'

There was an objection on the grounds of relevance. The judge advocate general overrode it and I was told to continue.

'It would be treated as a case of theft and investigated by the Royal Military Police.'

'If I was to tell you that the report of such a theft was made and an investigation by the Royal Military Police was held and the tapes were not recovered, what would you say?'

An objection rang out from the prosecution. The advocate general overruled the objection.

I answered. 'I have no idea, sir.'

'Thank you, Captain. So, we should have the other copies. Where would they be?'

'With the other evidence and the transcripts of them.'

'I'm pleased to say they are, as you said, in the evidence bundle and we will hear them to see if they confirm what you've said.'

I wondered what that was all about.

'Oh, just one more point on the tapes. Do you have a transcript of the tapes?'

Again, there was an objection. This one was upheld.

Roland continued, 'Why did Corporal Munro shoot Major Carmichael?'

'To save the lives of the thirty-odd soldiers bogged down in, I think it was called, Al-Zilfi.'

'That pronunciation is near enough. What did the soldiers call it?'

'The Al-Filthy.'

The tension that had been building in the court broke. It was like a sigh of relief. I realized that Roland had intended that.

'You're going to have to explain to the court how Corporal Munro shooting Major Carmichael was going to save lives and why Sergeant Phillips killed him.'

This was going to be tricky. 'The platoon was bogged down. There was a second platoon about a mile away under the command of Lieutenant Gillen – he's now a captain – but they were not, as far as Major Carmichael knew, under attack. It was one of those stupid situations that sometimes happen – radio contact problem. They could send but not receive.'

'Who are "they"?'

'The platoon that was under the command of Major Carmichael could send but not receive.'

'So, Major Carmichael could have called for help but chose not to.'

'That is my understanding, sir.'

'It follows that Captain Gillen did not know the situation because Major Carmichael did not tell him the situation.'

'Not quite true, sir. HQ knew the situation because Lieutenant Mortlake had told them and, at some stage, they told Captain Gillen. But it's true that Major Carmichael did not tell him the situation.'

'I see. On the other hand, Major Carmichael did not know the situation with Captain Gillen's platoon, as there was a problem with reception by the radios at Al-Zilfi.'

'Yes, sir.'

Roland Parsley was making sure the position was crystal clear.

'Go on.'

'Major Carmichael decided to fight his way out toward the other platoon. On the face of it, that seemed okay, except they would have to carry the four wounded. Assuming one-to-one, that was eight men out. That left, at best, twenty-four armed fighting men and their movements would have been hampered by the wounded. The insurgents had automatic weapons, grenade launchers and at least two machine guns, and they had fired some rocket-propelled missiles. Their strength was unknown and they held the high ground that the platoon would have to cross. HQ had recognized that the platoon was in trouble and was in the process of reinforcing the other platoon and launching a rescue mission. Major Carmichael and the soldiers at Al-Zilfi knew this.'

'How did they know? They could not receive information.'

'Yes, Lieutenant Mortlake had radioed HQ outlining his position and said that he would sit tight. It's usual in such situations for an assessment to be made. The action required would be obvious. No problem, sit tight and wait, but Major Carmichael did not want to be rescued by Captain Gillen. They had a personal antipathy.'

The objection rang out.

Roland said, 'I'll call a witness, Captain Cooper, on this point. Please continue, Captain Robinson.'

'The platoon commander, Lieutenant Mortlake, was one of the injured and he proposed sitting tight in accordance with the general recommendation from HQ. Major Carmichael accused him of being a "cowering, fucking wimp", if I remember correctly what one of the men told me. I wrote it in my notes – yes, sir, here. He also said he would have Lieutenant Mortlake "court martialled for cowardice".'

'So, if we call some of the men who you say gave you this information, they will confirm it.'

It was clear to me that Roland was flying by the seat of his pants. The information about what the major said was not in my report and the soldiers were not at the court martial.

'Yes, sir, the men believed Lieutenant Mortlake was anything but a coward. In fact, he had been wounded rescuing one of his men, who unfortunately died. Major Carmichael ordered Sergeant Cooper to prepare the men to move out.'

'Sergeant Cooper?'

'Sergeant Cooper was on attachment to the platoon. He was newly promoted and this was his first patrol in Iraq.'

'Inexperienced then.'

'No, sir, he had considerable experience as a corporal; he was just new to Iraq.'

'You're going to have to clarify something for me, Captain. Who was the senior sergeant?'

'Sergeant Phillips, sir.'

'Why wasn't he ordered to prepare the men to move out?'

'I don't know, sir.'

'What was Sergeant Phillips's relationship with the men?'

'He was their leader, sir. By that, I mean they would follow him into anything.'

'Objection. This is a conclusion and not elicited information.'

Sir Nicolas allowed it with the reprimand that only information from my report was to be elicited.

'So, if he told them to move out, they would have moved out?'

'Definitely, sir, and the converse is also true.'

'I see, I see.' He was allowing the court to reach its own conclusions as to why Sergeant Cooper was given the order to prepare the men. 'So, Sergeant Cooper was ordered to prepare the men to move out. What happened?'

'Sergeant Cooper reported that the platoon was below minimum in small arms ammunition and had no other weaponry available. He was accused of being a liar and a coward and was threatened with a weapon: an SA80.'

'An SA80? That is the standard infantry rifle?'

'Yes, sir.'

'By whom was he accused and threatened?'

You plank, Jake, you should have said. 'Major Carmichael.'

'Go on.'

'It was at that point that Corporal Munro pointed his rifle at Major Carmichael and requested that Major Carmichael lower his weapon or he would be shot.'

'Requested, Captain?'

'I do not have the exact form of words, sir, but I have them here. Yes, he said, "Lower you weapon, sir, or I will shoot you." Corporal Munro was ordered to be quiet and to lower his weapon. Corporal Munro shot Major Carmichael to prevent the shooting of Sergeant Cooper. Major Carmichael then fired two shots at Sergeant Cooper. Sergeant Phillips shot twice and killed Major Carmichael.'

'Let me be quite clear Captain. Major Carmichael pointed his rifle at Sergeant Cooper and threatened him. Corporal Munro told Major Carmichael to lower his weapon. Major Carmichael refused and Corporal Munro shot him. The Major then fired two rounds at Sergeant Cooper. Sergeant Phillips then shot and killed Major Carmichael.'

'Yes, sir.'

'What happened next?'

'Two hours later, an assault by the second platoon began, supported by some American gunships, and the whole thing was cleared up in about four hours. The soldiers knew from the intensity of the battle that they couldn't have fought their way out.'

'Captain Robinson, have you been in similar situations to the one this platoon were in?'

'Yes, sir.'

'Given the information that you gathered and using your experience in Iraq and in similar situations to the one this platoon was in, what do you think of Major Carmichael's decision to fight their way out?'

Again, the objection rang out. A discussion ensued as to whether, as I was not there, I could answer such a question. Roland Parsley argued that he had established that I was an expert witness and had direct evidence from the soldiers present; therefore, I could reach a conclusion. The prosecution argued this was insufficient and Roland asked the judge advocate general whether he could be given leave to establish my credibility. The judge agreed.

'Captain, we have established that you believe you've been in similar situations to that at Al-Zilfi. I notice your medal ribbons. Have you ever received an award for bravery?'

'Yes, sir.'

'What was that award, Captain?'

'The Military Cross, sir.'

'I see. Was that in Iraq?'

It was evident to me that Roland had done his research on me.

'Yes, sir.'

'I would like you to briefly outline the circumstances of that award.'

Oh, shit, how much do I say? 'A platoon was bogged down. The relieving unit ran into heavy resistance. The bogged down platoon had to hold the position for strategic reasons. They had a number of serious injuries and were running short of ammunition. It was similar to Al-Zilfi. I was at a hospital when I picked this up. I took a truck loaded with arms and ammunition. We put on medical supplies. A doctor decided to go with me and some of my men volunteered. I could only take four of them. We ran the gauntlet and got through. I became the ranking officer as the platoon officer was seriously wounded. We held the position.'

'Thank you, Captain. Not only have you been there, you were awarded a medal.' He turned to the judge advocate general. 'Your Honour, I think that establishes the captain's credibility.'

The judge advocate general told Roland to ask the question again.

The recorder read it out, 'Given the information that you gathered and using your experience in Iraq and in similar situations to the one this platoon was in, what do you think of Major Carmichael's decision to fight their way out?'

'Given the information available and given the state of weaponry, it was not the wisest decision to make.'

'A neat, political answer, Captain. Let me approach it a different way; if you had been in charge in such a situation, given the information available at the time, would you have ordered the platoon to fight its way out?'

'No, sir.'

'Why not?'

'In my opinion, it would be reckless and likely to lead to considerable loss of life.'

'But surely, Captain, it would be brave.'

'Sir, bravery is no excuse for stupidity.' I just knew that would result in an objection and I was rebuked by the judge advocate general. But, interestingly, he made no judgment that it was not to be considered in deliberations.

'I'd like to explore your response, Captain. When you took a truck full of arms ammunition and medical supplies, were you being brave or stupid?'

Another objection was presented on the grounds of relevance. Roland Parsley gave some answer that was not particularly meaningful and the judge advocate general allowed it.

I answered, 'I didn't consider it either brave or stupid, sir. It was necessary.'

'Necessary? Why necessary?'

'The purpose in battle is to win with minimum casualties. Without arms and medical aid we would have failed on both criteria.'

'So, in the opinion of the experienced sergeants in Al-Zilfi, neither of the criteria you state would have been met.'

'I agree, sir.'

'Captain, can I get some perspective? After Major Carmichael was killed, how many men at Al-Zilfi were killed or injured?'

An objection rang out and the judge and barristers had a discussion.

'Objection overruled. You can answer, Captain.'

'None.'

'I'm sorry; did you say none?'

'Yes, sir.'

'Of the attacking British and American forces, how many were killed or injured?'

'Two Americans were killed and four American and British soldiers were injured.'

'That is a total of two dead and four injured?'

'Yes, sir.'

'Of the Iraqi forces, how many were killed or injured?'

'Twenty-five killed, thirty-five injured and eighty-seven captured.'

A gasp and muttering could be heard in the court. Silence again descended.

'I make that a minimum of one hundred and forty-four Iraqis who the major would have gone up against.'

'Yes, sir.'

'I have a feeling that your analysis of the situation was correct. What made the massive difference?'

'Shock and awe or, more simply, helicopter gunships and a very large number of heavily armed American soldiers.'

He let what I'd said sink in. It was clear that the platoon could never have fought its way out.

'Let me just go back. Corporal Munro shot Major Carmichael. Major Carmichael then fired two shots at Sergeant Cooper. Could the shots fired by Major Carmichael have been a reaction to being hit by a bullet?'

'Yes, sir, but Major Carmichael intended to shoot Sergeant Cooper.'

The objection rang out. Clearly, the prosecution did not like the way my evidence was going.

'Let me rephrase my question; apart from Major

Carmichael threatening Sergeant Cooper, is there any evidence to show any real intent?'

'Yes, sir; for the weapon to fire, the safety catch must be in the "fire" position. With the SA80, the safety catch is moved to the "fire" position by the trigger finger. Therefore, it must have been set to fire and the major must have had his finger on the trigger. This would be very unusual in the close confines of the defensive position with the weapon not facing the enemy. Another consideration is that the major fired twice. That means he pulled the trigger twice. The second shot is probably unlikely if the trigger was initially pulled due to a reaction. It's more likely to be intentional.'

'But surely, Captain, if the weapon had been selected to automatic, then two rounds could have been fired.'

'It's possible, sir. I would suggest that there are two arguments against that. The first is one of discipline. In a defensive position, the weapon should be set to repetition, not automatic. British soldiers are usually very careful about such things. The second point is that if the weapon was in automatic and was discharged due to a spasm-type reaction, it would be likely to discharge more than two rounds.'

'Thank you, Captain. Wouldn't the argument you've just used apply to Corporal Munro?'

'Definitely, sir, but Corporal Munro was intent on saving Sergeant Cooper's life.'

'Yes, Captain. It's different. Let me make sure I'm clear and the court is clear; Major Carmichael accuses Lieutenant Mortlake of being a coward and then Sergeant Cooper of being a liar and a coward. He's threatening Sergeant Cooper with a weapon, a weapon that is primed to be fired, and he has his finger on the trigger. Corporal Munro requests Major Carmichael to lower his weapon or he will shoot him. Major Carmichael refuses. Corporal Munro shoots Major Carmichael. Major Carmichael's gun discharges two bullets and only two bullets. Sergeant Phillips shoots and kills Major Carmichael with two bullets.'

'Yes, sir.'

'So, Captain, all we have to do is ask Lieutenant Mortlake and Sergeant Cooper their version of events and we will have a clear picture. Is that not so?'

'No.'

'No? Why no?'

'Lieutenant Mortlake left the army on a medical discharge and Sergeant Cooper transferred to the US Marine Corps and is now in the USA.'

'I see, but this court martial could ask Lieutenant Mortlake to be a witness.'

'No. He's in a high-dependency medical facility.'

'What exactly do you mean by that gobbledygook, Captain?'

Why the hell didn't he leave it alone?

'A mental hospital dealing with severely physically and mentally handicapped people.'

'So his wounds caused his deterioration.'

'No, sir.'

'Explain please, Captain.'

'A bullet fired at Sergeant Cooper by Major Carmichael ricocheted from a wall, hit Lieutenant Mortlake and caused brain damage.'

For the first time, I noted a response from the observers in the court.

'That would be after Corporal Munro shot Major Carmichael.'

'Yes, sir.'

'It sounds like the gunfight at the O.K. Corral.'

The prosecution barrister was on his feet protesting.

'I apologize. Let me see if I have this correct. A platoon under the command Lieutenant Mortlake had taken a number of serious casualties: four, to be precise.'

'No, sir. They were the wounded; there were also four dead.'

'Thank you, Captain. The platoon was short of ammunition. The choice the senior officer faced was to wait for reinforcements or fight their way out.'

'No, sir. They were waiting to be rescued.'

'Yes, quite. Major Carmichael took command as the senior officer and made the decision to fight their way out.'

'Yes, sir.'

'I'm at a loss; why was Major Carmichael there if it was Lieutenant Mortlake's platoon?'

'I don't know, sir. Apparently, he arrived with two men – Privates Holt and Wright – after the fire-fight that had pinned down the platoon.'

'I notice you didn't interview Holt and Wright.'

'That is correct, sir.'

'Why not?'

'They had been transferred out, sir.'

'Come on, Captain. This is the British Army and we are dealing with a murder inquiry. Surely you would be able to interview two soldiers who were present at the alleged killing.'

'My request was blocked. The two men had been transferred and then I had no idea where or why.'

'You said "then"; do you mean you know where they are now?'

'No, sir. By "then" I meant at that time and I now believe it was to prevent me getting vital information.'

The prosecutor was on his feet, objecting.

The judge advocate general was glowering at me. 'Captain, you're implying a conspiracy.'

'I apologize, sir. I should have said that as I couldn't get access to these two men I couldn't question them. I've no understanding of why my access was blocked.'

There was a rumbling from the people observing. I had

no feel of what they were thinking, but there had been a shift.

The judge advocate general looked at me, long and hard. I was beginning to see that a defence barrister could look like he was defending the accused and could actually get them found guilty. Thank God for the change of barrister. The chief inspector's call was spot on. Jase Phillips and Mike Munro would have been trussed up like turkeys. And the colonel was correct; I was right out on a limb.

The judge advocate general said, 'I'm having some concerns about this case. There are many inconsistencies. Let me ask one question of you, Captain. You said in evidence that both Sergeant Phillips and Corporal Munro shot at Major Carmichael, but the autopsy report said it was Sergeant Phillips's bullets that actually killed him. Why is this not in the report I have?' The old bugger was testing the evidence being presented and he was using me to do it.

'Your Honour, you have the post-mortem report done here in the UK. I'm referring to the autopsy report done by the Americans in Iraq.' I knew he knew this.

He turned to the prosecutor. 'Why do I not have that report?'

The prosecutor shook his head. 'I have no record of such a report, Your Honour. The post-mortem report refers to an initial autopsy, but gives no detail.'

The judge advocate general turned to Roland Parsley. 'Do you have this report?'

'No, sir.'

I kept my face as blank as I could. I knew he had a copy. 'Captain, you have this autopsy report?'

'I have a copy. Yes, sir. The original was sent to the Army Prosecuting Authority offices.'

The judge advocate general spoke to both the counsels, 'I will see you both in my chambers.'

Now the shit will hit the fan, I thought. I was sent for and asked to hand in all my documents, including my personal notes, to the judge advocate general's office.

15

Days passed. People turned up at the court... Nothing. I was then given a date. I turned up on time at 10.00 a.m. and there appeared to be some activity. I sat in a waiting room. The clock had a loud tick and seemed to be going excessively slowly. It reached 11.25 a.m. and the court orderly told me to attend the judge advocate general in his chambers. As I entered the chambers, I noted that the judge advocate general was behind a desk. A long, matching table jutted out from his desk so that it formed the leg of a T. The prosecution and defence advocates and two men in suits that I did not know sat at this table. The court recorder sat to one side of the room.

The judge advocate general said, 'Come in and sit down, please, Captain.' He indicated a chair at the end of the table, at the bottom of the T, so I directly faced him. On my left were Roland Parsley and next to him the prosecution barrister, Major Nigel Reynolds QC. The two men in suits were on my right.

'Let me introduce Superintendent Alex West and Mr Singh Kohli of HM Crown Prosecution Service Inspectorate.'

They nodded to me. The atmosphere was stiff. The judge advocate general was clearly in total control and was not a happy bunny.

'We have a real problem, Captain,' he said. 'Murder cases are never simple, but this one did not did not seem complex. The facts appeared to be relatively clear, but the circumstances were a bit, shall we say, um, difficult to understand. The reasoning behind some decisions was open to question and there were elements that would appear to include the concept of mutiny. Your evidence complicated matters; there is an implication in what you said of tampering with evidence. I must say a quick check of what appears to be the main discrepancies confirms what is written in your initial report. I have to make some decisions. I've already made one decision and that is to initiate an inquiry into the whole conduct of the investigation and the preparation of the materials for this court martial. Superintendent West of the Metropolitan Police, Special Branch, will conduct the first half of that inquiry.'

That seemed odd, as it was a murder inquiry. Or if it were an investigation of me, I would expect an anti-corruption squad investigation.

He paused. He expected me to say something.

'I understand, Your Honour.'

'Good. What I'd like you to do is outline the process of your investigation. I want no content, only process. Are you clear, Captain?'

'Now, Your Honour?'

'Yes, now, Captain.' There was some irritation in his voice.

'Yes, Your Honour.' I was feeling distinctly irritated by the 'Your Honour' thing. And now I had to talk through the investigation with no preparation. Where the hell should I start? 'I am – no – I *was* responsible for a large Royal Military Police unit based in Basra, Iraq. I had three responsibilities. The first was the field training of Iraqi police. To that end, I had men posted at local police stations. Secondly, I had a contingency group, fifteen strong to patrol and handle police emergencies in my designated zone and, thirdly, it was my responsibility to lead any criminal investigations that related to British servicemen in my designated zone. For the first two responsibilities, I reported to Major Blackstone. For the third responsibility, I reported directly to Lieutenant

Colonel McCabe. On the twenty-seventh of October, I received an order to report to Colonel McCabe's office. I was briefed that Major Carmichael had been shot and killed and that an initial investigation indicated that it was suspected murder. The body was at an American military hospital.'

'Major Carmichael's body?'

'I apologize, Your Honour; Major Carmichael's body was at an American military hospital. All the injured were there. The two men, Sergeant Jason Phillips CGC and Corporal Michael Munro, were being held with the rest of the soldiers at a small camp under restriction by the RMP. The soldiers were being kept in close confinement.'

'So the death of Major Carmichael was outside of your designated zone?'

'Yes, Your Honour.'

'Why were you appointed to undertake the investigation?'

'I don't know, sir, but the Americans were first on the scene. It was their zone and I liaised with them and then took over.'

The Superintendent made a note.

'Go on, Captain, please.'

'I asked the US medical authorities to conduct an autopsy, but they had already conducted one. Not only that, the US Military Police had conducted some forensic work with their medical authorities. They had produced a report and talked my sergeant and me through it.'

'Your sergeant was a Sergeant J Billinghurst?'

'Yes, Your Honour.'

'Why didn't he render your original report to the court?'

'Sergeant Billinghurst is female, Your Honour. I don't know who or why the decision was made to exclude her. She has first-hand knowledge of the whole investigation and is a first-class investigator.'

'I think that is something else that needs to be looked into, Superintendent and Mr Kohli.'

'Yes, Your Honour.' Both Superintendent West and Mr Kohli were now making notes.

'So, Captain, you had an autopsy report and I assume you then interviewed the accused and witnesses.'

'Yes, Your Honour.'

Superintendent West looked at me. 'Have you a list of all those interviewed?'

'Yes, Superintendent.'

The judge advocate general intervened, 'Why would you want that? It's the process you're investigating and not the inquiry. You will be given copies of all of the investigation materials. I believe you can assume Captain Robinson is a competent police officer.'

'Yes, Your Honour. Thank you, sir.'

I'd an uneasy feeling about Superintendent West.

Sir Nicolas Ross's sharp eyes turned to me. 'Let me see; your inquiry done, you produced your report and that went to Army Prosecution Authority. Was that you, Major Reynolds?'

'Yes, Your Honour.'

'As I understand it, the report you received differed from the one written by Captain Robinson and did not include the autopsy report but did include a later post-mortem report.'

'It seems that is the case, Your Honour.'

'Well, Superintendent, it seems you have something to get your teeth into. Mr Kohli, something fell down the cracks here. Major Reynolds, did you conduct any pre-liminary examination to clarify the evidence or to assess the credibility of witnesses?'

'The information I received seemed complete, Your Honour. It was, as far as I was concerned, a complete case.'

'But you did not review it with Captain Robinson or Sergeant Billinghurst?'

'No, Your Honour.'

'Why not?'

'They were unavailable in Iraq and the case was accelerated.'

Now he was under pressure. It was unacceptable not to review the information. No report was ever complete and this was likely to be a high-profile murder case.

'Yes, it was brought forward. Why?'

'I don't know, Your Honour. I'd assumed that was your availability. I was put under considerable pressure to be prepared for the dates of the court martial, sir.'

'Mr Bartholomew, you were similarly, um, pressurized?'

'Unfortunately, yes, Your Honour.'

'It seems we have an unduly expedited case. That is something else that needs to be investigated, Mr Kohli.'

'Thank you, Major Reynolds. Thank you, Mr Bartholomew. Captain, I expect the superintendent may wish to ask you further questions at some time. Just one question, out of interest: what is your personal view of this case?'

What does the old bugger mean? That is so ambiguous.

'Your Honour, this was a very dangerous situation. In such situations, people may not behave in ways that seem sensible or logical in the cold light of a courtroom. Sergeant Phillips, Sergeant Cooper and Corporal Munro were the most experienced men there. They are battle-hardened veterans. They are the sorts of people I would listen to when in a battle situation. Sergeant Phillips and Corporal Munro had good reason to shoot Major Carmichael. I hope in a similar situation that I would have that courage. They knew where it would lead.'

'Thank you, Captain, but surely Major Carmichael was more experienced.'

'No, Your Honour. In that situation, he was just more senior.'

The judge advocate general stared at me. 'A very useful insight, Captain. You may go.'

'Thank you, Your Honour.'

'Before you go, is there any other comment you want to make or question you wish to ask?'

I'm sure he expected a 'No, sir'.

'Yes, sir.'

I was right; he looked surprised.

'Ask away, Captain.'

'Why are the Met dealing with this and not the Royal Military Police?'

'Ah! Do you doubt the competence of the Metropolitan Police, Captain?'

'In this circumstance, yes, sir.'

'Can you tell me why?'

'The Metropolitan Police is a civilian body, sir. It has no experience of dealing with military matters, no combat experience and no experience of Iraq. In a reversed situation of a murder trial from, say, the West End of London, the RMP would not be called in to assess the processes.'

'I see you challenge the competence of the Metropolitan Police.'

'In this circumstance, yes, Your Honour.'

'Then you deserve an explanation. You're correct in all you've said and it was those points that were put to Home Office and the offices of the Military Criminal Justice System. The Home Office professional standards unit recommended complete independence. The Adjutant General Lieutenant General PR Mackenzie agreed to this recommendation. How this officer was appointed,' he dismissively waved his hand at Superintendent West, 'is to do with the mysteries of the Home Office. It seems eminently sensible that Mr Singh Kohli looks at the internal processes that led to the APA having different information from that which you say you provided. You don't appear satisfied.'

'I have a second question.'

'Ask it.'

'Superintendent West, is Special Branch, does he have experience of investigating murders?'

'Now that is a very interesting question, Captain. Yes, Superintendent West is in Special Branch, or whatever it's called these days, but, Captain, he's only looking at process, so perhaps he doesn't need real experience of investigating a murder.'

'Thank you, Your Honour.'

It was clear that the judge advocate general was no happier than me. Perhaps he could smell the same political interference that I could or perhaps he thought for some reason that I had produced a false set of documents.

16

The court martial was reconvened the following Wednesday. I was sitting with the other witnesses at the back of the court. The court was called to order and the judge advocate general came in, followed by the president and other lay members; they sat at the bench. This was odd. This was the normal structure for sentencing, but the case was incomplete.

The judge advocate general banged his gavel: another odd thing. There was silence and he began to speak.

'It's not unusual for a court martial to be faced with a unique set of circumstances. It could be said that every court martial has some unique aspect. What is unique is for a judge to be faced with a situation that has in law no clear direction. Such a situation has arisen in this case.

'The investigation of the death of Major Carmichael had been carried out thoroughly and appropriately, providing the information from which the Army Prosecution Authority could have made an appropriate decision. The decision to prosecute was taken appropriately and all evidential tests had been met within the limitations imposed on the Army Prosecution Authority. It's essential when faced with such a situation that we revert to first principles. The prime principle in this case is that the accused are presumed innocent until proven guilty. What has emerged is information that leads me, after discussion with the president, to either dissolve this court or to discontinue. My decision is to discontinue.'

A buzz arose. Sir Nicolas Ross let it subside.

'Both the accused, Sergeant Jason Phillips CGC and Corporal Michael Munro, are acquitted of all charges and any associated charges that may have been brought, given the evidence compiled during the investigation into the death of Major Carmichael. The events leading to my decision will be investigated.'

The judge advocate general and the lay members left, and the court orderly closed the proceedings. There was a buzz of speculation. I would have made my way to Jase and Mike, but reporters were besieging them.

I was unhappy. I had an unhappy feeling that an hon-ourable judge was going to be hung out to dry. I had a feeling that I would be implicated in something, but what I did not know and I needed to talk to Josey Billinghurst to find out what sort of shit she was in and whether it involved me.

17

When the proceedings were over I decided to make my way to my new home. I'd never shared a flat on a platonic basis before, but life was full of change. I must admit, I'd tried it at university, but it didn't work. I just ended up in bed with one of the female flatmates and I was never quite sure how that happened. There used to be a song in one of the musicals from the 1940s that had the words, 'A boy chases a girl until she catches him.' It seemed to me that I just got caught in the honey trap, but I seemed to escape in the nick of time. I reckoned I would make a lousy husband.

I jumped into my brand-new, second-hand BMW, well brand new to me, and it just sang down the A12. It was a beaut. Only two years old, but it had 40,000 miles on the clock. That may sound a lot, but it wasn't for a 3-litre, series three coupe and I would get a new one in a year. The only thing wrong was some trolley scratched on the doors. I supposed that was the penalty of parking at a supermarket. Frances helped me get it from somebody in the car pool named Mac. Apparently I didn't rate a car of this elegance.

As I approached Chelmsford, I pulled into a service station, complete with a Little Chef, filled up my beautiful, blue dream car and went for a coffee. The waitress brought my drink over on a tray and I immediately noticed a folded sheet of paper lying on it.

It said, *I think I am going to have to take you seriously. You have won the first round. You will lose if you upset me again. In the meantime, I leave you a small symbol of my friendship.*

What kind of childish nonsense was this? Was it a serious threat or some kind of joke? I slipped it into my pocket.

I finished my coffee, paid at the desk and went into the car park. My car, my beautiful dream car was wrecked. I couldn't move for a moment, I just couldn't believe it. My beautiful car was absolutely totalled. It was an unrecognizable pile of junk. Two policemen were standing by it.

'Is this your car, sir?'

'I think it was my car.'

'I think you must have upset somebody. Can I see your licence and insurance?'

I pointed at the wreck. He made a note.

'How did this happen?' I asked.

He looked around the car park.

For the first time I looked around. It was empty. Well the restaurant area was empty.

'It happens, sir.' The policemen shrugged.

It would seem that nobody saw anything. In a large, open car park a car was totally wrecked and nobody saw a thing.

He took my details in a calm, neutral way, and was remarkably offhand. He smiled, gave me a card and said, 'I expect your insurance company will want some paperwork, but we are very busy at the moment, so it may take some time.' He gave me the number of a scrap dealer and then said, 'Have it removed.' I was getting a tiny feeling that the policemen knew exactly who had done this.

The weather was improving and it was turning into a nice day despite it being Wednesday. The sun was shining and the breeze was unseasonably warm. It was an ideal day to have your brand-new, second-hand car wrecked.

I rang Frances, left a voicemail to the effect that I was stranded on the A12 and would she give me a call. I then phoned BMW and told them what had happened. The very polite man on the phone clearly didn't believe me, although he maintained his professionalism. My next call was to the insurance company to tell them what had happened. The girl was polite, formal and suggested I get the car moved to a BMW garage, where one of their surveyors would assess the damage.

After a short wait, a BMW mechanic arrived from a local BMW garage. He stood and looked at the wreck for some time. I think he figured out that he was not going to get this wreck on the road, so he made a call and a large lorry, complete with crane from the local scrap yard, arrived. The mechanic and the scrap man had a conversation more of a personal nature than anything to do with my car, then the scrap man came to see me and the mechanic got back on the phone.

'Christ, what 'appened, mate?' This seemed an appropriate question.

'I upset somebody.'

'Looks like it, mate. Was she worth it?'

I smiled at his assumption. 'I think perhaps it was.'

Moments later, Nikki's white 8C Spider pulled up with the black soft-top down. The 4.5-litre engine rumbled and the exhaust burbled. Nikki alighted (she didn't just get out; she alighted), swung those exquisite legs, knees together, through the open door, placed her very high-heeled shoes onto the tarmac and gently rose. The car door swung closed with a well-engineered clunk. The scrap man watched her walk toward us.

'Fuck me, mate. She's fucking worth it.'

'Oh, Jake, what a shame,' she said in her mellow, husky, middle-class accent. She took my arm in a very familiar gesture, kissed me on the cheek and smiled at the scrap man. 'Good afternoon,' she said to him, giving him a dazzling smile, and I'm sure he blushed. She was definitely in the wrong profession; the cinema had lost a gem. The embarrassed scrap man left to supervise the loading.

'So, Jake,' she said, 'they've surfaced and you've only been on board a couple of weeks. Let's go and talk to the staff in the restaurant.'

The girl who served me was no help, as the woman on the cash desk had given her the note. The woman on the cash desk described the man, but it could have been anybody, 5ft 10in to 6ft, blond hair cut short, going bald and about twenty-five years old. We then checked the CCTV. There were three cameras and one had a shot of a man who could be our man, but it was very poor quality. With no leads to follow, it was back to London. As we drove down the A12, I told her what happened at the trial.

Back at the office, the whole thing amused Frances, but Mac was less than happy. He got me another car, almost identical to the first one, except it only had 30,000 miles on the clock. The age was the same so I would get a new one in a year. Altogether, it was a zero sum game for me. Wrecking my car was just spiteful. I'd upset a well-designed and executed plan and so they wrecked my car. No, it wasn't just spiteful; it was childish as well.

18

I'd been working in my new job about three weeks and had been appointed as an intelligence officer, just to get my feet under the table, while one of the officers who normally did this job was away on holiday. I had the impression that it was normal for newly recruited operatives to have this initial spell as an intelligence officer.

The best thing about the job was the hours: nine to five. I'd never had a nine-to-five job before and, as I was temporary, I was not on the duty list. It also followed, more or less, the same routine every day, which started with coffee at 9.00 a.m. while my computer went through its checks and downloaded emails. While that was happening and between sips of coffee, I listened to the voicemails.

This particular morning, my last day in this position, I had a message from Azif. He was monitoring the telephone calls of one of our targets: a UK businessman who was suspected of having links with a South American businessman in the oil industry and was believed to be connected to the illegal drug trade. I wasn't clear what this was all about, but it seemed to be part of Barrow's domain. The businessman also had some sort of political links, but what they were I wasn't privy to. Azif had called to let me know that our suspect was expecting a visitor from overseas and had arranged to meet this person the next morning at 11.00 a.m. at Victoria Station. I asked Sara, an admin assistant, to run the name of this visitor through our databases. Bingo! The visitor was a member of a Bolivian drug group based in France. This triggered a link to the Serious and Organized Crime Unit. As Sara started a file on the visitor, she also checked the visitor's mobile number, which came up during our target's conversation. A second hit: the number had come to our attention before. I triggered the surveillance section to find out whether it was possible to cover this meeting tomorrow. It was and they wanted me at a briefing at 2.00 p.m. I told Frances and she told me not to bother, as one of the other sections would handle it. The good thing about this job was that I was getting to know who did what and how the machine worked.

As I was leaving the building, pleased that it was the end of my last day when my phone rang; it was Frances.

'Jake, go to the Duke of Clarence on Old Brompton Road.'

'Okay. Now?'

'Yes, I will see you there.'

'Okay. Bye.' That was short and to the point.

I nipped down onto the tube and in about ten minutes I was off at Gloucester Road and walking toward my target pub. Frances appeared at my side.

'Let's go to the Drayton Arms.'

'Okay.'

I supposed the Drayton Arms would call itself a traditional pub, but to me it was the modern equivalent of a traditional pub. The worst thing about it was that it welcomed children. Well, it said *kids*, but it was more modern than that, so I expected it meant the brats whose favourite two words seemed to be 'I wanna.' Come back, Herod – all is forgiven! But enough of my prejudice.

We had no sooner settled into the comfortable seats, which I was sure traditional pubs could never afford, when in walked Jase and Mike.

'What's yours, Captain?' Jase was in first.

'Sit down and behave yourselves,' Frances commanded. 'Two pints of bitter, is it?'

'Yes, ma'am,' they both said together.

She smiled and headed for the bar.

'Your new boss, Captain? Or something more?'

'I could tell you, Jase, but then we would have to assassinate you. So, for what nefarious exploit do we owe the pleasure?'

'How can I describe this, Captain? Yes, I know – we're in the shit.'

'Not again. Who did you shoot this time?'

'It's the same case.'

'But it was dismissed.'

'Different angle; something about failing to obey an order in the face of the enemy and something about conspiracy to pervert the course of justice.'

'No, Jase, the whole thing was quashed. The judge threw out the whole kit and caboodle.'

'To whom have you been talking?' Frances had re-joined us with the beers. She was in superior mode.

'Nobody. Two coppers have been talking to some of the lads. A sergeant in Army Legal Services tipped us off.'

'And?'

'And they want to talk to us tomorrow.'

'Where?'

'MOD.'

'How strange. Have you a solicitor?'

'No. Well, not yet anyway.'

'Ring Keith Todd.'

'Suppose he can't do it.'

'Ring me,' said Frances. She started rummaging in her handbag, 'But whatever you do, don't take the duty solicitor.' She handed them each one of her cards.

'Why?' I asked.

'Because this smells fishy and if it's the duty solicitor he may just be somebody you don't want.'

'What do we do then?' Jase sounded worried, as well he might.

I answered, 'I'm going to give you a crash course in buggering a police interrogation. Pay attention. This is going to be quick and dirty, and you're going to have to remember what I'm saying. The upside is that Frances is going to buy you dinner in this luxurious establishment. Okay?'

'Yes, sir,' they both spoke together and laughed.

Frances just smiled and shook her head. 'Clients are supposed to pay their consultants, not the other way round.'

'Okay, fellas, start listening. If you don't understand, ask. If you have other questions about something I say, ask.' I looked at each of them. They nodded.

I started, 'The police will attempt to put over an impression of having greater knowledge of your activities than is true; don't be fooled. They will tell lies. Hints may be dropped that they have evidence that can't be revealed yet. They are looking for confirmation of their suspicions or something to use from what you say. So the less you say the better. It's best that you say nothing at all. If asked a direct question and you don't know the answer, or you don't want to tell them, or it seems like they are fishing, just say, "No comment".'

'Won't that make us look guilty?'

'Yes and they will say that to you. Ignore it. If they ask you something you can answer and you see no problem in answering, ask them why they want to know. Let's try that, okay?'

They both nodded.

'How did you come here today?'

'By Underground.' It was Jase.

'No, Jase. You have to ask me why I want to know. Let's try again. Did you come by the Underground today?'

'Yes… Um, no… Um, bollocks,' said Jase.

'Okay, Mike, I'm going to ask you another question and you're going to ask me why I want to know. Do you want another pint?'

'Yes.' He shook his head. 'You bloody bastard.' Mike was laughing.

'This is serious, Mike. These guys, guys like me, are trained to get confessions from people or create an evidence base that can lead to your conviction even if you've done nothing wrong. It's their job and don't believe they are honest. One more time; are you finding this difficult?'

'Why do you want to know?'

'Great, Mike.'

'You're a slippery bastard. I nearly said yes.'

'You get the message then; these policemen are, as you described them, slippery bastards. They will pull other tricks. Beware of statements getting you to agree. You do understand, don't you?'

'Yes.' Jase had dropped in. 'I've got it. They will ask me a number of questions or say things I agree with so I'm used to saying yes, and then they slip me a crippler.'

'Spot on, Jase. It puts you in a frame of mind that makes it more difficult for you to lie or to disagree. If you do attempt to change out of a yes mode, then they will leap on it with increased pressure.'

'So what shall we do?'

'Being vague sometimes helps. Think of the thickest person you know and respond like him. So what sorts of responses would he give?'

'I don't know.'

'Great, Jase.'

'No, I really don't. Someone is going to kill you soon, Captain, and it might just be me.'

Both Jase and Mike were laughing.

'If you want to break up that sort of questioning, some of the things you might use are, "I don't know," "Tell me again," "Ask me that again," "Do you think I'm thick?" and "Can we have something to eat?"'

'Okay,' said Frances, 'I'll get a menu.'

'Tell me what you think of this so far.'

'Is this another trick question?'

'No, Jase, but if it was, you gave a spot-on response.'

'It's like a game,' said Jase. 'They are trying to catch us out and we are trying to stop them.'

'And the best way to stop them is what, Mike?'

'Don't tell them bugger all.'

'I do believe he has it. The coppers will be sharp and pick up on things you might not have realized you'd said, so say nothing.'

'What about "no comment"?' Mike asked.

'What about it?'

'Well, it sounds like you're guilty or have something to hide.'

'Yes. So what?'

'I bloody hope you're not our bloody interrogator.'

'If you remember, I was your interrogator and you were open and straightforward about what you'd done. You hid some things from me, but I got what I wanted and you went to trial. This time is different. Someone is trying to nail you for something you haven't done. Doesn't matter what the coppers think. They can think you're as guilty as hell, but without evidence they're buggered.'

'I don't really like "no comment".'

'So say something else. Go on, try something else.'

'I will say nothing.'

'So, you've something to hide?'

'No.'

'Then answer my questions and show you're honest and innocent.'

'No, because you will twist what I say.'

'What are you doing wrong now?'

'I'm bloody talking. You got me justifying myself and the more I talk, the more likely I am to say something I shouldn't.'

'Okay, fellas, let's eat.'

Frances offered them menus. We ordered and ate, but I had this nagging problem. Why was the Met – I assumed it was the Met – gunning for these two guys?

'What are you doing now?'

'We are at an Aldershot training camp, supposed to be preparing people for Iraq.'

'And?'

'So far we've had no real trouble. There was silence.'

That concerned me. They were having trouble but not real trouble.

Frances picked this up.

'Are you happy in the army?'

'S'pose,' said Mike.

'Jase?' I probed.

'It's not like it was.'

'What isn't?'

'Well, we're side-lined with a bunch of no-hopers and that makes us look bad.'

I recognized the problem as I had seen it before.

'Do you want out?' asked Frances.

'S'pose,' said Mike.

'Have you any dependents?'

'Like kids and stuff?' asked Jase.

'Yes, like wives, kids, grannies. You know – dependents.'

'No, well, not anymore,' said Jase.

'What happened, Jase? You were married?'

'Yes – well – I still am, but – well – I went to Iraq and then I thought I was going to prison and – well, yer know – we sort of broke up.'

'And you, Mike?'

'Sort of,' said Mike.

Frances turned to me. 'Have you ever realized how tough it is pulling teeth?'

I laughed.

111

'Try this,' she said. 'If we wanted you two to go and do a job in Mozambique for six months, would that create any problems?'

'Only problem is that I don't know where the fuck that is,' said Mike.

Frances laughed. 'Okay, I've got what I wanted.'

19

The following day, I got a call at about 4.30 p.m.; it was Keith Todd. I had been on tenterhooks all day, but I shouldn't have been because I knew that Frances had phoned a friend while I'd been briefing Jase and Mike, and he had phoned Keith Todd, who had agreed to represent them as their solicitor.

'I need to see you today, Jake,' Keith said urgently.

Now that was a surprise, so I just agreed.

We met in the City Inn on Millbank at 6.00 p.m. I arrived first and then Keith came in, smiled, walked over and said, 'Let's walk.' So, we walked. We crossed over Lambeth Bridge and along the embankment. We were not followed.

'Okay, what's the problem?'

'They're not interested in your two soldiers; they're interested in you.'

'Me?'

'I reckon they are trying to set you up on a conspiracy to pervert the course of justice.'

'But why? I know they want to show that Carmichael was whiter than white and that my evil left a black smear on The Family.' I thought for a moment; if they could pin a conspiracy on me they could then get Jase and Mike. 'Got it. Who are the policemen?' I asked.

'That is interesting. West and Alleyne.'

'Alleyne?'

'Oh, he's an inspector that works with West.'

'But they were asked to look into the process I used to gather information on the killing.'

'Right. If they can show you cocked up or tampered with

113

the evidence, two things happen: one, you're a dead duck as far as the army is concerned and if it's the second option, you will go to prison and Major Carmichael again becomes a hero. But I'm not clear why someone would want to do this or who that would be.'

'How can they get me? I've done nothing wrong.'

'But think of the story this way: you do the inquiry, you write two different reports. One report you send to the Army Prosecution Authority. The court martial begins but you, bless your cotton socks, are not available and strangely your sergeant is not available either. So some gullible lieutenant, who is as pure as the driven snow, presents the information. You pop up and blow holes through the evidence. The defence barrister feeds you some prize questions, the judge advocate general gets all confused and your mates get off.'

'Okay, let's assume some plank buys that story. What's in it for me? How on earth would I benefit?'

'A good question, Jake. I bet the opposition is working on it. Let me just make one other point. Your opposition has already manufactured the evidence to get the trial in the first place. Don't you think they may just be able to generate some clinchers?'

I was feeling distinctly unhappy. 'I come back to why. I know Antony Bray wants to show that Carmichael was whiter than white, but this is going a bit far, isn't it?'

Keith thought for a minute. 'The why is easy; over and above Carmichael being related to Antony Bray, we have the political dimension. Bray is the personal private secretary to James Bradshaw, our current home secretary, and is destined for high office. Can't have anything messy in The Family or related to the government, but I'm thinking there are links we know nothing about. There's something special about Carmichael. Either Bray or Bradshaw is orchestrating this.'

114

'Why would West and Alleyne get involved?'

'Personal gain of some description?'

'It could be, but they would also have to be sold some organizational reason. They are not criminals.'

'Not criminals in the normal sense, but they could be doing a favour for a politician.'

'Not sure. I can think of a reason, but it's far-fetched.'

'Tell me,' said Keith.

'I'm army seconded to a special MI5 outfit that nobody knows about. I'm working with a bunch of nutters who have special dispensation to do things nobody else is allowed to do and the minister doesn't control it. This unit is an anomaly and The Family is its prime target. I know you know about it; otherwise, why would you be here? And you mentioned The Family, so you know more than other solicitors.'

'Okay, I slipped up, but I'm not a member of Barrow's unit or MI5. Tell me what I'm into.'

'Okay, Barrow's outfit is sort of part of MI5 but separate and works with MI5 and the Met. Both sides are a bit itchy that they don't control this unit. They're itchy because this unit has political corruption as its *raison d'être*. Now the government also needs some control to limit the extent of any investigations that might be embarrassing. We saw that in the inquiries into weapons of mass destruction, and that scientist guy supposedly committing suicide.'

'Dr David Kelly,' said Keith

'That's right. The Hutton inquiry turned over all the information, but because of the terms of reference, the government and Blair in particular were exonerated.'

'So, if you turn out to be a bad boy, the unit is embarrassed to the extent that it comes directly under MI5 or the Met, and the home secretary regains control. Then West will be a hero and probably get a promotion or knighthood or something.'

'Perhaps not a knighthood.'

We both laughed. Keith stared at me.

'What?'

'Who *did* tamper with the evidence? Somebody did and by looking at the process that started with you it should show who that could be.'

'Don't ask me.'

'It has to be in the MOD or the Home Office.'

'Look, I'm in the shit and I don't know what to do about it.'

'Oh! But I do. You just keep your head down. I will visit an old friend of the family; he will talk to his friend Judge Advocate General Sir Nicolas Ross and I think this could either explode or just quietly slip away.'

'Can I ask you why you've become involved?'

'Easy; I was at school with Carmichael and Bray, and Bray was a bastard: a very clever, bullying bastard who made the lives of some of my friends hell.'

'And Carmichael?'

'He was the muscle. He was a bit strange in the friends he had, but okay generally. But if anybody threatened Bray, they had Carmichael to deal with.'

'Strange friends?'

'Yes. He was the all-conquering sports hero: rugby, boxing, cricket, athletics, cross-country and basketball. You name it, he was the star. There was this little band of followers. We called them the homos. They were the arty ones. A lot of the young kids in the school worshipped him, but he favoured the homos.'

20

The next day, Barrow sent for me. When I arrived, his secretary told me to go to conference room 4, where I was confronted with a number of people: Judge Advocate General Sir Nicolas Ross, Barrow, Frances, Superintendent Alex West and some people I had not met. I knew one of them, but I'd never met him. It was Sir Antony Newham-Taylor, the newly appointed head of MI5, or TNT as he had been christened sometime in his career.

'Ha, you will be Captain Robinson, the centre of the turmoil that is disrupting my life.' TNT said this in an easy way that demonstrated he did not blame me for whatever the problem was and that his life was not being disrupted.

'Good morning, sir.'

'You know most of the other people here, but not Lieutenant Commander Philpot of the MOD or Mr Coxhead of the Home Office.' We shook hands.

'I'm going to review the progress of the investigation into the death of Major Michael Carmichael DSC. This is less an inquiry into his death and more an inquiry into the investigation carried out by the military police. I welcome questions and I will occasionally call upon individuals to confirm or maybe explain what the findings are. Now the faithful Nina will bring us all up to date.'

For the first time, I noticed a very serious, young, flat-chested woman, who could have been the model for the ideal librarian: very large, horn-rimmed spectacles, mousey brown hair in a bun, no makeup and no smile. Ian Fleming had some great descriptions of Russian or East German women who were evil personified, like Rosa Klebb, who

defected from the Russian secret service, the KGB, to join
SPECTRE. Nina, likewise, was an ideal that nobody could
invent. I could imagine she had first-class honours from
Oxbridge and all the necessary experience to be the ideal
person for the role she had, but I didn't know what that was.

The young woman stepped forward. From the way Sir
Antony had initially spoken, I'd assumed he would do the
talking, but this was not the case. Nina quickly gave the
background: Major Michael Carmichael DSC had been
shot; two soldiers shot him – Sergeant Jason Phillips CGC
and Corporal Michael Munro. She outlined the case, the
anomalies and the judgment of Judge Advocate General Sir
Nicolas Ross. She dealt with his instruction to Superintendent West to review the process that I'd used and Mr
Singh Kohli had reviewed the APA process. She then moved
toward some conclusions.

'Mr Singh Kohli has concluded that there is nothing
wrong with the process and the only way that the problem
could have arisen is by deliberate falsification. He reached a
tentative conclusion that this occurred by Captain Robinson
falsifying information separately from that rendered to the
APA, or the information received into the APA was falsified.' She paused to let that sink in. 'The findings by
Superintendent West were that this was a textbook investigation. In fact, it was so clean that he believed there must be
something seriously wrong and that there had been tampering with evidence, perverting the course of justice and
leading to a miscarriage of justice. From the narrowness of
his remit, Superintendent West was unable to identify
exactly who or how the perverting of justice occurred. It
would seem that Superintendent West and Mr Singh Kohli
are to some extent in agreement.'

I interrupted, 'May I ask a question?'

'Yes, you may, Captain.' It was Sir Nicolas Ross who
responded.

'You said there was some evidence that there was tampering with evidence, but we know evidence went missing, such as the autopsy report, and witnesses became unavailable to me – including Privates Wright and Holt – and later to the court, namely Sergeant Josey Billinghurst.'

Sir Nicolas spoke, 'In terms of the process of your investigation, no problems were noted by Superintendent West.'

'Then why am I the subject of investigation?'

'Captain, you're not, as far as I'm concerned, the subject of investigation, but I hope to show that somebody is.'

Superintendent West intervened, 'With respect, Sir Nicolas, I disagree. If some malpractice took place, then I believe it was during the Military Police investigation.'

So, West was going to lay down the bait that would lead me into a trap.

Sir Nicolas Ross fixed him with his eye. 'Superintendent West, belief is not necessarily the truth. Secondly, if some malfeasance occurred during the investigation, it does not necessarily imply that Captain Robinson was the architect of that malfeasance.'

Westy was clearly batting for some team and it was definitely not mine.

Sir Antony Newham-Taylor moved the meeting forward, 'Nina, I would be grateful if you would continue.'

Did she smile? Did I detect a minimal movement around the lips? Or was it a sneer?

'Yes, Sir Antony.' She recommenced her narration. Strangely, she had no notes; she was just telling us. 'As the process was, from Captain Robinson's point of view, complete, the information he had gathered went to the Army Prosecution Authority. They decided upon the information they had been given to progress with the court martial of Sergeant Phillips CGC and Corporal Munro. During subsequent proceedings, it was demonstrated that the information upon which the decision to prosecute was made was incomplete or was complete and subsequently tampered with. This also raised the question of whether or not the information presented by Captain Robinson was correct.'

Here we go. Jake Robinson did it.

'Discussions with the Judge Advocate General Sir Nicolas Ross and Brigadier Sir Humphrey Ballington resulted in the decision to reinvestigate the case. Lieutenant Commander Philpot of the Royal Naval Special Investigations Branch was given the task.'

Sir Antony said, 'Commander, please give us a very brief account of what you found.'

The naval officer nodded and started, 'I found my team was blocked at every turn. We were denied access to witnesses. When we got access, the witness was accompanied by a commissioned officer who spoke for the witness. We would arrive to interview a witness to find he had been transferred the day before. Eventually the problem we were having escalated and all the witnesses were posted to Whale Island, even those from the United States and those on active service abroad. With no interference, the evidence we gathered matched that found by Captain Robinson, even the information given by Privates Holt and Wright. Their information was very illuminating.'

'Illuminating, Commander?' Sir Nicolas did not miss a thing.

'Yes, sir.'

'Well, illuminate us.'

'What they said about the action that resulted in the death of Major Carmichael supported what other witnesses said, sir.'

'Commander, what else did they say that the other witnesses did not?'

'Sir, I'm not sure it's relevant.'

'Commander, we will decide on that.'

'Yes, sir. They said – I quote Private Wright – "The major was hyper: as high as a kite."'

'What do you understand by that?'

'That he was either intoxicated by the excitement of battle or he was drunk or on drugs, sir.'

'And which of the three was it?'

'Cocaine, sir.'

'You can't possibly know that,' West jumped in again.

'But he can,' I said.

'How?'

'From the autopsy report. The Americans check for drugs now, sir.' I was addressing Sir Nicolas.

'And it says that he had taken cocaine?'

'Yes, sir.'

'Can you explain the loss of the autopsy report, Commander?' asked Sir Nicholas.

'I checked its progress, but the exact point of loss can only be surmised. I gained a copy direct from AMEDD.'

'AMEDD?'

'Yes, sir. Sorry – US Army Med Department.'

'I see. No chance of falsification then?'

'Only if it occurred in the hospital in Iraq, sir. Mr Coxhead has a view.'

'Please, Mr Coxhead.'

'There is a record of the documentation of this case being sent from the APA to the Home Office and being sent back. I was given access to the APA records with the help of Lieutenant Commander Philpot and Mr Singh Kohli. The APA record of the documents included in the file lists the autopsy report. It also includes one or two other documents that are missing but have not been subject to notification of a problem. The records indicate that the request for the documents came from a Home Office department that no longer exists and has not existed for two years now, sir. I attempted to find out who requested the documentation and drew a blank. This is most unusual. There was also no authorization to return the documentation. When I pursued the matter, I was told in no uncertain terms to stop.'

'Who told you?'

Mr Coxhead was clearly perturbed by the question. 'My superior, sir.'

'Who is?'

'Mr Graham Mason, sir.'

I noted that Nina was on a mobile.

'May I ask a question, sir?' I asked.

Sir Nicolas looked at Sir Antony, who nodded.

'Were the dates of the transfer of the documents from the APA to the Home Office and back again before the decision was made to prosecute Phillips and Munro?'

'Yes, I'm sorry, Sir Nicolas,' said Mr Coxhead. 'It would appear the documents came from Captain Robinson on the third of January, or that's when they were logged in. They were allocated to Prosecution Barrister Major Nigel Reynolds QC on the sixth, but he was on holiday until the seventeenth and it was in that period that they went to the Home Office, sent out on the fifth and back on the fifteenth.'

'That means that Major Reynolds could not have seen the reports until he got back from his holiday and only then could he make any decisions,' said Sir Antony.

'So,' said Sir Nicolas, 'if we take out a weekend, that's nine days that they were actually missing for. It would appear in that time, the autopsy report went missing and some minor changes to the other documents occurred that changed the balance of evidence.'

'Or,' said West, 'the autopsy report was mislaid or the information rendered by Captain Robinson was the doctored information. Or the autopsy report was in the contents list and not in the folder.'

West was certainly gunning for me, but why?

'Yes, Superintendent West, your view on this matter is crystal clear,' said Sir Nicolas.

Sir Antony closed the meeting and said that it would be reconvened.

It would appear, on the face of it, that the tampering with the evidence occurred at the Home Office, but equally it could, as West had implied, be me. I could see the case against me building, but why? By whom?

21

I heard nothing, so I noodled around with the new team I was in, interviewing a series of civil servants (apparently in the Home Office, but with links to the Foreign Office and to Brussels) about a scam they were pulling, but it didn't seem to be going anywhere. They had this beautiful blocking mechanism. They would under interview say that something was in the memorandum, a specific person quoting something specific such as chapter four, para eight, sub-para eight point six. Faced with this information I looked it up and it was as they had said, but it was not applicable or was applicable but some other factor made it not acceptable. Hidden with this was a message that needed a mechanism to decode it. I could see exactly where the writers of *Yes, Minister* and other government-based farces and comedies got their stories. What amazed me was that anybody could write all that bureaucratic mumbo jumbo and I was even more amazed that anybody had read it, let alone remembered any of it.

I wasn't clear why Barrow had put me on this job. Here we had a department of apparently hardworking civil servants all at one to two grades above what the job, on the face of it, merited and they apparently produced nothing, but nobody in the civil service hierarchy was prepared to tackle this unit. The unit was costing a fortune and it was just accepted. I was the wrong person for this job; it needed a forensic accountant.

Then Barrow sent for me. I arrived at his office to see that Frances was there and she was frosty.

'Sit down, Jake. Frances and I have just been discussing a small problem that has been floated our way by six.'

I assumed he meant MI6.

'Frances is unhappy about it and so am I, but it's the best we can do in the circumstances.'

I waited.

'You're off the hook about your soldier friends. They have agreed to an honourable discharge from the army and have been set up with good jobs by five. Interesting, ah?'

'So it's a cover-up to protect the guilty at the Home Office or MOD.'

'Probably.'

'What about the block on Mr Coxhead?'

'Yes, another case of fog descending so nothing can be seen. Mr Graham Mason, the manager of Mr Coxhead, said he had received a message by phone from the office of the home secretary. However, he did not know who gave him the message or instigated the message. We felt it would be fruitless to attempt an inquiry at that august level.'

'So it's another cover-up.'

'I couldn't possibly say, but your conclusions are your conclusions.' He smiled a wry smile. I waited. I detected some discomfort in Barrow. 'Yes, six wants to borrow you for a... um, project.'

'A project?'

'Yes, Jake. Initially it's to do with your interrogation skills and some new stuff that some boffins have dreamed up. I just wondered if you would be interested.'

'Sounds to me that this is some sort of put-up job.'

'Well, it is and it isn't.'

Frances snorted but said nothing. Clearly she thought it was a put-up job.

'Let me paint some background. We are a special unit. In general terms, we do our own thing and we cherry-pick jobs. However, in order to retain that freedom, we must respond to a maximum of four Code Reds a year. It's unusual to get four. This year so far we have had one.'

'What is a Code Red?'

'It's normally what is called a wet job, but nobody is ever going to admit that, sometimes it's an infiltration; it can be anything that we have the specialist skills for.'

'So we do *do* wet jobs?' I nearly said assassinations, but stopped myself in time. I had had a feeling about that since my interview with Frances and the fact that I could be armed as I was complete with a shoulder holster and a 9 mm SIG P229 that I could sign out and had practised with.

'We will talk about that some other time, Jake.'

'Okay, so what is wrong with this one?'

Frances could be contained no longer. 'It's not a Code Red or anything like a Code Red. There is some political game playing here. It's simply an interrogation technique to be used on some dodgy American.'

'That may be true, but we have never challenged a Code Red.'

I was concerned. 'Tell me even more.'

'Look, we pick up jobs from five, six and SO15; that is Counter Terrorism Command. To be classified as Code Red, it goes to the leadership team of the Joint Operations Committee and a unit is designated to lead it or to do it.'

'Okay, so this has been cleared as a Code Red. Tell me.'

'Six have picked up some rumours from their CIA friends, but six wants us to handle it. I think that is so they can say it was nothing to do with them – clean hands and all that stuff. There is also some Foreign Office involvement to do with Islamists in Bolivia. For some inexplicable reason, you were asked for personally. This has never happened before and they also dangled a carrot, which was again very odd.'

'That is?'

'Well, the bargain is this: you do a little job for them and they will ensure you and your soldier friends are all sweet and smelling of roses.'

126

'This little job is just the interrogation then?' I knew it wasn't, but wanted to be sure.

'Um... Well, no. If the information turns out to be what we think it's likely to be, you'll go to Bolivia.'

'I see. A real out-of-the-way place for something to happen to me.'

'We are in totally uncharted territory.'

'You trust them, Barrow?' I asked

'Well "trust" is not a word I would use, but six has always delivered on a promise. I believe the Bolivia job should be ours anyway, but Frances is not keen that we get involved overseas.'

'Why should it be ours anyway?'

'Because it involves The Family.'

'So why were six involved?' asked Frances.

'They were working on a mafia thing and it drifted into The Family.'

'And as soon as that happened, the bastards ran for cover.' Frances really was an unhappy bunny over this one.

In for a penny, so I said, 'Okay, Barrow, I'm tired of doing not very much, or rather, not really understanding what I'm doing.'

'And by the way, Frances will be in the, um... in the mix with you,' said Barrow.

I felt a shiver of pleasure. I wanted Frances with me but at the same time I wasn't sure I should feel the way I did. 'It's best never to walk alone.' I started to sing, to hide the way I felt, silly really. 'When you walk through a storm, hold your head up high. And don't be afraid of the dark... But you don't seem happy, Frances.'

'Oh, do piss off, Jake. I don't like being mixed up with stuff six doesn't want to do. I like it even less if there is any hint of political interference. If there is one group of people who will renege on an agreement, it's the politicians.

They lie for a living and lack any moral code, but if Barrow is guarding our arses, then I'm in.'

That was that then, me pleased about going to Bolivia with her and she was pissed of at six and politicians.

22

A couple of days later, Frances and I were in Cambridge to see Professor Verling, a visiting psychology professor from the States. We met him with a Dr Michelle Tilley, who did not look old enough to have a GCSE, let alone a doctorate. Her thesis was something to do with the way blood flows in the brain under different psychological conditions.

'Please come along to my office,' said Dr Tilley. 'I need to explain to you a methodology for the detection of lies using an fMRI scanner.'

'I know what an MRI scanner is; what does the "f" stand for?' asked Frances. She looked at me, daring me to say something, but the consequence would be horrific for me.

'Functional MRI, or functional Magnetic Resonance Imaging, is a type of specialized MRI scan. It measures the haemodynamic response related to neural activity in the brain or spinal cord of humans or other animals. It's one of the most recently developed forms of neuroimaging.'

I could see Frances' face going blank and so could Dr Tilley.

'Let me explain,' said Dr Tilley.

I had this feeling of dread. I had listened to people like this as a student and then I never understood a word. Dr Tilley set off at a high rate of oral discharge and I didn't stand a chance.

'Blood-oxygen-level-dependent or BOLD fMRI is a method of observing which areas of the brain are active at any given time. Neurons do not have internal reserves of energy in the form of glucose and oxygen, so their firing causes a need for more energy to be brought in quickly. It

129

follows that the haemodynamics are closely linked to neural activity.'

Frances had given up and I was struggling. Now in her stride, Dr Tilley was totally oblivious to our lack of understanding and she ploughed on.

'The active nerve cells consume oxygen carried by haemoglobin in red blood cells. Haemoglobin is diamagnetic when oxygenated but paramagnetic when deoxygenated. The magnetic resonance signal of blood is therefore slightly different depending on the level of oxygenation. These differential signals can be detected using an appropriate MR pulse sequence as blood-oxygen-level-dependent contrast. Higher BOLD signal intensities arise from increases in the concentration of oxygenated haemoglobin, since the blood magnetic susceptibility now more closely matches the tissue magnetic susceptibility.'

I wanted to smile as the look on Frances's face was a picture of total bewilderment.

'By collecting data in an fMRI scanner, with parameters sensitive to changes in magnetic susceptibility, one can assess changes in BOLD contrast.' She paused. I think she was absorbing the blank faces. 'In summary, in the haemodynamic response, blood releases oxygen to active neurons at a greater rate than to inactive neurons and the difference in magnetic susceptibility between oxyhaemoglobin and deoxyhaemoglobin, and thus oxygenated or deoxygenated blood leads to magnetic signal variation, which can be detected using an MRI scanner.' She knew she was pushing water uphill with her nose, but clearly had a problem stopping. 'This haemodynamic response rises and then falls back. So we can read this on our instruments.' Her pace of delivery had slowed considerably.

Frances laughed out loud. 'Right, I'm supposed to understand that, am I?'

Dr Tilley looked bemused.

'Can I have a go?' I asked. I got a worried nod. 'fMRI is a box of tricks that uses strong magnetic fields to see what part of the brain is active. You stick a person's head in a magnetic field and using some technical gear, you can see on a screen which parts of the brain are working.'

'Sounds right to me,' said Frances. 'Over to you, Doctor.'

Dr Tilley was smiling. 'I need to explain our work and how you can benefit from it.'

My heart began to sink again.

'Let me tell you a story. It's probably easier to understand it that way.'

I could hear her thinking, *We have some people here with the mental capacity of children, so I will tell them a story.*

Oh, goody, goody! A story! Do pay attention, Jake.

'A white man – we can call him Brian – was accused of killing a black man – shall we say his name was Leroy.'

Aha, no racial stereotyping here then.

'Brian claimed he didn't do it. The police thought he did. He was known for his hatred of black people. He was known to hate Leroy in particular. The police had evidence and witnesses to that effect. He admitted to being in the area the night Leroy was killed. He offered to take a polygraph to show he didn't do it. It proved unsatisfactory. Whenever Leroy's name was mentioned or any oblique reference made to him, the response went off the clock; Brian's hatred was so intense. Brian was asked whether he would agree to some other tests. He agreed and they were carried out. Okay so far?'

We agreed.

'As Jake said, the fMRI scan shows what parts of the brain are working. When people are lying, the test indicates a different pattern from when they are telling the truth. Basically, more areas of the brain light up when people are lying. The test showed that Brian was telling the truth. The consequence was that the police went back to square

131

one and eventually found it was a black-on-black gang killing.'

Frances nodded. I wondered why it was nearly always 'white-man-hates-black-man' and not the other way round. I also wondered why black-on-black killing was a description frequently used, but not white-on-white killing; that must be more common. Why was white-on-black killing a race crime, but not when it was the other way round and, I wondered, why I was getting all hooked up by this? Just pay attention, Jake, I told myself.

'Okay,' said Frances, 'how do you know this is, well, correct?'

'Good question. A little scepticism is valuable.' This very young and clearly naïve girl with a doctorate looked very pleased with herself. I'm sure she had no idea what she had just said; I'll pat you gently on the head and tell you you're a good girl.

'With volunteers in tests, there is an accuracy of ninety-seven per cent. The tests, however, are conducted using made-up, unpractised lies. In people volunteering to prove they are not guilty of a crime, it's difficult to have accurate figures, but there are strong indications that it's an accurate predictor. The problem is that some people who have practised a lie can fool the test. There may be intelligence or personality factors also. Another problem is that movement of the head, even coughing or waggling of the tongue, can disrupt readings. Because of these objections, the tests are not admissible in any law court, and in the legal world we would need permissions to use the test.'

Dr Tilley looked at us in turn. Frances took the invitation to speak again.

'I'm not sure why you're telling us this. It seems like an interesting experiment, but so what?'

I waited for the condescension, but it didn't come. Perhaps I'd misjudged Dr Smarty-Pants.

'To some extent, we have overcome many of the problems. At a crude, descriptive level, we can say that by
physical restriction of movement and using very sensitive
movement monitoring that has been developed for the
Royal Marsden Hospital fed into a computer program, we
can virtually eliminate physical movement disruption from
the readings. Secondly, by the administration of particular
drugs, we can enhance the effect of the readings and this
gives us a better reading with practiced liars. Where we see a
use is in debriefing defectors, collaborators and double
agents. The security services in the USA and now in the UK
see this as a means to eliminate misinformation.'

It seemed to me that this was a gross oversimplification,
but I could figure out the reality.

Frances intervened. 'So why are you telling us this?' she
asked again.

The academics looked at each other and this time it was
the professor who responded.

'We don't know. We will set up the tests and analyze the
results. We will not hear the questions or the answers. Our
understanding is you will do the interrogations.'

I asked, 'Do we need to know anything about the interrogation technique itself?'

'Yes,' the professor again answered. 'It's important to ask
questions in discrete bits rather than continuously. The
reason is that it allows the brain to come back to – shall we
say – rest before the next question.'

'Does the type of question make a difference?'

'How do you mean?'

'I can ask a simple, closed question that will get a yes or
no, through to very open questions that are so vague that
the answerer has to work out what he or she thinks the
question is.'

'Yes, I see. Simple questions that are clear give better
results.'

'What about probes, such as, "Tell me more about X"?'

'They should work well.'

'In that case, seeking clarification and testing under-standing should give sensible results.'

'Sensible results, yes. You're probably correct.'

I'd passed into an area of expertise related to the work they were doing that they had little knowledge of. That has always been a problem. Academics know more and more about less and less; eventually they will know everything about nothing – obvious really.

'So, what now?'

'Ah, yes,' said the professor. 'There are some gentlemen in another part of the building. They will tell you about the... um, interrogation. Our technical people have been asked to set the equipment up and we will use it this afternoon.'

23

Dr Tilley took us through the building to a set of offices. She knocked and we entered. Four men in suits were in the office; one was Barrow. The atmosphere was odd. It was stiff, formal. The strangers looked arrogant and unfriendly. They looked at us as if we were beings from the forbidden planet, like an old duchess used to authority facing badly behaved hoodies. I realized they were frightened of us. But why? They were aggressive, because of fear? They felt superior, but we were dangerous, so there was uncertainty. How odd.

Dr Tilley said, 'I've briefed Ms Portello and Captain Robinson,' and she left.

Barrow did the introductions. The three men were Mr Frank Chambers, Mr George Mertzellos and Mr Peter Clerk. I found the 'Misters' odd and being introduced as Captain Jake Robinson even odder. It was all a little taut. I really had no idea who these people were, but it seemed that Frank Chambers was the man in charge.

He started with no welcome and no pleasantries. 'We are going to brief you on the serious situation that we have.' He was very serious and starchy, schoolmarm-ish. His pomposity got under my skin. His fat, white cheeks wobbled when he spoke.

'Our technologists, Professor Verling, from the University of Columbia, and Dr Michelle Tilley, who have conducted a briefing with you on haemodynamic response in neuroimaging, will advise you as to the veracity of the information you will have extracted from the informant in answer to your questions.' He paused between each part of the sentence as if explaining to some five-year-olds. My conclusion

135

was that this man was prat. Then, I thought, is he for real or is this some sort of elaborate joke? I supposed it was the precise way he spoke to us, as if we were infants. No: he spoke to us as if he were a superior being and his rigid, upright stance, buttoned-up, tweed jacket and precisely cut hair added to this prim and proper image. His hands were on his lap. I assumed they were clasped from the angle of his arms, but I could not see them below the level of the desktop that separated us. He had horn-rimmed glasses and pursed lips as if he were about to kiss me (well, not me in particular; anybody really).

'Excuse me,' I intervened and he looked at me in surprise. I could see his mind working: *My word, these untouchables speak. Whatever next?'*

'Yes?' His 'yes' was sharp and clipped.

'My name is Jake and this is Frances. How do we address you?'

A faint smile flicked across Barrow's face.

'For the purpose of this meeting, you can call me Mr Chambers.'

I tried not to laugh. After all, it would be rude to laugh. He just continued as if my interruption was a mere irrelevancy.

'This is quite complex. Are you comfortable?' There was a long pause. I was tempted to say, 'Please, miss, I wanna pee,' but I said nothing.

He started again. 'Let me tell you a story.'

I had to grin. Frances saw my grin and suppressed a giggle.

'Have I said something funny?' Frank – oops! – Mr Chambers was irked.

I asked, 'Is this about the white guy named Brian and the black guy named Leroy?' Frances was now fighting to contain herself.

'If it is, we've heard it already.'

Frances had her hand over her mouth.

Chambers turned to Barrow. 'I'm not sure you've given us the right people for this job, Barrow.' He noticed then that Peter was also smiling. 'And what is it you find so funny?'

The whole thing had taken on such a level of farce that I also had to suppress a giggle and that set off Peter. Frances was also barely holding it in. It was like *It'll Be All Right on the Night.*

Barrow said, 'I think we should get some coffee.' He stood up, took me by the arm and pushed Frances through the door with his hand in the centre of her back. She immediately ran down the passageway to a sign that said *Ladies.* Barrow and I walked on to a coffee area.

'I'm sorry, Barrow.'

'Go on.'

So, I explained about the fMRI briefing being done as a story and the fact that this guy, Frank Chambers, was such a stuffed shirt: 'Let... me... tell... you... a... story. Are... you... sitting... comfortably? Then... I... will... begin...'

Barrow smiled. 'I see.'

'Wait for Frances and have a coffee. I will calm it all down and I will come and collect you. What am I going to do with you two?' He smiled that smile of understanding and I felt like a ten-year-old with an indulgent headmaster. About ten minutes later, he came and collected us.

When we went back in, Frank Chambers watched us warily.

'Jake and Frances,' he began, 'I'm going to tell you what we know and what we believe. What I say may be true or some distortion of the truth. Jake, it will be up to you to discern the truth. Whatever you decide, Jake, you will be involved in whatever the next step is and I believe Frances will be in charge of that next step.'

The over-use of first names was on the verge of making me giggle again.

'Let me begin.'

I was now fighting for control again and I dared not look at Frances.

'We have a defector: a man named Edgar Klimt.'

I switched into listening mode. The word 'defector' evoked focus in me.

'He's an American. He has defected from the mafia. His erstwhile companions believe he's dead.'

I was now totally focused and indicated that I wanted to speak. Chambers adopted an air of surprise.

'Is Edgar Klimt his real name?'

'Does it matter?'

Oh, shit, he hasn't learned. I needed control – control of me. I stood and walked to the window and looked out and counted to ten. I heard a little cough in the silence; it was Barrow. I turned and walked back to my chair and sat. Apart from the sound of quiet breathing you could have heard a pin drop. Only then did I look at him.

'Yes it does, and let me say this, and I will say this only once.' I sounded like a character from *Allo, Allo* on TV. 'If you want me to do this job, you will not treat my colleague or me as fucking idiots. You will answer the questions I ask with facts. If you don't know the answer, say "I don't know." If you have a best guess, say "I think so-and-so," or "I believe so-and-so." This will prevent confusion between fact and conjecture. Fuck me about and you can get somebody else.' His mouth was hanging open and his eyes were large. There was a long pause as Frank Chambers got control of himself. He was definitely frightened. His colleagues were also looking very uncomfortable. He looked at Barrow. Barrow shrugged and smiled.

Now back in control of himself, you could see his mind working. He spoke, 'I apologize, Jake. I will answer your questions. Edgar Klimt is his given name. His companions, for self-evident reasons, knew him as Shiv. Shall I continue?'

I don't think anybody had spoken to him like I had in years, if ever, and he was very wary of me now. The balance of power had shifted.

'Please.'

'Klimt was a very junior member of the mafia: an associate, although he claims to be a soldier. He worked in a tourist district of New York. His job was to ensure that there was no petty crime and gangs did not penetrate the area.'

Frances interrupted, 'Explain that, please.'

'The bit about petty crime?'

'Yes.'

'In tourist districts, the American Costa Nostra make enormous sums of money from gambling, hotels and transport, mainly taxis and entertainment, such as theatres, restaurants, gambling, protection, prostitution and drugs. This is mainly done by what in legitimate businesses would be insurance or by franchise. For example, hotels don't want theft, so the local capo ensures that thieves in that line of business go elsewhere. Similarly, they protect prostitute groups. The authorities won't let the mafia run a casino or a nightclub, so, through third parties, they own the casino. Then it's franchised to a legitimate operator and they take legal returns. There is a whole mix of these things. They don't like what might be called "normal" crime, such as robbery. The people who pay for protection get protection. It requires policing and that is done by the soldiers and associates.'

'So they keep crime down.'

'True, but what they do is criminal and they do it by criminal means, but they have a set of rules to prevent their own people going into business for themselves.'

'Thank you, Frank.' Frances was being very polite, perhaps to make up for my forcefulness.

'Where was I? Yes; Klimt was sent on a job to guard and be a driver for a consigliere – that's an advisor, fairly important rank. This consigliere's name was Peter Milano, a long-established mafia family. They went to see a senator, Paul McGreevy. McGreevy is a high-level mafia associate. He does things for the mafia in return for political funding, but nobody can prove that. McGreevy has connections in Bolivia. Bolivia has three things that the mafia wants: cocaine, natural gas and silver. It also turns out that in the UK, a prominent underworld consortium with, we believe, connections in parliament, the House of Lords, and in the city has an interest in cocaine, natural gas and silver from Bolivia. The natural gas and silver are legitimate businesses, but the connections within Bolivia seem to be controlled by a criminal fraternity. All that is needed is agreement between the parties. Klimt knows the whos, the whens and the wheres, but can we believe him?'

'Is there anything else we need to know?'

'I'm not sure. I was asked to give you only the basics.'

'Good. Let me ask a couple of questions then. How did Klimt find out about this event?'

'He was asked to do some work for an associate of the senator. This entailed him being given the information he has passed on to us. When the senator's people realized that Klimt was not who they thought he was, they told the mafia capo and Klimt had a contract put out on him. He ran to the FBI who used a death in New York as a cover and shipped him over here.'

'Frank, you said, "passed onto us." Who are "us" and how did he make contact?'

He looked at Barrow and Barrow nodded.

'The FBI had an undercover agent or a defector working within a mafia cell in New York; they also had one in Washington. The Washington agent told the FBI and the FBI is the "us" I referred to.'

This was only a part story, but it was enough.

'Why isn't there an American presence here?'

140

'Ah!' Frank turned to Barrow.

Barrow smiled his enigmatic smile. 'Because the FBI now think he really is dead, but a CIA special unit knows he's alive. The one way we can keep a lid on any leaks is if there is deniability, so we are doing the information digging bit and we will feed to the CIA what we want them to know, and they are okay with that.'

'I want to make sure my thoughts about why we took this job are correct. I assume it's The Family connection.'

The suits looked blank. Barrow nodded. 'That's correct, Jake.'

So these people knew about criminal connections in government, but they didn't know about us in relation to The Family.

'I'd like to backtrack, natural gas and silver, is that the cover for the cocaine?'

'We think so but the natural gas and silver are lucrative in their own right.'

'Thank you, Frank. I'm hearing leaks in the FBI and maybe leaks in the CIA. Who is guarding our arses here?'

Frank looked at Barrow. 'That is a good question, Jake. Have you any particular concerns?'

'Well, yes. We know we have some dodgy officers in the special branch. We know this is a CIA project, so there are two potential sources of leaks. We are a small bunch and I don't know the extent of MI5 knowledge. We have the security complication of civil service involvement and with that politicians can get to know things.'

'And why should we trust you?' snapped out Frank.

'Exactly. Frances and I are the ones who are going into the lion's den and we might leak everything just to stay alive. What's your excuse?'

Barrow intervened into the tense silence in the room, 'Oh, I'm pleased we all trust each other. Let me reassure you. I know all the people in the know.' He paused, looking at me. 'They are all briefed to tell nobody anything and are to only communicate and liaise through my unit; that is you, Nikki and Howard. As from today, this small group…' Barrow waved his arm at the three suited men, smiling in the slow way he had. 'They know what Nikki will do to them if anything leaks that puts you two in any danger.'

I'd not seen this side of Barrow before. I found it reassuring. It also gave me an insight into Nikki's role, which I'd guessed at but not fully appreciated before. I was sure two of the three swallowed. No wonder they had a fear of us two. As far as I was concerned, our joint arses were covered.

'Thank you, Barrow. Thank you, gentlemen. I think Frances and I have a job to do.' I turned to Frances. 'Is that right, boss?'

She smiled. 'That's right, Captain Robinson'

24

We went to lunch. I didn't feel like talking, nor did I feel like eating.

Barrow said, 'Tell me, Jake.'

'I've an uncomfortable feeling that there are too many loose ends and we haven't really started yet. How is it that those jokers did the interviews?'

'Um. . . I agree, but this often happens. It's quite common that nobody knows where to park something. It's passed around with people ducking and diving to avoid it, or two or three groups are trying to grab it. It's the penalty of freedom. The strange thing is that if the papers don't get wind of it, it stays secret.'

'You're talking about normal situations, Barrow. We have an enemy on the inside.' I was uncomfortable about the bozos we had been talking to. They didn't feel right, too insular, too full of their own importance, too blind to day-to-day realities. 'Who are they anyway?'

'Ah, I was hoping you wouldn't ask.'

'But I have.'

'They're Foreign Office. They second-guess what is going to happen from information supplied to them and they use that information to advise ministers on potential options.'

'Okay, so they are very bright with high cognitive power and a long time span of discretion and forecasting ability. But they are not security conscious and are likely to trust people like ministers with information.'

'That is true, Jake. Do you want out?'

'No, he bloody doesn't,' said Frances.

'I have another problem, Barrow.'

'Go on.'

'They know who we are – by name and what we do. It's powerful information.'

'Jake, they are frightened little men and their fear of us is much greater than their fear of anybody else.'

'Okay?' asked Frances.

'No.' I had an itch I wanted certainty. My stomach was in a knot. I felt their fear was not enough for them not to trust somebody they shouldn't trust.

'Tell me what you want Jake,' said Barrow.

'I want them to know I will personally kill all of them if one of them leaks anything.'

'Jake, that's paranoid.'

'Spot on Barrow, remember, in this job only the paranoid survive.'

He laughed. 'Okay, I'll explain it too them in language they will understand.'

Well, that was that decided then. I trusted Barrow. The chances were, if I had said I wanted out, Barrow would be in the difficult position of persuading me to stick with it.

'Okay, Jake?' asked Frances.

'If she goes, I go.'

'Thank you,' said Barrow. 'See; democracy does work.'

I had to laugh at the absurdity of the thinking.

Barrow got a message and he took us to a small interview room. Sitting at the table was a small man. This was Klimt. We introduced ourselves. He looked tiny on his chair. I suppose he couldn't have been more than 5ft 2in. He had black, straight, greasy hair, greasy, sallow skin and a pointed rat face with a pimple on his neck. He was a greasy, little, un-likeable runt of a man. His clothes were untidy. They may have been clean but looked – well – greasy. I disliked him on sight. I suppose others felt like this about him, so I suppose he was used to it. No; how could you get used to being disliked?

I could see from her face that Frances felt the same as me. The interesting thing was that he generated menace. How was it that somebody that small could generate menace?

We got underway. I was the lead.

'We have been asked to talk to you, or rather asked to ask you to talk to us. Will you talk to us?'

He gave a sneering movement of his head and said, 'I've bin talkin' and no fucker has bin lis'nin'.'

'Yes, that's the problem; they are all deaf to what you want to say. We're not deaf.'

'They wanna put me on a machine.'

'What do you think about that?'

'Okay, I s'pose.'

'Okay. S'pose we have an ordinary talk and then you can go on the machine and we can see what we get.' I was trying to match his language, pace, emphasis and a modicum of pronunciation, but I needed to be careful in case it sounded like mimicking.

'Okay, I s'pose. Why don't we just get on the bloody machine?'

'Okay, let's just do that.'

Frances left and was back in two minutes with a large woman in a white overall, white stockings and flat, white shoes; Rosa Klebb strikes again. She spoke to Klimt in a warm and motherly tone, encouraging him to come with her rather than telling him. I found her hard face, bob-cut hair and cold character chilling, but Klimt responded to her.

She led us silently down through a maze of passageways and into a room that contained the scanner. She pointed, wordlessly, to a glass booth and we went to it. She took Klimt away.

A couple of minutes later, Professor Verling and Dr Michelle Tilley appeared in a similar booth, except their booth seemed to have lots of cabinets for electronic gear.

We just had headsets and microphones. Then Barrow joined them. I suppose that was to make sure they didn't hear the interview.

The large woman brought back Klimt dressed in a hospital shirt and shorts. He looked even more like a human rat. The track marks on his arms were clear and blended in, to some extent, with his tattoos. The woman arranged him flat on his back on the machine bed. She attached pads onto various parts of his head and body and connected wires as if he was to have a cardiograph, but they must have been movement sensors. She then put headphones on him, closed a sort of cage around his head and slipped a shaped, padded pillow under his knees. Dr Tilley gave him instructions and told him what she was going to do and to press a button if he was disturbed. It was all systems go and the bed he was on was rolled into the machine. We were given the all clear to start asking questions.

'Are you ready for questions, Klimt?'

Frances wrote a *1* on her pad and the time, *1427*.

'Yeah, but I doun like it in here.'

'Okay. Who is Milano?'

'He's the consigliere, yer know what I mean?'

'Yes. Who does he work for?'

'Il capo dei capi, he's the boss, yer know, the big boss.'

'What is the name of the capo dei capi?'

'I dunno.'

'You are a member of the American Costa Nostra.'

'Yeah.'

'You're an associate.'

'Yeah, but they're gonna make me a soldier, I told em that.'

'How did you make your bones?'

'I did a stoolie in Brooklyn. Didn't bother me nun.' A touch of bravado. So it did bother him.

'So you, a member of the American Costa Nostra, who has

146

made his bones, doesn't know the name of the capo dei capi.'

'Well, I do, but... Well – yer know – I can't...'

'Why not?'

'Cos... Well – shit – I made the vow; they'll kill me.'

'That will be a bit difficult as they think you're already dead, so you can tell us his name.'

'Oh, shit – yeah, shit – his name is Gumbello, yeah, Alessandro Gumbello.'

'Is that the name he's generally known by?'

'Chrise' no! Mos' people know him as Mr Alexander Prichard.'

'Not the Alexander Prichard who owns a string of stores and is a big wheel in food manufacture?'

'Yeah, that's him. Them stores, stuff like them stores is jus' small stuff.'

'So why did Milano go and see McGreevy?'

'Well, it was all about Bolivia. Il capo dei capi wants ta make a deal with some snake down there, yer know what I mean?'

'About what?'

'Christ, I told them other guys all about this.'

'Just tell me. Just start at the beginning and tell me.' Sod the short question bit; we'd be there a week.

'Well, okay. Well, this Bolivian guy, he's got an in with the big wheels, yer know, they are the real deal down there and they gotta fix on in the government, yer know what I mean?'

'The Bolivian guy's name?'

'Will yer let me tell yer the fuckin' story? His name is Machacamarca. And before you fuckin' ask, his first name is Jorge, right. Can I tell this fuckin' story now? Yeah, well, right, we need stuff from this guy, so they want the senator to go have a chat with him, right; kinda diplomatic and all that shit, yer know what I mean? But this guy has already gotta deal with some limey guy named Earl Carmichael, right; must be a black guy with a first name like Earl. Don't trust black guys, yer know what I mean.'

My head was spinning. Rupert Carmichael, Earl of Charnforth was Major Michael Carmichael's father. He sat in the Lords and ran a big financial business: insurance, pensions, accountancy and all sorts of financial stuff. Doggie Cannon's brother worked for him.

Klimt was ploughing on, 'Anyways, this guy Earl is sendin' over one of his guys to do the talkin'. I know you're going to ask me his fuckin' name, right. Yeah, it's Randy Mabry, right. He's some big wheel in the government over there, yer know what I mean?'

Klimt was right; he was a minister in the Foreign Office.

'You can't trust these fuckin' politicians.'

I had to laugh; mafioso saying you can't trust politicians. Klimt and I agreed on some things.

'What the fuck you laughing at? It's no fuckin' joke in this fuckin' thing, right.'

'I'm sorry, Klimt. This is great stuff.'

'I've been tryin' to tell you lot for... Oh, shit! I need outa here!'

'Just finish for me, will you, please, Klimt.'

'I'll tell ya when I get outta here.' I could hear the edge of panic in his voice and his breathing was shallow.

'Klimt, I'd like you to do something for me. Shut your eyes.'

'Why?'

'We need you relaxed to bring you out. Please. Are they shut?'

'Yeah.'

'Breath slowly ... deep breaths.'

'What the fuck for?'

'It helps.' He started to breath deeply. 'You ever been to the beach by the sea.'

'Yeah, as a kid. So what?'

148

'I'd like you to think about it. Do you remember?'

'Yeah.'

'And the sun was shining, and it was warm can you feel it.'

'Yeah.'

'Can you see the sea?'

'Yeah.'

'And it's sort of blue with sort of green and has waves. Is it like that?'

'Yeah.'

'And the waves on the beach make a sort of rushing sound.'

'Yeah.'

'And you are feeling good, kind of calm.'

'Yeah.'

'Now breath in and now out slowly and feel good like that day on the beach.' I paused, I could hear his breathing; he was relaxed. I must admit I was surprised. I never thought that would work. 'You were saying this guy Jorge Machaca-marca is going to talk to the senator and he already has a deal with a British guy named Earl Carmichael and this guy Earl is sending over one of his guys Randy Mabry.'

'Yeah, that's it. Anyways, if they're gonna meet, the Bolivian guy says it's gotta be in Bolivia, right, yer know what I mean, so they need security. They need protection, right, so each of them has to hand over somebody to the other two: a hostage; sort of protection, yer know what I mean. Anyways, this Brit guy has a wife and a sister. His wife will go stay at the senator's place and his sister will go to stay with Machacamarca, 'cept she can't on account of her bein' a nun, yer know what I mean?'

'A nun?'

'Yeah, a fuckin nun, right?'

'What is her name?'

'Yeah, Mabry, right.'

'Her name as a nun?'

149

'I dunno.'

'Her Christian name?'

'Annabelle, and I think her second name is fuckin Jane. Christ, it doun matter.'

'What about the senator's security?'

'He's doing the same, right. His wife is going to stay with this Earl guy and his brother is staying with Machacamarca, yer know what I mean?'

'Machacamarca's security?'

'Dunno. Well, his wife and daughter, but which one is going where I dunno.'

'When?'

'Christ! Why the fuck do you think I've bin tryin' to tell yer? Eight weeks. Yeah, that will be on the twenty-third for three days, okay.'

'Where?'

'I dunno. All I know it's somewhere in fuckin Bolivia, but it can't be hard to find as this guy Mabry's sister is goin' with a bunch of nuns from over there, and the senator's brother is travelling in the same bus.'

'Bus?'

'Yeah, a fuckin bus. It's some sorta holiday bus that's takin' them.'

'Anything else?'

'No. I wan' outa dis fuckin thin'.'

Barrow's voice came over the headsets. 'Okay, folks, that's a wrap.'

We went for coffee and met in the conference room. Barrow had the results sheets and Frances and Dr Tilley quickly decided that Klimt had been telling the truth.

'Well, you two are going on holiday. I'd better get that in motion.'

25

Why would anybody go on holiday to such a God-deserted place, where nuns sing hymns on buses? Yes, because the nuns were singing it drove away both God and holiday-makers. My philosophy lecturer at university would call that a non sequitur. 'Robinson,' he would say, 'that conclusion does not follow from the premises.' In this case, though, it was two conclusions based on a single premise. Although, like this case, I was usually just questioning the underlying logic or illogic, depending how you wanted to phrase it, but I was rambling due to the bloody dust. Hot, damp and smelly in the valleys; hot, dry and dusty in the desert, and now bare hills.

Compared to this place, Iraq was heavenly, apart from the problems of bombs or Improvised Explosive Devices (or IEDs as the Americans christened them) and getting shot at of course. When I left, the Shiite militias were using EFPs (explosive-packed cylinders that the US asserted were being supplied by Iran). It was amazing how three-letter abbreviations caught on. I wondered how many people reading a newspaper knew that EFP stands for Explosively Formed Penetrator. Only a small fraction of the roadside bombs used in Iraq were EFPs, but the device produced more casualties per attack than other type of roadside bomb. I hoped the troubles in Bolivia didn't get hot and those sorts of weapons were used. Sweat trickled down my face and dust stuck to it. No, on balance, I think I preferred the risk of IEDs and EFPs than TFD, which the Americans would be bound to christen 'This Fucking Dust'.

From the angle the bus seemed to be travelling, this was

one hell of a hill. We were grinding upward and the noise obliterated the nuns' singing. Just as I thought that, we levelled out, as in an aircraft. All we had to do then was wait for the descent, which was probably a lot more risky than the ascent, as we would, on occasions, rely on the brakes and I was uncertain that this bus had any. Whoops! We were descending. The engine scream was different. It was still screaming as if in pain, but it was a different pain and, consequently, a different scream. Oh, my God! We hit a bump that drove the barely sprung seat upward, jolting my spine, and then dropped away, leaving my stomach behind. If the engine scream was anything to go by, we were speeding up as we descended and we were lurching round bends. I was thankful that I couldn't see clearly out of the windows. I hung on; not in fear, you understand – no – more in total terror. Couldn't hear because of the noise; couldn't see because of the dust; disoriented because of the jolting, jumping and swerving; I needed a pee. One more heavy jolt, then I was sure I would provide some liquid – no – a lot of liquid, which would mix with the dust to form a wet cement that would set rapidly in the heat. My God, I realized I was hallucinating. I thought, perhaps, we should sing like the nuns.

'A life on the ocean wave! A home on the rolling deep! Where the scattered waters rave and the winds their revels keep! A life on the ocean wave! A home on the rolling deep!'

I felt a sharp dig in the ribs; it was Frances's elbow.

'Shut the fuck up; you're worse than the fucking nuns.'

What sort of language was that from a well-educated, middle-class lady? Ah, well, that had me put in my place and there was me thinking a rollicking sea shanty would match the rolling and pitching of the bus.

The descriptor Frances used about the nuns had to be wrong. I was fairly sure nuns didn't have carnal knowledge. God, I was bored. I expect you guessed that.

The bus seemed to be on the level, the dust clouds seemed to be clearing and with less clinging to the windows with every bump in the road. I could finally see out again. We were in a valley that was widening as we progressed. There were fields of cattle, clumps of trees, streams and no smell that I could detect; well, not the overpowering stench there was in the arable fields. I had the smell of bus, the smell of hot oil and diesel fumes and the smell of damp fabric and bodies – normal smells.

The bus was pitching and rolling like a dingy in a harbour, not like it was negotiating a choppy sea, so I relaxed. The muscles that were tense were no longer tense and I still needed a pee. The nuns started singing again. I wondered if they needed a pee. I assumed nuns had normal bodily functions; they couldn't be so pure that they didn't. I wondered if that was an element in confession. 'Please forgive me, Father; today I had three pees and a poo.'

Frances snapped at me, 'What are you grinning at?'

'Nothing really. Just my bizarre thoughts.'

'Yes, the psychiatrist said you were mad.' She smiled. 'I hope this bus stops soon; I need a pee.'

'I was just thinking the same thing.'

'What thing?'

'That you will also want a pee.'

'Oh, shut up and return to your bizarre thoughts. No, I think you should think about something that doesn't make you grin. There is something faintly obscene in a man grinning to himself while nuns sing hymns.'

I ignored the implications of that statement.

The bus pulled into a service area. I was amazed; there was a concrete forecourt and signs for parking and fuel. The signs were in Spanish, English and a local language. There was a very modern brick and glass building. It clearly had a restaurant, toilets and everything you would expect from a modern service station.

As we drove in the direction of the refuelling area, we stopped and were invited to disembark. At each bus were two attendants who guided us toward the entrance of the building in faultless English and, I assumed, a local language. The restaurant area was not air-conditioned, but had gently rotating fans in the ceiling. Each bus group was led to tables set out for us. It was good organization; they knew we were coming, but something was not right. These were normally a gentle, quiet, smiling people. In the restaurant, they were gentle and quiet, but definitely not smiling, well not in the way they usually did. Perhaps it was just me.

I headed for the gents. They were easy to find due to the international symbols pointing the way. The nuns had formed an orderly, very long queue to the ladies. Frances was in the middle of the queue of nuns, and other normal people were scattered down the queue. That was an odd thought, that nuns were not normal.

There was a French woman complaining loudly to a German woman, and that did not surprise me. French women seemed to me to think they had some privilege over all other women. Not that I was biased, of course. I could tell what the German woman wanted to say by the look on her face and the second word in English would have been 'off'.

There was no queue to the gents. I could remember a friend of mine, Shirley, facing a similar problem to the one these women were facing; she just went into the gents. She had an advantage over other women; her mother was French and her father was Irish so she had learned the French arrogance and didn't have English hang-ups.

Suitably relieved, I returned to our table to find a first course of some local fruit was being served. Eat up, Jake, I thought. There was a basic instinct in the army, and that was to eat and sleep as much and as often as possible because you never knew what was going to happen to deprive you of either or both.

There were three courses and the food was excellent. It was a real puzzle that in a poor country there were magnificent resources, such as this, for tourists. I wondered how many local homes in this, one of the poorest countries in the world, had electricity, running water and the general amenities that this complex had.

We headed back to the bus. I settled into my seat and Frances was alongside me as before. It was amazing how we adopted territorial rights and did things like sit in the same places. I suppose the British naturally do things to avoid confrontation. The French woman and her male companion sat where the Germans had been sitting, and the Germans were complaining to no avail. Of such things wars have started.

I was relaxed, refreshed and replete, but I still had this nagging feeling that something was not right. Perhaps it was the incongruity of the service station in this simple basic society. Or maybe it was the number of Toyota vehicles of the Land Cruiser type that had arrived and were parked facing the buses. Some were new and some were battered, but all were the same. Funny, I thought. Dudley Moore, the pianist and comedian, used to say that: 'Funny, I thought.'

Settle down, Jake, we will be on our way soon. Perhaps I was wrong, but then a man in smart, camouflaged fatigues got on, three pips on his epaulets, a captain. He was small and dark skinned with the features of the local people. Two men in shabby fatigues followed him. All were armed. The captain had a 9mm automatic in a holster. It looked like a Glock 17 with a standard 17-round magazine. The other two had AK47 semiautomatic rifles. One of the shabby ones had gone to the back of the bus. His fatigues were at least two sizes too big for him, so he had to use one hand to keep hitching his trousers up. The bottoms of his trouser legs were rolled up as were the sleeves of his jacket so that his hands and feet could protrude. This did not detract from the threat that he exuded. In an odd way, it added to it. I felt my buttocks contract. The other man was standing in the doorway at the front. Physically, he was the same size as the man at the back, but his trousers were so short that his ankles showed. His jacket was too long and, like the man at the back, his sleeves had to be rolled up so they were free of his hands.

Oh, shit! was my first thought; this should be funny, but it's exactly the opposite. I felt Frances's tension. She was reading what I was reading.

The captain spoke. 'Ladies and gentlemen, I would like to do an identity check. Please have your passports ready. If you're not a citizen of the USA, the UK or Israel please leave the bus. The French couple next to us started to talk to each other rapidly. The woman spoke to the senior man. Perhaps her male companion did not speak English.

'Now, you! What authority have you got to–'

She got no further with her question. The captain pulled out his gun; it was a Glock, as I'd thought. I heard the click as he prepared to shoot. I don't quite know how I did it, or whether Frances helped, but she ended up kneeling on the floor with her head on the seat between my legs. I was bent over her with my chest pressed down on her back. I've fired one of those beasts. The gun emptied the magazine in a blink of an eye. The easiest way to describe shooting one is that it feels just like turning on a high-pressure water hose. The gun bucks and just starts pushing straight back into your hand while you notice a stream of ejected brass cases arcing up and over your shoulder. The whole thing is over in a second or two. If you haven't practised, accuracy is non-existent, but with seventeen bullets in the general direction of your target, who cared? Well, I did if I was the target, but nothing happened. I then heard people getting up and leaving the bus. Frances did not move and neither did I. I felt a tap on my shoulder. It felt like the barrel of the gun.

'I don't think this is the best time for a blow job,' he chuckled, not unpleasantly. 'Please sit in your seats.'

I sat up and Frances extricated herself, short of breath.

'I think I prefer to be shot than suffocate in your crotch,' she said.

The officer laughed. I'd decided he had to be the officer in charge with his pips, his sound grasp of English, his better weapon and smarter uniform.

'Ah, well, you can't blame a man for trying.'

She smiled, 'You're incorrigible.'

'Identification please,' the officer said. He glanced at the back page that held our photos and then said, 'You're not married.'

'No, partners.' I prayed Frances would say nothing.

'Partners,' a big smile showed his beautiful white teeth. 'The UK tax system has a lot to answer for. You better stay together then.'

Frances still said nothing. The officer was appraising us with his very dark eyes.

'Okay,' he said and shook his head. Something was puzzling him. He then walked down the bus to check on other people.

Frances said quietly to me, 'What do you think this is about?'

'Diplomatic hostages, I would have thought. Otherwise they would have taken all of us. Must be some negotiations somewhere.'

She smiled. She, like me, knew there were negotiations going on to do with human rights and the place and rights of Muslims. But more important were the criminal negotiations and that required their security hostages – one nun and one American man.

'Button it!' The order was crisp, clear and directed at us. This guy must have been educated in the UK or US and probably in the military.

The officer left the bus and two other men got on. One was the driver and the other seemed to be some sort of NCO, as he wore corporal's bars on his epaulets. His uniform more or less fitted him.

The bus joined the convoy and we saw our former travelling companions standing in a group, watching us leave. I realized they had no luggage. The Toyotas were between the buses, so we were a convoy: Toyota, bus, two Toyotas, bus, two Toyotas, our bus, two Toyotas. Only the nuns and UK/US citizens had been taken hostage, or that's what it seemed like. There were no Israelis. I suppose the uneasy feeling I'd had in the service station was because the staff knew this was going to happen.

The nuns were not singing. I was now missing the company of their hymns.

We travelled for two half days and one nights, the drivers changing every three or four hours. The only stops for any time were to meet our natural functions and to refuel, and sometimes refuelling was from jerry cans. On the second day, we arrived at our destination, hungry, dirty, dishevelled and smelly. Our guards were in little better condition. Assuming we averaged something less than twenty miles an hour and we had been going for twenty-four hours, we were probably 300 miles as the crow flies from the service station. We were in a heavily wooded mountain region. By guessing, and with my limited knowledge of the geography, this was the Paraiso region, the home of the independence-seeking Hastaqbeli group. My conclusion was that a radial Islamist group of converts from Christianity had abducted us. Why? The criminal negotiations to secure the negotiation hostages were the most likely reason, but was that the only reason? In that case, they only needed to take two people: the nun and the American.

Everyone we had seen was a member of the indigenous population. They were apparently Muslim, but this was a predominantly Roman Catholic country, apart from some relics of past religions in such places as this. The thought sprang to my mind, 'There are none so pure as the purified.' This country had always been in turmoil and the Islamic dimension was just another layer on the mound of discontent and hatred. I'd read that the government had tried to suppress the growth of Islam, so I expect that fuelled a number of converts from the anti-government population.

Our original mission was now out of the window and we were just a couple of bodies on the flotsam of a turbulent, terrorist-ridden political sea.

'Let me go home. I wanna go home. I feel so broke up. I wanna go home.'

Frances looked at me and shook her head. 'You're singing songs to yourself again, aren't you?'

I nodded. She shook her head, leaned back and shut her eyes.

It was only when we reached our destination that I was sure this was the plan to ensure Jorge Machacamarca secured the negotiation hostages for his safety, but now he also had additional hostages as bargaining chips.

26

The accommodation was not bad, but it had clearly not been used for some time. I presumed it had been some sort of safari hotel for tourists. This was an ideal place for tourism, given the forest and the mountains; there was loads of wildlife in the area. The most modern change I could see was the razor-wire fence and camouflaged watchtowers. If this had been modified for us, I would have been surprised. It seemed the fences were designed to keep something out rather than to keep us in.

The nuns were settled in a dormitory-style block also within the enclosed compound. There was a growing area just outside the compound and already there were some nuns, the Mother Superior and guards looking at it. I imagined they intended to grow vegetables or something there. They were clearly preparing for the long haul or they knew something we didn't.

In only three weeks, life settled into a routine. The nuns, forty of them, had taken charge. The whole camp – or was it a prison? – was running like clockwork. At daybreak, chanting and singing of hymns awakened us. A small group of nuns then attended to breakfast and cleaned the restaurant. Some went into the garden, where they had already dug it over, with minimal help from the likes of me, and planted things. I assumed they were vegetables. They had a laundry and staffed that. A couple of us helped them with making and repairing things, so most people were contributing. By the sixth day, a Wednesday, a small committee had also emerged and, for some reason, the Reverend Mother co-opted Joe McGreevy, the American security hostage (who had not mentioned that he was the brother of the senator), and me onto it. I'm not a committee person really. Frances was, if only because you had to be to survive to the ripe old age of thirty-seven in the security services.

Frances, Joe and I represented the Brits and Yanks. Reverend Mother, Sister Teresa (a lovely woman who must have been seventy and was as sharp as a pin) and Sister Veronica (a young girl who couldn't be more than eighteen) formed the rest of the committee.

We received a message for the committee to come to the dining hall. We arrived at the appointed time to be greeted by the man we now knew as Captain Wayna and a couple of his ragged army. They were quite relaxed.

'Señor Machacamarca will be here shortly to speak to you,' said Captain Wayna.' As he spoke we heard the gentle crunch of the gravel outside as a car pulled up. The door opened. He was a powerful looking man, in his fifties, five foot eight or nine, with broad shoulders, olive skin, a dark seven o'clock shadow, and dressed in a double breasted pin striped dark navy suit. Incongruously he was wearing light brown shoes. Two equally powerful-looking men in suits accompanied him. There was a bulge of weapons under their jackets.

'Good afternoon, please be seated.' He waved his arm towards some seats at one of the tables. He had a Latin accent but his English was clear and his pronunciation was good. We sat and he joined us at the table. He remained standing with his suited men at either side of him and looked at each of us. Almost inspecting us. 'You will be Sister Theresa the Mother Superior; I am very pleased to meet you.' She nodded but said nothing. He looked at the other nuns. 'Sister Teresa and Sister Veronica.' He smiled and nodded to them. He then looked at Frances, almost inspected her. 'You will be the mysterious Ms Portello, a person that disappears and then reappears. Spanish name but not Spanish.'

'Good evening, Señor.'

'Ah, this one speaks.' He turned to Joe. 'Joe McGreevy who apparently has a famous brother who I have met on a few occasions.' He turned his penetrating gaze on me. 'Now you are also interesting. A Royal Military Police Captain who attempts to get people he has arrested freed and then comes to Bolivia at a time of turmoil as the, I think it is called, the partner of Ms Portello.' He smiled and ran his eyes over us again. 'I apologise for the inconvenience you find yourselves in. Unfortunately we had to abduct you to aid us in achieving our ends. We will not harm you. We hope you enjoy your sojourn here. Please treat it as a short holiday. If you need anything please ask. As I said, we wish you no harm and hope you enjoy your stay. You will be released,' he paused, 'eventually.' He paused again and smiled. 'This is a very remote place so it is difficult to travel to or from. I wish you a pleasant stay.'

'Excuse me, Señor Machacamarca.' I heard myself speak. He turned towards me. 'Yes?'

'Are we all prisoners or can some of us be released now?'

'Unfortunately, due to the political situation and some imminent negotiations, we need the opposition to us to believe we have hostages.'

'Do you need all of us to demonstrate your criminality?'

'Clearly Captain Robinson we have different perspectives. You are our protection not hostages. If we could let you go we would do that immediately. We understand you are inconvenienced but we wish you no harm. We will supply all your needs and I would like you to enjoy your time with us.

He turned and walked to the door, followed by his entourage, then turned and faced us again. 'Good after-noon and please have a pleasant day.' With that he left.

There was silence until we heard the vehicles pull away and then babble broke out.

The days dragged on. I was relaxing after a long day of

not doing very much. In reality, Frances and I were still recovering. We had had dengue fever and it had not been clever. I was still weak and not good to live with and there were a number of other people in the same boat, including a few of the nuns. It was really bad for about seven days with fever, bladder problems, constant headaches, eye pain, severe dizziness and loss of appetite, and then about two weeks of slow improvement. But we were through the worst and well on the mend trying to nurse each other. The nuns had set up a nursing regime that had kept us hydrated and fed us food that we could cope with. The local doctor, who I'm sure was liaising with a witch doctor, provided some smelly brew that kept the fever in check and reduced the headache from blinding to just agony, and some stuff called Ribavirin that it seemed was an antiviral. He assured us that this was a mild version, so what a full-blooded version was like I'd hate to think. Some of the nuns were put on a drip, but Frances and I were not that bad. Machacamarca visited the sick and it seemed he was concerned and he was paying for the doctor who it turned out he had brought from the nearest hospital.

Sister Veronica came to our suite and asked us to come to the chapel. She was distressed, so we went in a rush or as much of a rush as we could manage. It was evening and the chapel was dim. In the short time we had been in this place, they had done a great job and the chapel had a feel about it. I was an atheist, but even I could feel a presence there. Sister Veronica led us through to the committee room. There was a tension there. The Reverend Mother and Sister Teresa were close together in mutual support. There was also a local woman, Naira, who served in the rebel leader's house. She was standing close to Captain Wayna, who had been the officer on the bus, and was in obvious distress. From the looks on their faces and the way they were clustered, something very serious had happened.

'It can't be this bad,' I said.

'It is.' As usual, Reverend Mother was the spokesperson. 'Tell us.'

Reverend Mother turned to Captain Wayna. She wanted him to give us the bad news, whatever it was.

'Please. It must not come out that I told you.' His voice quavered.

Frances picked up the control. 'Captain, you have our word. You're distressed. Please take your time and tell us whatever it is from the beginning. If things are in order, it will be easier for us to understand.'

The sweat was running down his face. At the armpits of his shirt were large, damp patches. My first thoughts were that this man was scared, but then it seemed more like he was horrified.

'The commandant sent for me.'

'The commandant? Who is the commandant?'

'Señor Machacamarca is the commandant.'

'Yes, I understand,' said Frances.

'I have to make preparations. Let me start again; the commandant sent for me. There were some men there who I know are leaders of our movement. They have been negotiating with the government so that we Muslims have legitimacy. That is so we can have mosques and can stand for government and those sorts of things. We had asked that representatives from the Islamic countries be arbiters and they said yes, if diplomatic representatives from the USA and UK could be there also. Agreement was achieved some weeks ago. Shortly, the negotiations will reconvene.' He stopped and drank some water. So far, everything seemed positive. 'We captured you as a safeguard that the government would stick to the agreement.' He stopped again. He was having trouble.

'I understand so far, Captain. We have come to no harm. Something has changed. Just tell us in your own words.'

He swallowed hard and continued, 'There is a rumour that the Americans will drop out. There has been some leak in an American newspaper and some politicians are saying the USA should not be involved. The newspapers say we are criminals and we do deals with the mafia.'

'But it's only a rumour. No decision has been made.'

'Yes, yes, it's only a rumour, but our leaders have responded with a threat.'

'That threat is?'

Captain Wayna again sipped some water. His hands were trembling and the water splashed about in the tumbler.

'They said that the nuns will be marched naked from where they are being held to the town. They will be filmed and the pictures sent around the world.'

'What does Machacamarca say?'

'He is against it but the Imam says it will happen.'

'But what of the Ulama?'

'We lack the law Captain.'

'What is Ulama, Jake?' asked Frances.

'It is their lawyers that interpret the Quran,' said the Reverend Mother.

'Let me be clear, Captain; this act will only occur if the Americans do not come to the negotiations?' I asked.

'That is what they have told the Americans, but they are going to do it anyway, whether the Americans come or not.'

'Why?'

'I don't know.'

'When?'

'The day before the negotiations start again.'

'That is?'

'In two weeks.'

'That is the twenty-third.'

'No, that is the twenty-sixth.'

'Who leads the American group?'

'It's Secretary of State, Mr Bloomington.'

165

'Who else?'

'Who else? Yes, he will be Mr McGreevy; he's a senator and is friend of Señor Machacamarca. He's coming to visit Señor Machacamarca before the conference.'

'And for the British?'

'I believe it's the man who is foreign secretary.'

'Who else?'

'I not know.'

'Why is Naira here?'

'She heard and told me to do something.'

'She told you?'

'Yes, sir. She's my sister.'

'I see.' I had an overwhelming feeling of helplessness, then I realized they were looking to me for a solution. 'This is something I will have to discuss privately with Reverend Mother. It's best that nobody else knows what I have in mind until Reverend Mother agrees.' I turned to the Reverend Mother. 'Reverend Mother, may I talk with you tomorrow?'

'You can, Captain, and I will listen with interest and hope.' She had this calm exterior. She was standing upright and her voice was steady.

Frances and I walked back to our suite. We walked in silence and we were halfway there before Frances said, 'What are you going to suggest?'

'I'm going to suggest this is bullshit.'

'How can you think that?'

'Let's just think this through. There is a meeting here between Machacamarca, Senator McGreevy and Randolph Mabry. This is to make a deal on drugs, silver and gas. Assuming this goes well for the mafia, the aristocracy and the Islamists get UK and US support in their negotiations with the Bolivian government. If it goes pear shaped then the Islamists are buggered, so they want an ace to play. The nuns are their aces.'

'I'm not sure.'

'I'm saying the deal on the twenty-third will go well for the Brits and Yanks because the Islamists need that deal, both for their businesses and for their political ends.'

'But if it doesn't?' pushed Frances.

'Islam is a deep and profound religion. Their very theology would not allow this atrocity, that's why I asked about Ulama, and if they did go ahead with it, they would be condemned by the rest of the Islamic world.'

'But they blow themselves up.'

'True, but that's war. This isn't war but negotiation.'

We reached our apartment.

'Then, why is this rumour put about?'

'I only answer easy questions, and that's a hard one.'

'A hard one... Um, I guess we best go to bed then.'

'What a splendid idea.'

Frances laughed, 'Good things come to those that wait.' So, we went to bed. Life is strange. In the real world out there Frances is my boss but here she is now truly my partner. We had settled down in harmony.

The next morning, I went to see the Reverend Mother. I told her my thinking. She said she would talk to Machacamarca. I could see she was not entirely convinced.

'Supposing, just supposing, you're wrong and they... they... they...'

'Reverend Mother, let's consider that then. What's the real problem? If it's the dignity of your sisters you're concerned about, I would ask, where is your faith?'

'But, but...'

'Reverend Mother, the real problem is that your nuns will not march singing with their heads held high.'

She looked at me in surprise and realization began to dawn on her. 'Supposing they steel themselves, march and sing in unison. What matter that they are as naked as your God made them? The biggest problem is motivating them and them being fit enough to make the march as proud brides of Jesus. Look at the weather. It is unseasonably hot and if they can withstand the heat of the sun and the burning of their exposed skin, then they can march with pride and shame the people who would treat them badly.'

She was thinking. 'How can I convince them of this thing, Jake?'

Have you heard of Saint Ethelflaeda?'

'No. I don't recall that saint.'

'Saint Ethelflaeda was a nun in charge of a Benedictine house in a place called Romsey. She was sanctified for such acts as the chanting of psalms late at night, whilst standing nude in the freezing water of the nearby River Test. So if a nun who went nude into freezing water can be a saint your nuns could walk in the sun singing hymns.'

'So I must prepare them?'

'Yes, Reverend Mother, and how will you do that?'

'They must lay nude in the sun and become tanned, and they must spend time becoming fit for the march.' She was in deep thought.

'Problem?'

'Yes,' she paused. She was embarrassed; she pulled back her shoulders. 'There is nowhere they can sunbathe privately.'

'That is good then.'

'Why?'

'If they have to march naked, many people will watch them: people who are strangers. Better they are used to being seen by those who are not strangers.'

'May the Lord protect us from this evil and may we have the strength to be humble in our hour of torment.' There was steel in her voice.

'That's my girl.' I smiled.

'Tomorrow I will tell them of Saint Ethelflaeda and gain their agreement. I will take it one small step at a time.' I could now hear confidence in her voice. She was going to lead a brave band of martyrs.

I got back to our room and Frances asked how it went, so I told her. Her response was, 'You disgusting, perverted bastard. I bet you volunteered to train them, you... you pervert.' She spat the words at me.

'No, but you should.'

'I... I... Get the fuck out of here.'

'Whoa! Just think about this.'

'Think about it? Think about it?' She was incensed.

I retreated. That night I slept outside. In the early hours of the morning, I felt a gentle kick in the ribs.

'Come on in. I'm sorry. You're right. They have no choice and this is making the best of a bad job. I will go and see the Reverend Mother tomorrow. I doubt very much whether we can get them tanned sufficiently or fit enough in the time, but we can build their morale and we have an advantage in their belief system. And if you smile or say I told you so, you'll sleep outside again tonight.'

I said nothing. Discretion, Jake, discretion.

27

It was a couple of days later. I was shaving. The blade was not as sharp as it should be, but I seemed to have this compulsion to be clean-shaven. Silly really – who cared in our situation?

Suddenly, a screech of brakes and the sound of flying shale alerted me; in fact, it sent a shiver of apprehension down my back. I was heading for the front door, wiping away the soap from my face, when the banging began. It was the guard captain and he was chalk white. That was an exaggeration, given he was normally nut brown, but I'd never seen him so pallid and he was trembling.

'What's up, Captain?' That just sounded stupid, like the cartoon character Bugs Bunny saying, 'What's up, Doc?'

'Jake, I need you and bring Frances. Now!'

This sounded serious and my mind was full of questions that I suppressed. I shouted for Frances. She wasn't there; she was with the nuns.

'Stay here, Captain. I'll go and get her.'

I ran across to the nuns' area and into the yard at the back to be confronted by a large number of naked, female bodies.

'Frances! Frances! Where the devil are you?' It was not the best choice of words, but – ah, well – Frances appeared. 'Come on, we're needed.'

'But. . .'

'Bugger the but. Come on.'

Seconds later, we were haring down the road, bouncing about on the uneven surface and hanging on for grim death through the village and up the hill to the commandant's residence. It was palatial. The gardens were immaculate and

two gardeners were standing in the middle of a very unlikely, bowling-green-flat lawn. They were two of the people
who had abducted us on the buses. On the drive were soldiers, just standing about. The captain drove across this
lovely lawn.

A senior officer and two men in suits were standing
before the door. One of the suited men walked up to me
and held out his hand.

'I'm Detective Calammarca.' He was small and dark with
the flat facial features of the local people. His English
pronunciation was clear and correct with very little foreign
accent. He was clearly an educated man. 'This is Colonel
Irupana.' He indicated the officer. 'And we understand
you're Captain Jake Robinson of the RMP on holiday here.'

That was a neat description. He knew about me. I wondered how.

'This is Frances Portello, my partner.'

'Ah, yes, the mystery woman who disappeared some eight
years ago. I'm pleased to meet you, madam.'

Mystery woman, disappeared eight years ago? Somebody
had definitely been doing some research on us.

He turned back to me. 'We have a problem. It seems that
Señor Machacamarca has been murdered by the Mother
Superior of the sisters in retreat on the hill. This is a very
delicate matter and it was thought politic if you and your
lady friend would... um, would handle the Mother Superior.' He was ice cool. The Mother Superior had murdered
Señor Machacamarca, but this was only a 'problem' and this
'problem' is only a 'delicate' matter. His very distance and
coldness dissipated the shock I felt. The immediate con-
traction of my stomach relaxed and I was breathing normally again. I realized I had held my breath. Frances took
my hand; she was in shock. I put my arm around her and
that caring responsibility reinforced my calmness. 'Handle'?
I wondered what that meant.

'Would you like me to conduct an investigation of some description?' Even to my ears this sounded naïve.

'We would like you to work with us. We know you are on holiday here but it's essential that there can be no accusations of bias. It's important that it's conducted in English so everything is clear and understood. We are led to believe you are an expert in interrogation.'

'I see!' I wondered if his definition of 'interrogation' and mine were the same. 'Tell me what you've found so far,' I said, 'and what you think this is all about.'

'You'll work with us then?'

'Yes, of course.'

'It will be kept – how you say? – confident.'

'It will be totally confidential.'

'Yes. I apologize – confidential.'

'Now what happened?'

'It seems the Reverend Mother – um – stabbed Señor Machacamarca.'

'And?'

'It would seem that Señor Machacamarca – um – assaulted the Reverend Mother.'

'Assaulted?'

'Perhaps, um...' He was struggling for words and he was embarrassed. 'Raped.'

'Raped?' I could hear the shock in my voice.

'That is the accusation, Captain.'

'Action, Jake, my boy. Action.' I could hear my father's voice and that took me through my consternation into clear balance.

'Okay. Send somebody to get Sister Claudine, Sister Angelica and Sister Laurel.'

'But why?'

'Sister Claudine is a doctor and she can examine the Reverend Mother. Sister Angelica is a nurse. Sister Laurel is a psychotherapist and we may need her advice.'

'Yes, I see, and as they are sisters it will be – yes – confidential.'

'And we will have to consult with Sister Teresa to handle any protocol.'

'What is prot-o-col?'

'The code of conduct when it comes to the religious aspects.'

'I understand; it is to avoid offence and things that may be sins.'

'That's correct. If you send somebody for the sisters, I will go and see what I can find out. Okay?'

'Yes, certainly, Captain. We will stay here.'

I looked at Frances.

'I'll come with you, Jake.'

The policeman on the door stepped aside for us, though he seemed reluctant to do so. We were in a magnificent hallway with three doors on either side, a wide stairway to the left and a passageway to the right. The third door on the left was open; it was a sitting room and the Reverend Mother was sitting on the edge of an armchair. She was looking at the floor, so did not see us until I spoke.

'Reverend Mother.'

She looked up. She seemed controlled, probably numb, in shock or denial, or disbelief.

'Ah, Jake.' She went to stand.

A voice barked an order in Spanish. It was then I noticed two armed policemen.

'You two, out!' I ordered and pointed to the door. They turned their guns on me. I walked toward the nearest one so that his rifle, a 5.56mm Galil rifle of Israeli manufacture, was 6 inches from my chest. 'You, out, now.' I snapped out the command. A look of total confusion crossed his face.

A quiet, female voice spoke in what I assumed to be Spanish. The policeman, or he might have been a soldier, shrugged and lowered his weapon. I maintained eye contact. The policeman looked down and then walked away through the door that I had pointed to, followed by his companion. I watched them go. A young woman stood by the door.

'You're either very brave or very foolish, sir,' she said.

'Thank you. I'm sure I'm just plain stupid.'

'Yes, sir,' she smiled and left.

'Christ! You frightened me fartless,' said Frances.

I turned to the Reverend Mother.

'Reverend Mother, it seems you've been in the wars.'

Her left eye was blackened and was merely a slit. Her nose was also swollen and bruises ran down the left side of her face. She was in a cotton dressing gown that was tightly crossed over in front of her and secured with a tie. Her legs were bare and she had no shoes.

'Thank you for coming, Jake. I found the policemen rather intimidating.' She spoke with a flat, quiet reserve; not the depth and power of her normal speech. I was surprised that she did not appear distraught or anxious. I just wanted to go and hug her and tell her it would all be all right, but I couldn't, unfortunately.

I noticed blood smears on the front of the dressing gown where it seemed she had wiped her hands. I also noticed smudges elsewhere on the dressing gown and on the tie. It appeared that she put it on with blood on her hands. I guessed she was naked beneath the cotton material.

28

I went outside leaving the Reverend Mother with Frances. Detective Calammarca greeted me.

'We have been discussing our, um, ah, problem Captain Robinson. We agree it might be expedient if you and I interrogate the Reverend Mother.'

I was surprised and pleased, 'Why?'

'This is very difficult. There are the church matters and the...' He stopped thinking of the right words. 'There are political matters and we,' he paused, 'we are unsure what is the wisest way to progress given the negotiations due soon.'

I could recognise the problem with international observers and the press. If I did the interviewing then the Bolivians could construct an appropriate story.

'Perhaps you are right. So it might be better if I interview her and you are an observer. We do things slightly differently in England.'

He spoke to the small gathering of officials and I could see and sense the relief and the agreement.

I asked him to wait and went back into the room where the Reverend Mother was with Frances.

I'd never interviewed a Reverend Mother before and felt this was going to be difficult.

'Reverend Mother, I'm going to interview you as a policeman.'

'Yes, Jake. I understand.'

'Frances will be here as a chaperone and there will be a local policeman here also.'

She nodded.

'Frances, will you get Detective Calammarca? Only Calammarca.'

As she left, I placed a chair across the room to the left of where the Reverend Mother was sitting. He would be able to see her, but she would have to turn slightly to see him in her peripheral vision. I placed another chair to the left of where I would sit in front of the Reverend Mother. Frances would sit here, but not in direct vision, though she would be in view. Frances was a reassurance factor.

Frances came back, but with her were all three men.

'I'm sorry, gentlemen. Only Detective Calammarca.'

'But–'

I cut off the detective. 'I decide; you understand?' I sounded like the idiot English tourist in a foreign country. 'With all these people we are unlikely to find out what happened and it may be difficult to control what is told to people afterwards.'

The detective nodded. He had clearly recognized the uncertainty and the implications. He turned to his companions and in apologetic terms, or that's what it sounded like, asked them to leave. This they did. I pointed to the chair over to my right. He went and sat there; Frances sat in the other chair.

'Frances, Detective, I'm going to conduct an interview with the Reverend Mother. You will remain silent and you will remain seated. Do you understand me?' I looked at the detective; he nodded. I raised my eyebrows.

He responded, 'Yes, I understand, Captain Robinson.'

I turned to Frances. 'Yes, Jake.'

'I suggest you two make notes of anything that you think is significant.' I did not check that they had paper and pens. Frances walked across to a bureau against the wall and, after rummaging in it, came away with an A4 pad and a ballpoint pen. The Reverend Mother had sat with her head down with her hands in her lap all through the preparations.

'Reverend Mother.'

She looked up.

'How would you like me to address you?'

She established eye contact.

'Oh, Jake, you are a considerate man, but you ask me an impossible question. "Reverend Mother" is the official way to address me. It's my position. But this interview is personal. It's about the inconsequential, insignificant person who I really am. Perhaps you should just call me Beth.'

'Thank you, Beth, could I have your full name?' This was so uncomfortable. How do you question a mother superior of a sisterhood in a criminal situation?

'It's a long time since I had to answer that. Yes, my full given name is Elizabeth Joan Huxley.'

'What I would like, Beth, is for you to tell me exactly what happened from the time you left the centre yesterday evening until now. I will, on occasion, ask you to clarify what you're saying. I'll make notes of the main points and Frances and the detective will also do that. Are you clear what we're going to do?'

'Yes, Jake.' She thought for a few seconds. 'Yesterday, one of the staff of Señor Machacamarca delivered an invitation to dinner. I had requested to see him on a matter that you and I'd discussed. He said transport would be sent for me at six-thirty yesterday.'

'This was an oral invitation, not a written one?'

'Yes, that is correct.'

'At that time, did you ask why?'

'No, I assumed it was a business dinner and I assumed it was on the subject we had discussed.' She was being circumspect not mentioning the subject we had discussed.

'Did you have any concerns about accepting or going alone to dinner with this man?'

'No. Concerns did not cross my mind.' What innocence.

'Have you had similar invitations in the past?'

177

'Yes. Normally there is a group of people, so I suppose I assumed there would be other interested guests, but I didn't ask.'

'You said "usually".'

'Yes, I see; I've been invited as the only guest on two occasions. The first was when the archbishop invited me for dinner, and that was to ask me if I would like to become the mother superior of a small convent and headmistress of the attached school. The second time was similar and it was to take up this post.'

'This post?'

'Oh, yes, The Convent of Saint Catherine and the school. All the nuns here are of that convent and most are teachers. We also train novices who will become teachers or who are already teachers.

'When were you appointed?'

'It must be – let me see. It must be six years ago now.' She was now confident to answer my questions and had accepted the pattern of me seeking clarification about the things she said.

'So six-thirty yesterday is approaching. What are you doing?'

'I was dressed and ready. I was sitting with a small group of sisters. We were chatting.'

'What about?'

She smiled a small smile. She had anticipated the question. 'There was of course much concern about what may happen to us if the threat to make us walk to the village was carried out. There were some suggestions about what we might need and a question about when we would be released from here, that sort of thing.'

'What happened next?'

'A large car arrived; it was chauffeur driven. We arrived here at, I suppose, ten to seven.'

'Do you know the name of the driver?'

'Yes, it's Adolfo.'

'His surname?'

'I'm sorry, no.'

'You don't know or don't want to tell me?'

'Oh, I'm sorry, Jake; I don't know his name. I now understand I must be more specific.'

'Thank you, Beth. You arrived. What happened?'

'I was invited to have a drink. I took a small sherry. I regarded it as an aperitif.'

'Were you also offered food with it?'

'Oh, yes, Jake. There were crisps and cheese bits on a stick, that sort of thing.' She looked at me as if she was waiting for the next question. I stayed silent. 'We chatted.'

'What about?'

'The gardens.'

'What gardens?'

She was visualizing the conversation. 'Oh, yes, Jorge had been to the UK and had seen the Ascott Garden at Wing.'

'You referred to Señor Machacamarca as Jorge.'

'Yes. He asked me to.'

For some reason, this did not seem right, but I didn't know why. It was this funny instinct that I had when things were not correct.

'What did he call you?'

She looked surprised at the question. Why should she?

'Reverend Mother, of course.'

Why, of course, I was calling her Beth. I felt discomfort again.

'Ascott Garden at Wing; that's in Buckinghamshire, right?' I asked.

'Yes, my lovely, transparent, Jake.'

That response surprised me. Well, the word 'lovely' surprised me, but why, I didn't really know. But she was now reading my questioning pattern so that it was transparent to her. She was telling me, but why?'

'So he had been there?'

'Oh, yes, he knew all about the Dutch Garden, the Madeira Walk, the Venus Garden and the topiary sundial. Yes, he was familiar with the gardens and other gardens.'

'And then?'

'We went to dinner.'

'At what time was that?'

She was thinking. 'It must have been about a quarter to eight.'

'So, you chatted for about three-quarters of an hour.'

'Yes, I suppose so.'

'Long time. Did you have a second sherry?'

'Yes Jake, but I didn't drink it all.'

'Anything notable about dinner?'

'Not really.'

'You had some wine with dinner?'

'Yes, I know where you're going, Jake, and I probably had more wine than I would normally have in an evening at a formal, social dinner.'

'Why?'

'You mean why did I drink more than normal?'

I nodded.

'I suppose it was because it was exceptionally pleasant wine and the host was hospitable. The past few weeks have been stressful and...' She paused. 'I just did, Jake.'

'It must be difficult for you being questioned in this way, having a duty to be totally honest.'

'I suppose for some that is the case, but because of my calling, it isn't. If I tell it as I perceive it, then it will be. No, the truth will be my shield.'

I liked that; 'the truth will be my shield.' I'd been on so many investigations where innocent people have believed it was safer to lie than tell the truth. Equally, I'd see the innocent suffer and, on at least one occasion, be convicted for telling the truth because the prosecution bent the truth.

'Did you cover the topics you wanted to over dinner?'

'No, we talked about the political situation really. Jorge Machacamarca wanted to gain the perspective of a Christian about government, the law, democracy and Islam, and it was a wide-ranging discussion.'

'Why do you think he wanted to discuss this subject?'

'He's representing the Islamic people of Bolivia. He felt the need to gain an understanding of how the British and American observers at the discussions may interpret things.'

'So it was more political than religious.'

'I suppose so.' She paused. She was thinking. 'I hadn't really thought about it like that.'

'What happened next?'

'After dinner, we went into the lounge.' She paused as if searching for words. 'And it became difficult.'

'What became difficult?'

'Initially, the subject became difficult.'

'What subject?'

'Mr Machacamarca wanted to talk about sex in the church and whether being celibate gave the sisters a problem.'

I was having problems. It wasn't just the subject; I knew I'd have to tiptoe round it. There'd been a shift in where she was coming from. She had been up front; now she was not. There was a shift from Jorge to Mr Machacamarca: a distancing. Was it the subject or was it something else?

'So, that subject was difficult for you?'

'Yes, and he asked whether I was a virgin and whether I regretted not – as he described it – having experienced the joy of womanhood.'

Ambiguity? So was she saying she was a virgin or was she saying virginity was his assumption? There was something amiss here. Leave it, Jake, you can come back to it.

'So what did you do?'

'Thank you, Jake, you can be considerate.' She knew I

181

avoided the question. She was genuinely grateful. Did that mean a truthful answer would have been embarrassing? It answered my unasked question.

'I said I would like to leave.'

'And?'

'He said there was no transport available.'

I waited. The silence continued.

'Beth?'

'I know I must tell you, but it's difficult.'

'Would you rather tell Frances and I'll leave.'

'Despite being an atheist, you are a good man, Jake.'

Was she playing me? I decided to take it slowly. There was a long silence. Then the Reverend Mother swallowed and started again.

'He placed his right arm around my back onto my right upper arm at my shoulder. I went to turn away and he placed his left hand on my left breast.' This was so specific; not 'he touched my breast', but the whole nine yards. She was trembling. This was the first slip in her self-control. As she spoke, her voice cracked, 'I felt totally powerlessness: a feeling of helplessness. I'd never experienced anything like that before. I tried to say no, but my mouth was dry and all I could do was croak. It wasn't that I didn't want to. . . to, ah, to fight.'

The pause after 'want to'; what did it mean? 'Fight' was a strong word, not 'struggle', not 'escape', but fight. Fight whom? Him or herself?

'It was that I couldn't. It's all a blur, but it's also all so clear. He stripped me. He was not aggressive or rough; I couldn't stop him. I was – no – it was like I was paralyzed.'

The whole of this passage was dominated by 'he'. It was a personification shift. Was she seeing Machacamarca differently now? It wouldn't be a surprise, but it didn't feel right. She was crying. Her arms were across her chest, gripping her opposite shoulders and her elbows were on her knees, which were pressed together. Her head was bent forward.

The tears dripped from her nose onto her knees. She was silently sobbing. Frances went to get up. I shook my head and she sat down.

'Beth, you were naked, frightened and powerless. I'd like you to tell me what happened next. Take your time and we'll stop anytime you wish to.'

She looked up at me and smiled, a fleeting smile of thanks, then nodded. She looked at the floor, at my feet. She was not talking to me.

'He laid me on the floor, parted my legs and touched me. He was gentle. He was over me. He took my hand and placed it... and placed it...' Her hands came down on her knees. She raised her head and looked me straight in the eyes. 'He placed my hand on his penis and I held him. He then moved himself forward and backward, then he entered me and it hurt. And when he had finished, he went and got a wet flannel and a towel. He washed me and dried me and I couldn't move. He picked me up, put me on the bed and covered me.'

'So he carried you from here to the bedroom?'

'No.' She stopped. It was almost as if she didn't know the answer to my question. It was as if my question was a surprise. 'No, we were not in here.' She was thinking; didn't she know where the rape took place? 'We were in the small sitting room.'

I'd missed a trick finding out where they were, but she had corrected me. There was definitely something wrong. Yes. She had said, 'After dinner, we went into the lounge'. It was as if she did not know where the rape had occurred and she made up a place.

'Did he speak to you during this sexual encounter?'

'Yes, he spoke to me, but I did not hear him. And, Jake, it was rape. I didn't want this. I'd no choice in this and I had no control, no strength. Yet, in an odd sort of way, I had no fear, for my God was with me and I will be forgiven.'

Um, the past tense then future tense. Odd. Is her God not with her now? She will be forgiven in the future; is she in some sort of limbo? No, I was reading this wrong. But how? What? Press on, Jake.

The Reverend Mother was looking at me. There was concern on her face; for me or for her?

'What happened to you, Beth, is called the "freeze reaction". It's strongly linked to survival. It happens to most women and I believe to most men, when they are being raped and to many people when their lives are in danger. I've seen it happen to very brave soldiers in action.'

The Reverend Mother was looking at me. It seemed, for some reason, she was relieved. I was definitely missing something. The way she had told the events was as though it was a long time ago, not just last night. I knew I needed to take her forward gently.

'You're now in bed, Beth.' I paused. Her eyes held mine. 'You're warm. How are you feeling?'

She was there; her eyes were on me, but they were looking inward.

'I'm praying. I'm praying for forgiveness and I pray for his forgiveness. I feel selfish because I'm worried what the sisters in my care will think of me. I'm angry with myself for such arrogance. I'm confused by my anger. It's a measure of my arrogance and I pray for forgiveness and inner calm.' She stopped and came back into the room, and she was seeing me. She gathered herself and said, 'I must have gone to sleep.'

I felt the Reverend Mother was going to be okay. She had relived her time in bed as if it was now, in the present, in this room. Her profound belief was her support system and maybe she had previous successes in dealing with crises. But could anyone, irrespective of their inner and external support system, fully recover? Her words sounded right but ambiguous. I supposed they were bound to be in such a traumatic situation.

29

It seemed to me that the rape phase was over. I needed to move forward to the killing. 'Are you okay to continue, Beth?' I asked. I still didn't feel right calling her Beth. It seemed I was not talking to a person named Reverend Mother – the person I knew – but to a stranger named Beth.

'Yes, Jake.'

I wasn't too sure she was okay to continue, but I decided to move on. 'You were woken, Beth.'

'Yes. I heard angry voices and I was afraid. I knew they were arguing about me. I can't remember what I heard, but it was someone who wanted to... who wanted to... who... who...' She became silent. 'Then I heard Jorge Machaca-marca saying they had not agreed this and another man saying he didn't care. He wanted... he wanted... Jake, oh, Jake, this other man wanted to rape me again and I was terrified.' She adopted the curled forward position again and her body was shuddering.

I wanted to touch her, bring comfort to her. I was on the edge of tears myself. My chest was constricted and I could hardly breathe, but knew I must on no account touch her. Frances was on her feet and I stood and held up my hand to stop her. Frances was crying. I knew she was feeling pain, perhaps like my pain, but the Reverend Mother could not be touched; it could become a trigger for this deep, trau-matic emotion in the future. Frances sat down again, searching in her bag, and found a handkerchief. I sat and faced the Reverend Mother.

'Would other people have seen or heard the other man?' My police training had kicked in. If a witness or victim

185

believed somebody else had seen the same person as they had, they are more likely to tell the truth. Why did I think this pressure was needed? Something was not right. I didn't know what it was, but it wasn't right. Nothing the Reverend Mother said would be a lie, so I faced confusion. I was going to have to park my feelings and be analytical and very sceptical.

'I don't know.'

'But given what you do know, a chef or some kitchen staff, security staff, servants; is it likely?' I was pressing home the idea that her description could be verified.

'I suppose so.'

My sixth sense was registering that Beth was very uncomfortable but covering it.

'Tell me about the voice of the other man.' I was now a cold-blooded interrogator. I was literally cold. I was crystal clear, emotionless and focused. The Reverend Mother's emotion no longer touched me. I knew I needed this information, but I did not know why I needed it. Frances was looking at me in disgust. She turned her head away.

'It was English, upper-class, public school with a faint lisp.' She was focused on the very incident; she was there. I had the feeling she knew this person. Was it that somebody else might have seen or heard this person so she was being accurate?

'Then what happened?'

'I had to escape. I slipped out of the bed and crept into the kitchen. I saw them arguing.' She stopped. She was visualizing.

'What do you see?' I watched her eyes; they went up to the right. She was constructing the image, not remembering the image. She looked down at her knees to the right and then to the left. She was emotional and she was silently talking to herself. She looked at me and saw I was analyzing her. She shut her eyes, cutting off the window to her mind.

Her back straightened, she lifted her head and her hands rested on her lap. She had made a decision.

'He was tall, taller than Jorge, but slim.'

The 'Jorge' registered with me.

'Blond hair, fair skin, not burned red but tanned; somebody who spends a lot of time in the open air. Black trousers, lemon shirt – yes – silk.' She paused and then started again. 'Cruel face: it seemed to me aristocratic, handsome; it was the nose: aquiline with a bump. I'd seen him before.' She paused and thought. Why? 'In newspapers and on the television.' Why explain where? 'He's a Member of Parliament. Something important.'

'Do you know his name?'

'No, but he's the son of some aristocratic person and is in the news a lot. But he's not a minister, one of those they call a high flyer.'

For the first time, I really doubted the Reverend Mother. She knew this person. She knew his name, but she was denying it. Why? My trust in her was knocked. I believed her description was accurate because she knew him. Why deny it?

She was now calm, clear, precise, even cold. Perhaps she had caught my mood. The switch came when I asked his name. I knew she knew his name. More than that, she knew I knew she knew. This was so strange; why didn't she just tell me? I was lacking clarity and I didn't know why. Something was confusing me. I knew she lied, but I also knew she was a truthful person.

'What are you doing now?'

I watched the mental shift. It showed in her face as the fear returned with the different memory. Now she was remembering.

'I'm edging toward the kitchen. The man sees me and shouts. I'm running. The floor is cold and smooth. I grab a knife. It is a big knife on a magnetic strip. I killed Jorge

Machacamarca.' She was looking at me as if she wanted me to give her absolution or she wanted me to believe her. I didn't.

'Why did you kill him?'

'The other man had a chair; the legs were pointing at me. He was holding the seat of the chair. He held it so I would be inside the legs, so I let him come toward me. I didn't back away. I raised my arms. I don't know why; it was as if I was being controlled from outside of me. The rail between the chair legs hit my chest and pushed me back. I slashed at the man's hand and the knife sliced between the joints. He dropped the chair, and he screamed and ran away, holding his hand.'

'Which hand?'

The Reverend Mother looked at me as if I was daft. Then some enlightenment dawned on her. 'You *can* catch him?'

Was that concern I heard?

'Perhaps, which hand?'

She raised her hands and looked at her right hand. 'His right hand.' She had to work that out. Alarm bells were again ringing in my head, but I did not know why. I tried to picture the scene. There was something wrong.

'So, we need to look for a tall Englishman, who is a member of Parliament with a badly cut right hand between his knuckles. He's fair haired with tanned skin and an aquiline nose.'

The Reverend Mother just looked at me as if I was some kind of magician, but she also had concern. I wondered what the concern was.

'What colour were his eyes, Beth?' I was speaking fast. It blocked her time to think.

'Blue.' There was no hesitation.

'Other distinguishing features?'

'I don't know.'

'Hair?'

'Fair, receding.'

'How long?'

'It was long at the sides with bald patches on either side of a central clump in the middle. The clump in the middle was cut short, sort of stuck up.'

'Are you absolutely sure, Beth?'

'Yes, of course I am.' There was a faint trace of annoyance in her voice.

'Great. You've just described Randolph Mabry.'

Again, she looked at me with some sort of wonder. A shadow crossed her face. I was definitely missing something.

She asked, 'Do you know him?' There was something wrong in the way she said that.

'I'm very pleased to say I don't, but I'm going to.'

She smiled. It was, or appeared to be, a smile of resignation.

'You were naked.' I'd shifted the emotional temperature from positive to factual. It was as if I'd hit her. I was no longer a saviour but a policeman: a cold, interrogating policeman.

'Yes.'

'Why?'

My question had confused her. 'I don't know.'

'You said you were trying to escape, but you were naked.'

'I suppose I didn't think. I don't know.' She started to cry again. Her elbows were on her thighs, her head bowed and her hands on her face. Why was she crying? If you want to escape, surely you hide or find something to wear. It felt wrong, but I was not the one who had been raped and who was in fear of being raped again. I waited. She calmed and looked at me through reddened eyes. The bruises on her face were still red, but had started to turn a purplish blue. Her left eye was but a slit due to the swelling.

I turned to Frances. 'I think Beth needs a cup of tea and the very patient people outside need to be briefed. I turned

189

back to the Reverend Mother. 'While I sit here making sure you don't run away, the detective is going to make certain I don't talk to you.'

'I see,' said Frances.

'Well, you're my superior, so you should have the glory of briefing the wooden tops and ordering some flunky to get us tea.'

'You'll suffer for this, Jake Robinson,' she said as she went through the door. Frances was now calm and accepting of what I was doing. The detective was silent and inscrutable. I wondered what his agenda was.

I said to the Reverend Mother, 'Relax, I will start questioning you again when you've had some tea. Think about what happened. Think about what you've told me. You may want to add or clarify some things.'

Five minutes went by. The Reverend Mother was relaxed in her chair with her eyes shut when the tea arrived. A manservant brought it, poured it and left. There were also some tablets – painkillers – and biscuits.

I was disturbed. I thought over the Reverend Mother's answers. There was something wrong: odd emphases and odd nuances that gave implications, but of what? This was what triggered my sixth sense. In much of what she said, she was not lying, but I felt she was not telling the whole truth. What she said was the truth, but the emphasis was cockeyed. She did have sexual contact and it was not consensual in the normal sense, but it was rape? What she said seemed true and at the same time, it seemed untrue. There was trauma, but it was reconciled. Could any rape victim recover that quickly? Perhaps, just perhaps, she was describing a true situation that happened, but not this one.

I watched the Reverend Mother sip her tea. The cup was in her left hand, but she looked at her right hand when I asked her about the knife wound. I realized she was left-handed. So what, Jake?

30

Frances returned and said, 'Our police friends and notables are not happy bunnies.'

This registered with me; Frances was catching the phases that I used.

'It seems the important Randolph Mabry is well known to the local constabulary as a VIP,' she continued. 'I've a feeling they will not act. They were also a bit concerned that you've not yet dealt with the death of Señor Machacamarca.'

'Are you okay with this interview, Detective?'

'Yes, Captain. It has been an education.'

The Reverend Mother had been listening to this conversation.

'Good.' I turned to Frances. 'Okay, lovely lady, we will deal with that now.' I turned to the Reverend Mother. 'Are you ready to continue?'

'Yes, Jake.'

Frances moved the tray with the crockery to a side table.

'Let me just revise where we were. You had a knife. Randolph Mabry was defending himself and attacking you with a chair. You slashed his right hand. He screamed, dropped the chair and ran away. Is that correct?'

'Yes, Jake.'

'What hand did you have the knife in?'

A shadow passed over her face. Was it a realization or was she just surprised by the question?

'My right hand.'

'Explain.'

She was looking at me as if I'd betrayed her. 'I had the

191

knife and slashed like that.' She swung her right hand from right to left across her body.

'Wasn't that very awkward for you?'

She was alert; she now understood my question about the wound that had been inflicted. 'Yes, it was very awkward because I'm left-handed.'

'So why did you have the knife in your right hand?'

She looked at the palms of her hands; her head was bent forward. 'I don't know; it just was.'

'Tell me what happened next.'

'Jorge Machacamarca was shouting at me to drop the knife, so I did.'

'Why?'

'I don't know. I suppose to... I don't know.'

'What happened?'

'He charged at me; he was punching me and screaming at me. He knocked me down. I was on the floor. I picked it up and I stabbed him.'

'You picked up the knife and stabbed Jorge Machacamarca?'

'Yes.'

'Where were you when you stabbed him?'

'On the floor.'

'Where did you stab him?'

'In the leg.'

'Which leg?'

'I don't know.'

Good answer. She was thinking. She knew she must tell the truth.

'What happened next?'

'He kicked me and slipped.'

'Where did he kick you?'

'In the ribs.'

'Are you bruised?' She looked inside the dressing gown. It fell open, exposing herself on the right side. She moved her

192

breast. Her gown was now gaping; it had slipped off her lap. Strangely, she was not self-conscious. I could see all the bruising. It went from just under her breast to her waist.

'Yes, my ribs were red and are now turning purple.' She readjusted her clothes; it was only then that she became aware of me as a man. 'Oh, I'm sorry. Did I embarrass you?'

'Actually, you did.'

'Please accept my apology. It's only a body.'

I didn't think I'd ever encountered anybody as well adjusted before. This woman had been through an experience that would have destroyed the mental balance of some women for life and she was already on the mend. But I had a nagging doubt. My sixth sense wouldn't let me accept what my logic was telling me. But accept what?

'You stabbed Jorge Machacamarca in the leg and he kicked you in the ribs. How many times did he kick you?'

'Three. He stepped back and he was looking at me and holding his leg.'

'Which leg?'

She was thinking, visualizing. 'I know now; it was his left leg.'

'What happened next?'

'I tried to get up and he rushed at me. He was shouting, calling me names.'

'What names?'

She looked at me. She had a concerned, perhaps puzzled, look on her face. She seemed to be struggling with the words.

'Whore. Bitch. Slag.'

'This was in English then?'

'He also used Spanish words, but I'm unfamiliar with them.'

She looked concerned. So she should; this was just not true. A whole series of subliminal tells were informing me. I thought it was the change in breathing and direction of her gaze. I was getting to know her patterns of behaviour and the shifts were registering with me. He may have been shouting, but not names, or he was not shouting at her.

'And then?'

'I stabbed him in the stomach.'

'Which way? Straight forward, downward or upward?'

'Um... upward. Blood gushed out. He just collapsed and I realized I'd killed him. I need a priest. I need to confess.'

'It will be done. What did you do then?'

'I don't know, but I found this dressing gown and the driver came in. He was very upset and angry, and he called the police. They came with guns. Luckily, the captain was there. He took charge and then he went to get you.'

'You found this dressing gown where?'

'I don't remember.'

'You're in the kitchen. Jorge Machacamarca is on the floor. He's bleeding. You're now standing. You have a knife in your right hand. You are naked. Is that right?'

She nodded.

'Are you absolutely sure?'

She nodded.

'Let me run through this so I have it all neatly in a row. You are on the floor, naked. You stab Jorge Machacamarca in his left leg. He kicks you. You stab him in the stomach with an upward thrust of a knife. Blood gushes out. He falls to the floor, bleeding. You are on the floor. You stand up. Are you absolutely sure that is what happened?'

Her hands were clasped, fingers interlocked so tight they were going white. Her eyes were down. She was staring at her hands.

'Yes, I'm sure.' Her voice was quiet, controlled and firm. She was lying.

I waited. The room was silent apart from the normal rustles and creaks. The silence became oppressive. I could hear my breathing. I then spoke again. 'You've no blood on your body, but you have blood on your hands. Please explain.'

'I... I... I... don't know.'

'You said that you were naked. You said, "I tried to get up and he rushed at me." You said, "I stuck the knife in his stomach, upward, and blood gushed out," but you have no blood on your body. There is blood all over the floor, but you have no blood on your feet. Please explain.'

'I can't.'

Did that mean she didn't know, or did that mean she couldn't tell me?

'Did somebody else kill Jorge Machacamarca?'

'No, I killed him.'

'So you admit killing Jorge Machacamarca?'

'Yes.'

She was icy calm. The 'yes' was clear: no tremble: no mumble. The 'yes' was a lie. If she'd done this, she would be, at minimum, splashed in blood, but there was only blood on her hands and there was blood on the dressing gown consistent with being put on with blood on her hands. There was something seriously wrong here. I thought somebody else killed Jorge Machacamarca. I thought she was naked when she picked up the knife, but that was after Machacamarca was stabbed, and I was sure her fingerprints would be on the knife. Then she put on the dressing gown. I knew I could break her down and find out what happened. I was sure somebody else did this killing and she was protecting that person. Why?

'Frances, will you get the police and the others in here? No, wait, before that, Reverend Mother, where exactly were you when you were raped?'

'In there.'

'Show me.' I nodded to the detective and he followed us with Frances.

We walked into a small sitting room. There were pictures

on the walls, some easy chairs and deep-pile carpet with rugs.

'Detective?'

'Yes, Captain.'

'Could you look for evidence in here of a rape?'

'Yes, Captain.'

It was all too clean, all too tidy. Nothing would be found here.

'Okay, Frances, get the sisters and when I've spoken to them, we'll get the other police people.'

After a short while, Frances came back to the main room with the four sisters: Claudine the doctor, Angelica the nurse, Laurel the counsellor and Sister Teresa.

'Sister Claudine,' I began, 'please examine the Reverend Mother; please check her for damage and dress her wounds. I believe she has been raped. I want a report on what you find and your professional conclusions as a doctor. She may have a cracked rib. Will you help her, Sister Angelica?' I pointed out the way to the bedrooms. The sisters took the Reverend Mother out. Frances left for the police and Sister Teresa sat by the window.

31

The police came in with Frances.

'Sisters, gentlemen, thank you for coming,' I began, 'and thank you for allowing us to help you establish the facts. Please find yourselves a seat. I will outline my thoughts. The detective and my colleague will raise any observations that they have if they differ from mine.'

The men found seats. I waited and there was an expectant silence.

'In any information gathering, there are distortions both in what the witnesses, accused or victims say and also in the interpretation of what has been said by the interviewer or interrogator. What I do is listen to the information and then I analyze it. I then reach a conclusion. Sometimes I fail to reach a conclusion, so I need additional information, ideally from an independent source. I apologize for stating this obvious way of working, but I have two possible interpretations of what I've heard today. I will outline the two interpretations.'

I then took them through the rape by Jorge Machacamarca, the assault by Randolph Mabry with his description and wounded hand, the assault by Jorge Machacamarca, leading to the damage of the Reverend Mother's face and ribs and the Reverend Mother's defence with a knife, leading to wounds on Machacamarca's leg and an upward thrust into his stomach.

'You'll note the order the things occurred: rape, rest, the voices suggesting rape by a second person, the escape attempt, the attack by the second person who was injured, the attack by Señor Machacamarca and his killing in self-defence. This is a simple, logical, coherent order that, in my view, mitigates the action by the Reverend Mother. Are there any questions on this first view?'

There were no questions.

'There are some inconsistencies that at the moment that I cannot resolve. The inconsistencies are in the observed evidence. It could be due to the Reverend Mother suffering a traumatic loss of memory, or it could be the killing as described by her is a lie, and somebody else killed Señor Machacamarca.'

There were some mumblings then the detective spoke. 'What has been outlined by Captain Robinson is how I see it.'

This man was a detective, an experienced detective, but I thought that he had an agenda.

'Thank you, Detective. Any other questions or comments?'

There was no response from any other person in the room.

I continued, 'The inconsistencies rest with the lack of blood on the Reverend Mother's body and feet. The lack of blood on the feet could be explained, as there are no footprints in the blood. On the impact of the blade, the victim could have moved backward and collapsed, and the killer moved in the opposite direction, but there is evidence of splash on cupboards and other furniture and on the floor. The Reverend Mother was naked when she claimed she killed Señor Machacamarca. If she washed off the blood splashes, it could explain no blood on her body, but we then have the problem of blood on her hands. Further investigation will resolve these inconsistencies.'

There was an air of confusion in the room.

'It could be that the Reverend Mother did not kill Señor Machacamarca.' I paused, but nobody spoke, so I moved on. 'Let us assume that the Reverend Mother was not raped, but had consensual sexual intercourse.'

Both the detective and Frances objected, and others clearly were disturbed by the idea. I held up my hand. 'I said other interpretations could be put on the evidence given. It's the professional thing to do to explore at least one alternative, and one alternative is consensual sexual intercourse. This may be a repugnant idea to some of you, but we all know of cases of priests molesting choir boys, and that is even more repugnant in my view.'

I looked around. This was not a happy group, but they were prepared to listen. I continued, 'The first part of what the Reverend Mother said would be just as she said it, except for her acceptance.' I waited. No objections. 'The sleep and waking could have been exactly as she described it.'

They were now waiting for the other shoe to drop, having been disturbed by the first one.

'Supposing the voices were talking about something else; who knows? The Reverend Mother heard it. Perhaps she was disturbed or frightened by it.'

Everybody in the room was now actively listening. Jorge Machacamarca was a known Islamist. Reverend Mother may have needed to take some action.

'It could be exactly as she described it, except Jorge Machacamarca did not attack her; she attacked him with the same outcome. Now we have murder.'

There was silence.

'The final unknown elements still apply. There is a more likely explanation. For me, the evidence indicates that there was a violent clash. The Reverend Mother was injured. It would seem a third party was involved, and he was Randolph Mabry, who killed Jorge Machacamarca. Why would the Reverend Mother lie? Why would she accept the blame for something she did not do? Ladies and gentlemen, we have unfortunately no answers at this stage and further questioning is necessary.'

The silence could be cut with a knife. This was not what anybody in the room expected.

I spoke again. 'The Reverend Mother is being examined by a doctor. She, the doctor, will, I hope, give us some information regarding the alleged rape.'

'Jake.' It was Frances. 'Could this be a honey trap?'

'Yes, I suppose it could.'

There was a babble of Spanish and then the guard captain asked, 'What is a honey trap?'

'It's a technique used in espionage. Men are trained to seduce women to gain access to information or support.'

The babble of Spanish started again, followed by a laugh. The ice was broken.

The colonel asked with a laugh, 'How do you get such training?'

'Unfortunately, I failed the selection test.'

There was another laugh.

'What do you suggest we do now?' asked Colonel Irupana.

'Firstly, the detective's men must seek evidence of rape in this building, explore how blood could be washed off and work out the sequence of events from the information we have. Secondly, you need an all ports and airports warning to arrest Randolph Mabry.'

'On what charge?' asked the detective.

'I'm unfamiliar with your legal structures. I would go for something vague like conspiracy; you can sort something else out later. Thirdly, I would suggest all the staff are questioned: has the Reverend Mother visited here before? What do they know about last night?'

The unnamed man in civilian clothes spoke to the detective and left.

'Find out from the sisters if the Reverend Mother had made other visits here at any time alone.' I looked around. 'I will go and have a word with the doctor now and come back and report to you.' My sixth sense was quiet.

32

I was walking toward the bedrooms when I heard talking. I knocked on the door; Sister Angelica opened it and invited me in. The Reverend Mother was sitting on the bed. Her left arm was in a sling, she was dressed in a summer, cotton, print dress and she had bare feet. She looked much younger than when in formal attire. Her hair was short like a 1950s crew cut, and fair. I'd never thought about her as a blonde. The bruising on her face was still as pronounced and she held an ice pack against the side of her face.

'How are you doing, Reverend Mother?'

'I'm feeling much better and I preferred it when you called me Beth.'

'Ah, well, Reverend Mother, we can't always have what we may want.'

She clearly read a meaning in what I said that I had not intended. 'True, very true, Captain.'

Now we were back on a very formal footing.

'I came in to see Sister Claudine.'

'She's through there,' said Sister Angelica.

I went into the adjoining room and closed the door behind me. Sister Claudine looked at me. She was serious, perhaps a little nervous.

'What did you find, Doctor?' I asked.

'This is not easy, Captain.'

I waited.

'I found no evidence of trauma, no evidence that I might expect to find in rape or even rough sex.' She was looking worried. 'What I found was what I would expect to find in a normal sexually active woman. The Reverend Mother was not a virgin last night. I found evidence of a past pregnancy.'

'So you're not saying she was not raped; you are saying there was no evidence of rape.'

'Thank you, Captain. That is what I'm saying.'

'Why are you so concerned then, Doctor?'

'The Reverend Mother has been a sister since she was eighteen years of age. If she has not had sexual intercourse since then, some nearly twenty years, I would be astounded.'

'But she had sexual intercourse last night.'

'Yes, she did, with no trauma, not even bruising. It's almost inconceivable for a celibate woman of her age.'

'But it's possible.'

Sister Claudine looked concerned. 'Most alleged rape cases I've dealt with have been with sexually active women. I've dealt with a few cases of women who rarely have sexual intercourse. If it were not consensual in this group, I would expect some bruising, even if it was just because of inexperience.'

'Would the fact that she has had a child make the evidence more ambiguous?'

There were tears in Sister Claudine's eyes and they started to trickle down her cheeks. The evidence of a birth and the lack of evidence of rape had shaken her to the core. I'd seen how the sisters almost worshipped the Reverend Mother and for one of them, Sister Claudine, some of the illusion seemed to have been shattered. She was in shock. She could be wrong, but she didn't think she was and that was agony for her. She could not answer my question.

'Lie down there.' I pointed to the bed. She lay down. I put the pillow under her feet so she was flat on her back with her feet raised. I gave her a handkerchief. 'Okay, Doc?' I squeezed her hand. She tried to smile and dabbed her eyes with the handkerchief.

'Thank you, Captain.' She did not attempt to move, so I

left. I reported the medical findings to the detective. Well, I reported that the doctor had no concrete evidence of rape. He asked whether he could get that in writing and I told him to ask the doctor. It was up to her, not me.

'Detective, I need at some stage to continue the questioning to close off the unknowns.'

'Yes, Captain, perhaps tomorrow.'

33

I was totally cream crackered. All I'd done was interview a woman and she was easy to interview. This was not one of these long, drawn-out battles of wills and intellect, but something was eating at my brain like a caterpillar eating a leaf. No, that was a silly analogy. No, it was more like my brain was in a spin dryer and I couldn't separate the tangled elements. I had to think it through: go back to basics. One of the negotiators had been killed. Another negotiator had been injured. Two hostages were here and so was the killer of a negotiator. The killing of the negotiator was far from clear and that was extremely strange. The description was great, but the facts did not fit it. The stuff about the rape – or was it consensual sex? – just muddied the waters, as did the religious connotations. The problem was that there was no real evidence that sexual intercourse took place.

Frances and I had a whole bunch of information on the injured negotiator that could send him to prison in the UK and we had foundation information to start some pretty deep investigation into organized crime in the UK and perhaps the US. We knew we had better get the hell out of there. The local bad boys would soon be ordered to eliminate us. I reckoned the key was another talk with the Reverend Mother, or was she just Beth? I had a bond with this woman that said I wanted to help her, but why? Was she just a suspect?

I went into the bedroom. The Reverend Mother was not there, but Sister Claudine was and she was talking to the detective. They stopped and looked at me. I'd interrupted something.

'I was looking for the Reverend Mother.'

The detective responded, 'She's being taken to the local police station, and then she will be taken to La Paz.'

'Why?'

'This is a very serious matter and she will have to be tried for the murder of a Bolivian citizen. She's English and so will need diplomatic support. She's also a sister and I expect the Catholic Church will want to be involved. Yes, La Paz is the best place for her.'

'Can I speak to her?'

'What about?'

'Detective, she's still the Reverend Mother.'

He looked at me in a puzzled way. 'Okay.'

He walked with me to the garden. The Reverend Mother was sitting on a bench with two policemen guarding her.

She smiled. 'Another fine mess we're in, Captain.'

'Are you taking the mickey out of me, Reverend Mother?'

She smiled a happy, friendly smile. 'Of course, Jake.'

'Are you going to get out of it?'

'Oh, I've little doubt that I will be well looked after one way or another.'

'You are in the care of the police.'

'Yes, that is my main concern.'

'I have a small concern. Frances and I will be going back home soon and perhaps one or two of your sisters should go with us.'

'Yes, we have a problem. One of the sisters is vulnerable. One is to take care of her in one way, and one is to take care of her in another.'

'What is the sister's name?'

'The sister you need to help is Sister Veronica. Her school name was Annabelle Jane Mabry.' The waters became murkier; Sister Veronica was the hostage.

'Her protector?'

'Sister Felicity.'

'And the other one?'

'My best guess is Sister Theresa Anthony.'

'Choice of weapon?'

'Come now, Captain. I don't know everything.'

'Ah, Reverend Mother, I just want to stay alive.'

'Yes, Jake, I understand; probably a cord or perhaps a string of beads.'

'You are joking?'

'No, Jake, easy to hide in full view, expected on a sister and effective when used properly.'

'I'll take your word for it.' She spoke with such confidence that I wondered what she *did* know.

'May you be protected, for you've God's work to do, Jake. I will pray for you.'

'Thank you, Reverend Mother. It seems I'm now no longer part of the case that concerns you.'

'That's all to the good, Jake. May you have the protection of the Lord as the next part of your journey in this life may be very difficult.'

'Thank you, Reverend Mother.' She reached out and we clasped hands. She was up to her neck in this and was playing a dangerous game, but I was unclear what side she was on and what her role was. Whatever it was, I was sure she saw it as her God's work.

I picked up Frances and we travelled back to the compound. I was still struggling to find a name for our temporary home. Was it a compound, camp, prison, site, complex? I just could not adjust to an appropriate word. We walked to the sisters' area and asked for Sister Felicity. I had not been able to place her, but when she came to us, I recognized her. She was about 5ft 7in, round busted, slim hipped, firm bottomed and muscular. I was pleased she was dressed but she was not in the formal nun's habit but was wearing a plain brown close fitting tunic but no scapular or veil. My polite description might be athletic; my impolite one would be, 'Wow!' She was pert, bright and sharp with brown-cropped hair and hazel eyes. I immediately liked her, but – there is always a but! – she was challenging. When she spoke, her accent was West Coast Scottish: a tough, little cookie. I wasn't going to beat about the bush.

'Sister, we need to get out of here fast and you need to take your charge with you.'

Her face was blank. She was feigning lack of understanding or we had this wrong. The Reverend Mother may have pulled a fast one.

'Look, don't fuck me about. We need to get out and young Sister Veronica is vulnerable.'

'I think we are too late, Captain. You disappear and perhaps we can work something out later.' She nodded up the road. There was a cavalcade of cars heading towards the compound. Then she went back into their home. Frances and I nipped across to our residence, where we could watch what was happening.

The Land Cruisers braked hard and stopped. The six fighters rushed into the building and brought out the two nuns. Two of the fighters held each of them by their arms, not that peaceful nuns needed much restraint. Sister Theresa Anthony accompanied them.

That night we moved to another flat. If they came for us, we would have time to get away and we were packed. Frances slipped down to the village and spoke to Naira, Captain Wayna's sister. It seemed she was very frightened and upset at what had happened and her brother was frightened that the Muslims would find out that she was still a Roman Catholic. Naira said her brother would help us and would get the weapons Frances asked for if we would take her with us. Frances agreed.

The next night, he was at the agreed meeting point with everything we needed: two rifles with enough ammunition to start a war, two automatic pistols, Glocks, two pouches of grenades, smoke and high explosive, short fuses and, most importantly, maps. The maps brought home to us our precarious position. I hadn't thought much about where we were. It was only when we sat down and contemplated a rescue attempt and then an escape that the geography registered.

Jorge Machacamarca had positioned his base well. We had a local map (crude, but it seemed to scale) and an area map, which showed us that there was really only one way in and one way out by road. Wayna had also brought a Bolivian road atlas and even a compass.

The smell of fear wafted from him like a breeze over an open cesspit. His hands were trembling, his face pallid, his shirt soaked in sweat. His sister had told Frances that his name was Aniceto. I needed to calm him down.

'Aniceto I understand you are frightened, if we get caught we all die.'

'Sí Captain.'

'We are not going to get caught.'

'Sí Captain.'

'So tell me the problem.'

'Señor Machacamarca is difunto, no, dead.'

'Tell me.'

'Señor Machacamarca was, um, good man. He do bad things but he good man. He look after – look after those who um servicio, no, serve him.'

'Take your time tell me slowly the problem.'

'You will protect my sister?'

'Yes. We will take her with us.'

He was unsure and he had to trust us. He looked into the distance. I think he was working out what he had to say and as he did he was becoming calmer.

'La organización delictiva, si, the criminal organisation, yes, it makes business with La familia de Inglaterra, yes and, ah, la mafia.'

'Ok. We know that, Señor Machacamarca wants a deal with The Family and with the mafia, drugs, tin and oil.'

'Ah! Sí.' Now he relaxed. His eyes cleared. His breathing became more regular. He nodded, he was thinking and he smiled.'

'You know, you understand.' With the fact we understood he regained his grasp of English. How extraordinary.

'Tell me what is happening.'

'Colonel Irupana, yes, he had taken away Reverend Mother.'

'Where?'

'I don't know but he makes deals with, um Mister Mabry, sometimes, but sometimes he makes deals with el gobierno, yes, the government. With Señor Machacamarca dead the mafia has, how you say, go away and Mr Mabry he also go away.

'What are you going to do?'

'I stay here.' I decided not to ask why.

'So, we will take your sister with us.'

'Sí. Thank you.'

'Why are the nuns being held?'

'Mr Mabry and the mafia hold hostages. To get them back we need hostages.'

'The "we" concerned me.'

'We?'

He looked at me blankly then he laughed. 'I am one of the luchadores por la libertad, yes, you call freedom fighters, but my sister, she more important.'

'Why?'

'My sister, she Roman Catholic.'

'Right, where are the nuns?'

He went into a long and complicated explanation that boiled down to them being guarded by the local freedom fighters, and Sister Theresa Anthony was apparently in control of the prisoners. It seemed some form of negotiation was going on between the Bolivian organization and presumably The Family but it was unclear. The Bolivians had given an ultimatum: hand over Reverend Mother, or Sister Veronica and Sister Felicity die. They had three days, so we were right up against it. Wayna believed Reverend Mother could not be returned. Rescue from outside of the area was a nonstarter due to the terrain. It was down to us to make a rescue and an escape. The problem was that if we did, what would happen to the rest of the nuns?

Frances again did a survey. She spoke to Sister Teresa. Sister Teresa had a plan: a simple, agricultural plan. They were going to just walk out of the retreat with three bullock carts and three handcarts. The local smallholders, who were Roman Catholics, were their suppliers. Neither the nuns nor the farmers could envision a nun being shot. The nuns and farmers were preparing supplies and they reckoned that would take two weeks. It was a mad idea, so mad that I thought it could work. After all, killing three or four people was one thing, wiping out a whole bunch of nuns and farmers was something else and politically unacceptable in a tricky negotiating situation with international observers who, by now, knew about the nuns.

We returned and discussed our escape with Captain Wayna. Our task was, in theory, simple: rescue the two sisters from the armed guards, load them into transport that we didn't have yet and then drive 500 miles to La Paz in, say, 20 hours without any stops so that means, in reality, a minimum of two days and one night and, of course, the baddies weren't going to catch up with us. I was really glad we would have a couple of nuns to say prayers for us. Then we had to get a flight and fly out to the UK and the security service and police were going to ignore us. I found I was humming a tune from my schooldays when I was a boy scout, 'I'm riding along on the crest of a wave and the sun is in the sky.'

'Jake.'

'Yes, lovely lady.'

'Shut up.'

'Yes, oh, beautiful one.'

The captain smiled. This was the first sign of any relaxation since he had come to us. 'I will get you some transport. Behind the Old Catholic church is a barn; it will be in there.'

'When?'

'Tomorrow before dawn and my sister will be there'

'Thank you, Captain Wayna.'

He bowed his head. 'It's an honour, sir.'

Frances kissed him on the cheek. He blushed.

That was it then. Tomorrow night would be rescue night. We needed to move our luggage and weapons to the barn and the belongings of the two nuns. This was surprisingly easy; Sister Teresa arranged it under some pretext or another. She wasn't happy about the weapons, so we left them in the dell in the forest to be collected later.

The two captives would need to know. Frances went to visit Naira again. She would get a message to Sister Veronica and Sister Felicity. Two hours later, Captain Wayna's sister, Naira, came back to us. The message she had was simple; at 5.30 a.m., drive through the main gate and round the house's right side as if going to the garages, turn round and stop outside of the back door. Open the back hatch of the car. The sisters will come out, throw their gear in the back and get in. We were then to drive off. Don't rush. Keep it slow and steady.

At 5.00 a.m., I went to the barn, loaded up and drove down the road toward the area of the dell. Frances and Naira came out of the trees. The road was clear. We loaded the weapons and Frances and I armed ourselves with Glocks. Naira drove us toward the villa. She was driving and the guard would expect that. We reached the gate at 5.29

211

a.m. I had a Glock ready. No problem; the guard waved us through. We drove gently along the drive to the right-hand side of the villa. The tracks left by the car across the lawn were still clear. We turned round. I slipped out and opened the back hatch ready to jump in when we moved away. This was too smooth to last and it didn't. The sisters came out at a rush. Frances dropped onto one knee, facing the back door; aiming a pistol. A guard rushed out following Sister Theresa Anthony. The gun in Frances's hand spoke twice. It was silenced; the guard and Sister Theresa Anthony went down, but the guard got a bullet away and it made a very loud bang.

The driver's side door was open and Naira was hanging out – dead. Frances was pulling her clear and Sister Veronica was getting in the way, flapping and crying, so I helped. A burst of fire slammed into the rear door as Frances scrambled in to the driver's seat. Sister Felicity and I pushed Sister Veronica into the back seat. I ran round the Toyota and climbed in the passenger seat and slammed the door. It was then I realized Sister Felicity was shooting through the rear window.

We got away at a high rate of knots. The gate guard was out on the road and had a rifle. I fired at him from the passenger-side window and Frances drove straight at him. He dived for cover.

I could hear Sister Veronica praying for Naira.

'We beseech Thee, O Lord, in Thy mercy, to have pity on the soul of Thy handmaid; do Thou, Who hast freed her from the perils of this mortal life, restore to her the portion of everlasting salvation. Through Christ our Lord.'

We were away, but not in the quiet way that had been planned.

34

We set off at high speed and bounced around on the very rough road.

Sister Veronica had swopped into Latin: Actiones nostras, quaesumus Domine, aspirando praeveni et adiuvando prosequere: ut cuncta nosta oratio et operatio a te semper incipiat et per ta coepta finiatur. Per Christum Dominum nostrum. Amen.

I knew this one from school it was, I think, about doing things and inspiration. Ah well! I knew we were going to need help even if I didn't think it was going to come from that direction. Sister Veronica ploughed on with her prayers.

Sister Felicity looked through the back regularly. We had been on the road about an hour and a half when she said, 'There they are.'

We were sweeping up a steep incline and could see, across the valley, two Toyotas. A great cloud of dust surrounded them and they were closing on us.

'Don't rush,' she said to Frances. We need to find a good spot. How come you've a Land Cruiser?'

'Simple, we stole it and hid it,' I said.

'Aha, I see, and you have weapons?'

'Yes, they were donated to us.'

'And you know we are going to ambush our friends back there?' I could see in the rear view mirror she was looking at me and smiling.

'Yes.'

'That sounds good to me. Just before the bend up ahead looks like a good spot. Just round the bend out of sight please and drop us off,' she said to Frances.

213

Sister Felicity and I were dropped off with the heavy bag. 'Frances, it's up to you, boss,' I said. She made a little wave and was away.

We climbed the slope and settled among the brush and rocks. We each had an American military M16A2 rifle; a weapon designed for either 3-round bursts or single shot with four magazines. These were ideal for the situation we were in. I took control. This was my expertise.

'You take the lead car; I'll take the second one. Your first shot will be my signal to fire. Use the three-shot, burst automatic. Take out the driver. You follow up with the destruction of the first car. When we have achieved our objective, we will assist each other. Any questions?'

'No, sir,' she said and smiled.

We settled down to wait. It would probably be three or four minutes before they got to this point. 'You're handy with a gun for a nun,' I said.

'And you're a poet.'

I smiled, having just realized what I said. 'What's your name?'

'Sister Felicity.'

'Right, and your other name?'

'Dianne Murphy and we have company.'

The two Toyotas came roaring down the straight. I had a clear sight of the driver of car number two. I was approaching optimum shot position when a burst of fire came from Dianne's rifle. I squeezed my trigger, the windscreen shattered and the Land Cruiser veered toward us, hit a rock, tried to climb it and rolled over. I put a second burst into the exposed fuel tank and it burst into flames. Burning fuel ran under the car and I ducked. The tank exploded; a heat and pressure wave hit me. I doubted that anybody would get out. I then heard two bursts of fire from farther down the road. Dianne's target had hit a tree and she was in the road. A door was open and a body was hanging half out

214

on the left of the vehicle. The rear screen was shattered. She moved right, running with her weapon at her hips. It was like a scene from a comedy gangster film: the nun with the gun. I followed her down the centre of the road. She closed on the car and put a burst at an acute angle through the right quarter light and door window. I put a burst through the rear window. She drew abreast of the car, stopped, selected her target and fired another burst. I thought it was overkill. She then closed in. She signalled all were dead.

There we were, armed and on foot.

'Guess we walk then, Sister.'

'I think you've just guessed right, Captain and you can call me Dianne.'

I supposed we had been walking for about a quarter of an hour when we saw a cloud of dust approaching us. From it emerged a Toyota: Frances and Sister Veronica.

'Want to drive, Captain?' said Dianne.

Frances and Sister Veronica were in the back. Soon we came off the rough mountain roads onto a main thoroughfare.

35

I can remember somebody saying to me, when being briefed to come here, that travelling the roads in Bolivia was like playing Russian roulette. They were absolutely right. After about half an hour on a supposedly main road, I was hanging onto the steering wheel as if my life depended on it. I supposed, to some extent, my life did, but it depended much more on the mad truck drivers, the rock slides, washed-out roads, indigenous protestors, narrow mountain passes and broken-down trucks. Broken-down buses were the worst things. Not only did I have to manoeuvre round the bus, which was invariably at an angle on the road, but the passengers who had got off wandered about like lost souls. Mine was not to wonder why; mine was but to blast my horn and swear at them; I was definitely taking this very personally. The Bolivians must have the worst maintained buses in the world. One may believe that driving in some remote area of Southern Europe was adventurous; here each part of the journey was bringing new challenges and new adventures, but I felt that I was too scared to pass wind or I would fill my pants. My stomach had turned to liquid. It was not that we were travelling fast. In fact, we were travelling quite slowly. It just seemed very fast. In a civilized country, it was possible, with the minimum of attention, to forecast what may happen in a few seconds. Here, it was difficult to know what was happening right now. Forget the forecasting bit. It did not help that many of the roads in Bolivia were still unmetalled, and because of that, weather could have as much of an effect on travel time as anything. I now had no idea where we were going or how long it would take to get there. My navigator would take care of that. The route was easy though; there was only one road. I had total trust in Dianne; I just didn't trust me.

'We will go over a bridge in about a quarter of a mile; take the next left,' said Sister Felicity.

'Where are we going?'

'We are taking the scenic route. Our friends will have worked out that we will head for La Paz. They will be following down the main road and probably have spotters. This may just throw them off the scent for a while.'

I'd been driving for perhaps six hours with a number of very short stops for fuel, food and relief. I was bushed. Frances took over again. We pushed on until it seemed that it was dark. I crawled into the back and slept.

It was morning and I awoke as we pulled into a service station. 'Where are we?'

'Do you care?' It was Dianne in her direct West Coast way.

'Not really.'

'Good. Go and get cleaned up, and then we eat. We are about half way.' Dianne liked to be in charge.

It was a good station. I washed, put on some clean underclothes and socks, and joined the others in the rest area, well two of them; Frances was not there.'

'Wait here,' said Dianne. The two nuns disappeared into the ladies. I swear she was back within five minutes towing a reluctant Sister Veronica and trying to handle two bags. They were dressed like normal people: a smart, casually dressed woman and a girl in a summer frock. I did not believe any woman in any circumstance could get changed that quickly, and not only that; I could not believe the transformation. They looked nothing like the nuns who had walked into the ladies. I wasn't going to ask where the clothes came from.

'My word! Who are these beautiful, sexy women? I know you're the beautiful Annabelle, but who is your gorgeous companion?'

'Piss off,' said Dianne.

'Have you a passport?'

'Of course.'

'In what name?'

'I'll tell you if I need to.'

'Right. Where's Frances?'

'She will be out soon; she's feeling a little unwell. What shall we have?'

'Let's have this lomo montado,' Annabelle suggested. 'It's steak.'

So we ordered. When it came, it was fried tenderloin steak with two fried eggs on top, rice and a fried banana.

'Looks good, but I'm not sure about fried bananas, especially for breakfast.' I was sure I would suffer for this.

Frances joined us but did not look well. She had a coffee but could not finish it and took a bottle of water with her when we left.

Annabelle said, 'Can I drive?' Dianne and Frances agreed. I just bit my lip and prayed for a miracle, but one didn't happen.

The road was better than I'd expected and we made good time well probably up to 20 mph. We rotated drivers and I assumed we were heading toward La Paz. I seemed to have lost any idea of time but I suppose we had been on the road for about three hours and then, once again, we hit the main road. I sat behind Annabelle and had the best view of the road. It didn't look as bad from there. We passed trucks loaded with market goods, buses filled to maximum capacity, tankers filled with fuel and bikers taking part in the ultimate adrenaline rush of riding flat out, weaving between the other traffic. There were times when we faced oncoming traffic head-to-head and it was our duty to reverse up the mountain to a spot with a few more inches of room to pass within a breath of each other. I was amazed. Annabelle was a great driver.

The day wore on and I change places with Annabelle. Then we had some trouble; the engine was losing power. We descended into a valley and ran into the inevitable traffic jam. By the road was a garage and car sales place, so we pulled in. Dianne went to chat to the mechanic. He revved the engine, did much sucking of teeth and clearly was explaining that this was a difficult and expensive problem. Dianne was explaining to him something else entirely. Eventually, she towed the mechanic to a wrecked Toyota Land Cruiser and pointed to the engine. The mechanic shrugged.

Dianne came over to me and said, 'Have you got a hundred dollars US?'

I gave her the money. She went back to the mechanic. He smiled and nodded.

'What was that all about?'

'Simple. He said it would take at least a month for the spare that was needed. I said there would be one on that wreck. He agreed, but he would have to take it off and he couldn't sell it then. So we bought the wreck and, once he transfers the part, he can keep it.'

'But that's no different.'

'You know it's no different and I know it's no different, but it does mean he can say he conned some American because we couldn't drive the wreck away.'

'How long will it take?'

She shrugged.

So, we were in for a wait.

36

Frances wanted a walk. We out got out and we agreed to meet Dianne and Annabelle at a bar-type place we could see on the hill a mile ahead. I wasn't too sure, but Frances insisted.

We walked down the road. Midday early summer but with the sun blazing down is not the time to walk anywhere. The bar was set back from the road with a forecourt of empty canopied tables and chairs. The inside looked dark and cool from the road. 'Let's get a drink.'

'I'm not sure.'

'Christ, it's just a bar.'

We walked in, and it took a few seconds to get used to the darkened room. It was cool, but cigarette smoke curled around the tables and hit my nose. It was full of locals, just men and no women. The chatter had stopped; it was almost silent, and the men were looking at us. No, they were staring at us. Perhaps thirty pairs of eyes focused on just the two of us. Ha hum.

'Let's go,' said Frances.

'No, let's get a drink.' I walked to the bar, head up, shoulders back. Frances stayed in the doorway. This was unusual for her. The barman was drying glasses with a cloth, not a particularly clean cloth. Now I would have to muddle through with very poor Spanish.

'Que vais a tomar?' said the barman. Got it; he's asking what I want.

'Yo quiero dos cervezas por favor.'

'Si, señor, dos cervezas.' He was taking the mickey out of my pronunciation.

I smiled. When in doubt, smile. He pulled two bottles of beer from the cooler. At least I had that bit right. He opened them with a gadget attached to the edge of the bar and started to pour them.

'Let's go. I'm uncomfortable,' said Frances.

The silence of the men in the bar was becoming oppressive.

'I've ordered now.'

'Just pay, damn it.' There was irritation in her voice.

'Hang on a minute.'

The barman placed the full glasses on the bar. They looked cool and inviting. The condensation ran down the glass.

'Gracias,' I thanked the barman

'Bueno,' I think he responded.

I picked up the glasses, walked toward Frances, gave her one and went back to the bar.

'Cuanto es?'

I did not understand his reply, so I pulled out a $5.00 bill. The barman smiled and gave me a great pile of notes of various local denominations.

I noticed Frances had gone and the conversations among the men in the bar started again. They were now ignoring me. I went outside and she was sitting at a table in the shade of a canopy, sipping the beer.

'You bastard,' was all she said.

We sat there sipping beer and chatting about nothing in particular.

'Jake.' She had that tone that said 'pay attention'.

'What?'

'We're in trouble.'

A car rolled into the car park in front of the bar. It was the Merc and Adolfo was driving. Two men got out of the back and Adolfo got out of the front. Adolfo walked to the door of the bar and stopped just outside. Aha! Nobody's coming out then.

'You have any weapons, lovely lady?'

'I have some knicker elastic you could ping them with, but in the state I'm in, I'm not much use to you.'

The two men had stopped talking and were walking toward us. One was clearly a heavy, 6ft-something tall and as wide as a barn door. The other – the suit – was huge, but it was all fat. He could have rolled to us.

'Good afternoon, gentlemen,' I said.

'We have need to speak to you,' said the fat man.

'Yes.'

'I believe you are an English policeman named Captain Robinson.'

'Yes.'

'My name is Concepción de Lozada.'

'I thought de Lozada was the president.'

'Unfortunately, I am not the president and he's no longer president.'

'Being president is not a very secure job then?'

'No, perhaps it's not. We would like you to accompany us.'

'Why?' I loved the question 'why'. I always felt it gave me control.

'We have a suspicion that you've abducted some sisters; one is Sister Veronica. You must recognize that abduction is a grave crime.'

'Oh, we do. Are you a policeman?'

'Oh, no. I am a member of what you would call a security service.'

'I'm afraid we cannot help you. As you see, we are stranded here with no transport and there are no sisters with us.'

'Ah, yes, you will come with us.'

'I don't think so.'

'I am afraid I will have to insist.' He spoke in Spanish to the muscle standing with him.

We were faced with a dilemma. To go or not to go, that was the question. I looked at Frances. She smiled at the security man and said, 'No, we will stay here.'

I stood.

De Lozada, who was not the president, spoke to the big man again. The man with the muscles walked purposefully toward us, slowly. He took off his dark glasses and tossed them aside. His eyes were blank. This was going to be like stopping a train. I stood my ground. I could feel my pulse increase as my body prepared itself. Aggressive anger was building and I had to control it.

As he stepped past Frances, she delivered a swift punch to the man's testicles from her sitting position. It totally surprised him and me. He gasped in pain and clutched himself. I grasped him by his shirtfront and head butted him. His nose shattered; not that it made much difference to his looks, as it was broken already, but it would impair his breathing. Frances smashed the top of her beer glass on the edge of the table, buried the sharp edge into the big man's backside and twisted it. It cut through the thin cotton material and stayed in position; blood was running down the glass. I delivered a left hook that hurt my fist and did little else. I backed off fast. He trundled slowly forward. I hit him on the head with the clay flowerpot that had been on the table and he finally went down. I grabbed another pot and hit him again. That sent him into an enforced sleep and I stamped on the glass in his bum. Now I had to pick the spines out of my hand from the cactus that had been in the pots – no gain without pain.

The fat man laughed. He was holding an automatic pistol. 'Gee, well done. He'll be pissed with you two.' His English was good. The accent was strong, but I didn't think it was Spanish and it had an American pronunciation and vocabulary.

Then, suddenly, our Toyota pulled in and accelerated.

223

The bull bar hit the fat man, he was dead and I grabbed his gun. Frances and I scrambled into the back and we set off backward like a bat out of hell. Dianne then accelerated hard, shouting, 'Hang on!' and she rammed the Merc. The bull bars that had demolished the fat man now wrecked their car.

'I can't leave you two for five bloody minutes, can I?' she said as she wove onto the road, squeezing between a bus and a truck.

'Sorry, Sister, but the bad man wanted to take us away.'

'Who was he?'

'He said he was security service.'

'Oh, well, there's a hotel about ten miles down the road,' said Dianne. 'With luck, we should be okay tonight.'

'Are you bloody joking?'

'No, they will assume we are trying to get away fast. Anyway we need to rest up. And I think they were criminals, so I doubt there will be a police problem.'

'I hope you're bloody right.'

'I wish you two wouldn't swear,' said Annabelle.

'Sorry, Sister,' I said, trying to sound contrite. Frances just lay back with her eyes shut. 'The car got fixed quickly.'

'Yes, the mechanic decided to take the thing, whatever it's called, off this car first. When he did, he found some gunk and taking that out cured the problem.'

'So he *did* con us?'

'I suppose he did.'

The rest of the day and that night were good, except Frances was very tired and clearly unwell. I was worried about her. This was not me. I don't worry about people but I was worried about Frances. Dianne, Annabelle, and I did guard shifts, two hours on and four off. Dianne had her gun, and I had the fat man's gun. It was a Springfield Armory XD .45 ACP. She was probably right about the men being criminals. The Springfield had a 3-inch barrel, and the service issue weapons usually had the 4-inch. It was loaded with Pow'R Ball rounds. These bullets had polymer nose plugs that, on impact, caused the bullets to expand. This 165-grain, high-velocity round would make it a one-shot stopper. This would not be the choice of a security service organization.

37

The next morning, we set out again after a less-than-appetizing breakfast. Frances did not eat. Bolivian organized crime or, more likely, the mafia were tracking us but were probably wondering where we were as we had now been on the road, so to speak, for two days.

There was no sign of the Merc on the road, so it was probably a write-off, but we would be easy to spot. Progress was slow and eventually we reached a small village that we discovered was 50 miles from La Paz. My main concern was Frances. She was running a temperature, was clearly in pain and there was no chance of getting a doctor. We had some painkillers but that didn't seem to do much good. Still, under three hours didn't seem too bad.

As we approached La Paz, there were signs of commercial life everywhere along the dusty road: food stalls and families on the move, auto mechanics and fruit stands; the country was abuzz with excitement and verve.

I took over driving again. We were now on one of the roads called El Camino de Muertos, the Road of Death, these are reputed to be the most dangerous roads in the world. I must admit, this one seemed less dangerous than some of the roads we had been on. Perhaps I was just getting blasé as we had survived so far. This road was barely more than a single track cut from the side of the mountain, with ravines that plunged so deep that you couldn't see the bottom. Well, I wasn't close enough to see the bottom and I was glad about that. When we met a car coming down the mountain, it was forced to the cliff-drop side of the road. The drivers had to judge the matter of inches before the tyres slipped in the gravel and added to the statistically significant death toll of the road. We were going up the right-hand side, so we had the safe side. I did mention to Dianne that there must be a better route and she just told me to 'piss off' so there was a better route. The disconcerting thing was noting the various crosses and makeshift ceremonial altars set up by the families of those killed on this road. They were a poignant reminder of the risk we were taking with our own lives but, at the time, they felt more like an adrenaline boost to my weary body rather than their true, symbolic meaning.

We came to a stop. A police and rescue unit was blocking traffic in both directions. Ahead of us, a line of ten or twelve people stood staring down the side of the mountain at what we assumed was an accident. Dianne and I walked up past the line of cars. The young men on the side of the roadway assisted the rescue unit by pulling ropes and lending a hand where they could. Others stood by in bemusement at what was below. The limp body of a man was hoisted out of the ravine and onto the roadway. His body lay on the steel rescue sled, with a long line of dried blood coming from the corner of his mouth. His shoeless feet dangled behind him and his arms crossed on his chest, tied at the wrists, as the workers dragged his lifeless body past us, just a few feet from where we were standing. From the expressions of the people looking into the ravine, it was clear that there were no survivors.

My sixth sense kicked in. In addition to the accident, something else was happening. Two policemen were casually walking down the road, checking the cars and the occupants. The question 'why' was ringing in my head. We were in a stolen Toyota Land Cruiser. As casually as I could, I mentioned the problem we were about to face.

'Dianne, there are two policemen checking cars up ahead.'

'Yes, I know.'

'We're driving a stolen vehicle.'

'Yes, I know.'

'Have you a contingency plan, by any chance?'

'Yes, I think I have. Let's go back to the car.'

When we were back in the Land Cruiser, she got into the driver's seat and sat Annabelle beside her. She eased forward in her seat, removed her blouse then her bra and then put her blouse back on. She turned to Annabelle and said, 'You too.'

'I can't,' came the horrified response.

'Do it! You can tell the priest about it tomorrow.'

Reluctantly, she obeyed. Her square-cut neckline gave a view of her bust.

'Now hitch up your dress.' She was about to resist when Dianne snapped, 'Now.' Frances had already followed suit.

'Can I keep my trousers on?' I joked, only to receive an elbow in my ribs from Frances.

'Cash, who has any cash?' I realized I had a wallet stuffed with US dollars and now the local currency, so I gave it to Dianne. She extracted three large-denomination notes and put two of them under the windscreen in full view in front of Annabelle. The other she tucked in her cleavage.

'Were you trained to do this as a nun?' I asked.

'Ask no questions and you will be told no lies,' she responded.

The policemen arrived. They stood and admired the scenery inside the Land Cruiser. The policemen on Annabelle's side said something to her in Spanish. Dianne responded. The policeman leaned across Annabelle and, looking down her front, took the notes. The policeman on Dianne's side plucked the note from her cleavage, weighed her left breast in his right hand, said something to her and stepped away. The two policemen spoke across the car, laughed, and then moved on. Annabelle released her breath. I had the impression that she hadn't breathed all the time the policemen had been there.

Frances giggled and said, 'I needed a pee. I think I've picked up some infection.' My worry was she was becoming delirious.

'Thank Christ that's over,' I said.

Dianne smiled. 'So you are a believer after all.'

The tension was released and the convoy started to inch forward. Frances was looking better, well that's what I told myself. We found somewhere for her to relieve herself and eventually continued along the road. About two miles further on was a two-hour stop for construction workers to dynamite the road and clear a rockslide. A makeshift community had developed, including vendors, bus passengers, truck and cars drivers and the various other unfortunates who had to wait with us. Many had met at the accident. We ate rice empanadas, shared our snacks and talked. Mainly the language was Spanish, but a number could speak English and there were some other local languages.

Eventually, the road cleared and in a haze of blue exhaust fumes, we started to move forward in a convoy.

As we drove toward the city and entered what appeared to be a canyon, we were travelling along the city's main thoroughfare. It roughly followed the river and I noticed it changed names over its length, with a tree-lined section running through the downtown core. We got to the centre and Dianne got her bearings. She apparently knew this city and we had already discovered that she was fluent in Spanish. Now we had to find somewhere to stay and that didn't seem to be a problem.

38

Frances had been silent for a long time. She was pale and sweating and clearly in pain.

'What is it, my lovely?'

'I think I've dengue fever again.'

I could see the red blotches on her legs and exposed upper chest.

'We need a hospital, Dianne.'

I felt the Toyota do a sharp left turn as she swung across the traffic and accelerated, followed by a cacophony of horns blaring at us, as she wove the Toyota through the traffic. I knew she was heading for a hospital and I knew she was very familiar with this city. I also realized she was one hell of a driver. I asked myself again, what sort of nun has the range of skills she had displayed over the past few days?

We entered a road that seemed to be called Avenia Saavedra, but for some reason it was blocked by a red-and-white-striped pole. We found a parking spot and started to walk instead. I was supporting Frances, carrying her more than supporting her. Just then the rain started. In next to no time, the cobblestone street was so slick that I was slipping and sliding. In front of me, I saw Hospital de Clínicas. We entered what appeared to be a courtyard through a wrought-iron gate and, at that point, Dianne took over.

'You two disappear and give me some more of those dollars,' she said to Annabelle and me.

What little I saw did not impress me. It was an unsanitary-looking hospital, but there was a nurse, dressed in the 1950s-style white apron and little hat. Annabelle and I left and waited under an awning that, for no apparent reason, covered part of the pavement. After about ten minutes, Dianne reappeared. She hurried down a side alley to return five minutes later, down the road, past the barrier in a taxi. I was mystified. How did the taxi get here? We ran in the rain and jumped in. Five minutes later, Annabelle and I had been dumped outside a hotel and Dianne left with another bunch of my dollars to buy some medical stuff. She had a list of the things required that included medications, syringes and needles. Apparently, this was how hospitals were run in Bolivia. Dianne was concerned that the supplies would be too expensive and Frances would have to go without the treatment. Thank God for the NHS, was my thought.

Annabelle and I went to reception, but I wasn't sure about this place.

'Good afternoon. We would like some rooms.'

The little, old, very wrinkled lady behind the counter put her head on one side and said, 'Now that's a real surprise. I thought you might be wantin' tickets for a bullfight.' She spoke perfect English with a beautiful Irish accent.

I picked up a brochure from the desk. This was a rooming house attached to the Intrepid Travellers Backpackers Hostel. It seemed so unlikely, and I was so tired that I started to giggle, and so did Annabelle. The old lady just stared at us. I thought she was going to throw us out.

'We would like four rooms, please.'

'Now there's a polite, young man – that you are. Unfortunately, we only have one room available. But it can sleep four and it also has a bathroom.'

I looked at Annabelle, she looked at me and I knew we had a deal.

'We'll take it.'

We paid a deposit and lugged our suitcases and those of Dianne and Frances up the stairs to a spacious room with four wide, single beds. The door locked. It seemed to me that we had a safe and cosy environment.

'I'm going to have a bath,' said Annabelle. But it only had a shower and no lock on the door, so she made me promise that I would not come in.

I'd just settled, listening to the rush and gurgle of the shower, when I heard a knock on the door. It was a young woman.

'Mr Robinson?'

'Yes.'

'Tonight we will have a celebration and Doña Celia wondered if you would like to join us. Yes, only a small celebration. The...' She was searching for a word. 'The work males have finished the work, so we have a small celebration.'

'We would be delighted to come to your celebration. Do we need to bring anything?'

'Ah, yes, Mr Robinson. Ah, only yourself and your lady friends.'

'When?' Again she was struggling, so I showed her my watch. It showed 4.10 p.m.

She smiled. 'Yes, see,' she said and pointed to 7.00 p.m.

'Where?'

'No special wear, clothes like. Yes, like now.'

I then made a classical English mistake. 'No, not wear,' I said, pointing at my shirt, 'but where?' and I waved my finger in a circle above my head.

She smiled and had a little laugh, 'Yes, where.' She went to walk away. I didn't know what she had understood by my finger waving, but she didn't seem to have the message.

'Wait, please.'

She turned and looked at me inquisitively.

'At what place is the celebration?'

'Ah, but yes, it is up the...' Again, she was searching for the word and pointed at the stairs. Now I understood her misunderstanding.

'Upstairs? Thank you.'

'Yes, celebration up... um... stairs.'

I closed the door.

'Who was that?' Annabelle, wrapped in a towel, asked.

'An invitation to a celebration tonight.'

'Are you going?'

'We're all going: Dianne, you, me and, if Frances is out of the hospital, she's also going. We're going to celebrate.'

Annabelle looked dubious.

'Look, you may be a nun, but if you never see a sinner, how do you really know what one looks like or what a sin is?'

Annabelle looked at me as if I were the devil tempting her.

'Don't worry, pretty lady; I will ensure that Dianne protects you. But please don't tell anyone you're a nun, or that will certainly put the kibosh on any celebration.'

We waited. The clock crept on. I was worrying. And then Dianne appeared. I could have hugged her. I did hug her.

'How's Frances?'

'Okay. They'll have more definitive news in the morning.'

'But she'll be all right?'

'Probably. She's comfortable and they are pumping her full of stuff.'

'What stuff?'

'Don't worry. They have met this before and they know what they are doing. Frances is the least of our worries.'

I couldn't imagine we had worse problems. 'Such as what?'

'When I came out of the hospital to come here, the police were at the Toyota. They asked me if I'd seen who left it, so I said no and asked if it was stolen. It seems it was, and they were looking for an English man and woman. They gave a pretty good description of you and a very good description of Frances.'

'What do you think we should do?'

'Go to a party?' she said. So we did, and I then knew for certain that she was a very un-nun-like nun.

We had scarcely walked through the door when Doña Celia, the matriarch of the house, grabbed me firmly by the arm and thrust a large tumbler into my hand. Through glazed eyes, she scanned the room for the nearest of several opened bottles of various wines, beers and spirits. In the course of her unsteady attempts to fill my glass with beer, at least as much splashed onto the floor as into my glass. She was giggling and talking about someone called Pachamama. Dianne said he was the ever-grateful god of the earth and pleased to receive the beer that was spilt. The señora had clearly been drinking for some time.

There was a table loaded with local food and it looked great. But I was impeded in getting to it by the señora, deciding that she wanted to dance with me, very slowly with much rubbing of herself against me. Dianne seemed to find this amusing and Annabelle seemed to think it was disgusting. This bodily contact also seemed to enrage the family pet, a less-than-charming parrot that clawed its way up my arm to perch on my shoulder. A small dog took exception to this and started to bark at the parrot. I decided to stay in time with the dog rather than the music. It seemed safer that way. I wasn't sure if I was dancing with the señora or the dog. The parrot attack was okay, apart from the pain from its beak and claws, until it defecated down the back of my shirt, which was promptly washed clean with neat vodka. I was also helped to recover with a couple of slugs of the said vodka and a delightful cuddle from the young, and now very attractive, girl who had invited us to the celebration. Eventually, Dianne rescued me, although I wasn't sure I wanted to be rescued, and took me to the tables laden with food. The Bolivian dining treat was a delicious beef-heart shish kebab that tasted divine. Well, it was divine until I knew what it was. It was served with peanut sauce and a potato.

Apparently, this was the supreme anticucho, flame grilled on a street corner in Zona Sur.

The night wore on and I knew we had to leave when I rescued Annabelle from an American psychology student, who wanted to show her his latest thesis on some sexual matter. I was positive it wasn't his thesis he wanted to show her. I was also sure that if I'd not rescued her, she would have seen whatever it was he wanted to show her.

The next morning, I rolled out of bed wearing only a pair of baggy pants. Dianne shot out of bed wearing even less and ran for the bathroom.

'Me first,' she cried as she passed me, holding onto her breasts.

It was amazing how the student travellers' views of the world and enjoyment of its fruits rapidly took over, even if you weren't a student. Sod this, I thought. So, I dumped the shorts, followed her in and joined her on the wet square that formed the base of the open shower. It was all very innocent fun. We just soaped each other down, washed each other's hair and embarrassed Annabelle when she looked through the door. We were still wet, but clear of soapsuds and, by then, involved in mutual – um, ah – exercise. We gently dried each other and I had a shave, which was not easy, as Dianne kept cuddling me and touching me. As I said, the traveller sees the world and enjoys its fruits. I suppose it was also the release of the tension we had been through and Dianne's enforced period as a nun. I felt a little guilty about Frances, well more than a little but I didn't start this. Oh, shit, who was kidding whom?

I wrapped a towel around me and called out, 'I'm decent, Annabelle,' and walked into the bedroom.

She was watching me, sitting up in bed with just her eyes peeking over the bedcovers. Ah, well, even nuns needed sex education, I supposed, so I just dumped the towel and got dressed. I heard a scuttling and turned to see Annabelle disappear into the bathroom with a sheet wrapped around her.

'We need to go and see Frances,' I said.

'My thoughts exactly,' said Dianne. 'I'll brief Annabelle to stay locked in here and allow nobody in until we get back.'

39

The taxi dropped us at the iron gate and we walked in. Dianne spoke to the receptionist, but then all hell broke out from her.

'Her room! Fast! Now!' The 'now' was snapped out like a bullet. She might have been a physical-training instructor driving a bunch of new recruits.

I went up the wide stairs two at a time and I could hear Dianne behind me. Frances's room faced the end of the corridor. The door was open and two people were there: the American student from the party last night and a young American woman, who I remember was with him part of the time. They heard us. The big guy started to run toward us. It was the only way out. There was a trolley of crockery on the left side of the corridor; I moved over to the right to cut him off.

Dianne, behind me, panted, 'He's mine.'

I stepped sideways to the left, past the trolley, and the big man and I passed each other at high speed. Then, a few steps from the open door of Frances's room, I heard an almighty crash behind me, but I didn't turn. I came to a dead stop in the doorway, looking at a lady's handgun pointing at me. The American girl was holding it and it was rock steady. Her body was square to me with her feet wide apart and knees bent. She had her arms extended and was using a firm, double-handed grip. The weapon was pointing at my head and was brought down slowly to my chest. Now, this was worrying. I felt my stomach contract and my heart beating fast. Less worrying was the expression on her face, which indicated that she was at least as scared as me. The difference was that I'd been here before, facing people who weren't scared. This was silly: a bidding war on fear. I'm more scared than you, so there! I felt myself relax and I could no longer feel my heart beating in my chest.

'Have you shot a man before?' I asked.

Now, that may seem like a daft question in the circumstances, but it was the only calming opening I could think of. When I spoke, she raised the weapon to my head and then lowered it slowly to my chest again. This lady knew about accuracy and my chest was the target.

I could see the weapon more clearly now. It was a lightweight, .38 special, 2-inch revolver with snag-free configuration: probably an S&W Centennial Airweight (nice lady's weapon, not accurate due to the kick when fired, but a real stopper), but I didn't care; it was a gun and she had it. With luck, though, I could live through this, but perhaps not at this short range. Could she miss? I lived in hope. The real problem was her rock-steady grip.

She made an involuntary shake of the head and the gun wavered. That gave me some confidence.

'It's easy to kill somebody. The problem is the sleepless nights afterward, the waking up in a cold sweat, the shakes when you walk into a store and see the person you killed; only, it isn't him. No, the killing bit is the easy part.'

She smiled, well a sort of crook of her mouth, and said, 'Your boss nun will die.'

What the hell did that mean? Christ, she thought Frances was the Mother Superior. I just stood looking at her; our eyes were locked. Say nothing, Jake Robinson. Look brave; your life may depend on it. If she was looking into my eyes, she was not on target.

I could smell Coco Mademoiselle by Chanel. I knew Dianne was close to me. She didn't smell like that when she was a nun, more like carbolic soap. She was to my left, hidden by the wall.

She whispered, 'Step right when I say go.'

There was a pause.

'Go!'

I stepped forward and right. Two shots exploded on my left; a hole appeared between the American girl's eyes and her white blouse was turning red as she just crumpled. I could smell the propellant discharged from the gun. It was me who was going to wake up in a cold sweat.

Dianne then gave an order – crisp and clear. 'Main door. Walk to the hostel. Right side of the road. Steady walk. No rushing. *Go!*'

I skipped around the overturned trolley and jumped over the tangled, prone body of a very dead American. His head was at an odd angle. This Dianne was some nun; perhaps she trained in a Shaolin Temple.

As I reached the top of the stairs, a whole bunch of people were coming up. Another shot rang out. It hit a large, old-fashioned lighting thing above us and showered us with glass and plastic, and we all ran down the stairs again. It was like the Keystone Cops in the old black-and-white films, but not funny. I could remember an SAS sergeant saying to me when we were in what I thought was a very dangerous situation, 'It's okay, sir, just leave it to the professionals.' So I did and ten minutes later, we walked out. I obeyed the professional, did as I was told and just walked out.

I was on the main thoroughfare, heading toward the hostel. I was walking steadily, a bit tense, but gradually unwinding. My heart wasn't thumping and I had no trembling, but I could still smell the mixture of the pistol discharge, medical antiseptic and Coco Mademoiselle. That had to be a good sign.

A taxi pulled up beside me. I tensed. My heart rate increased again. A voice I now knew well, with a West Coast Scottish accent, calmly said, 'Hop in, Captain.' So, I did and

239

my hammering heart slowed down again. I could just smell Coco Mademoiselle. What a relief.

We got back to the hostel and everything was peaceful: no Americans, no police, no criminals; just an Annabelle who was mightily perturbed by her attraction to the American and was on her knees praying for at least half an hour after we got there. I supposed she had been praying since we left. I must admit I'd this evil thought that perhaps she was praying for something that she shouldn't be praying for. Just behave yourself, Jake. I, on the other hand, had a roaring thirst and a desperate need for something to eat.

Dianne was not in the least the worse for wear from the evening before. She must practise with holy wine. Killing two people in the past hour also didn't seem to have affected her in the least.

'We need to go back to see Frances,' I suggested.

'No. Not yet. The place will be packed with police. We wait.'

Dianne was right, of course, but it didn't feel right, but I wanted to see her.

'I will go with Annabelle. You will stay away.'

Again she was right and I felt bad.

To absorb some time, we went down into the town. It was now mid-morning. We went into one of the local dining establishments and had a salteña (a mid-morning pastry snack of chicken or vegetables in tasty gravy), but I struggled to master the peculiar technique of eating them without splashing gravy everywhere. Locals somehow managed to eat and suck at the same time, noisily slurping away all the gravy and leaving plates spotlessly clean, rather than leaving the whole area and me sprayed with gravy. Fortunately, my inability to do anything very active, and the raised adrenaline and testosterone levels, caused me to take note of what was happening about me. As I ate, I noted that we were being watched. Was this local criminal activity?

Unlikely. It was probably something more ominous. It was time to bail out.

I said to Dianne, 'Get us to the embassy.'

She never even blinked. We got up, stepped into the road and hailed a taxi.

40

Ten minutes later – most of which had been spent haggling about the fare – we were in the embassy. I ignored the various signs that directed people to the normal (or was it abnormal?) problems met when in a foreign country and found a desk with a woman at it.

'I'd like to see Mr Cuthbert Browne, please.'

The woman was local, smartly dressed with a perfect English accent and pronunciation, even if the syntax was a bit stretched.

'Yes, sir, and whom shall I inform him has called to see him?'

'Captain Jake Robinson.'

'And your companions? I require their names, please, sir.'

'I'll discuss them with Mr Browne.'

'Yes, sir, I am required at this time to enter them into the register.'

I gave their names.

'Are they citizens of the United Kingdom, sir?'

'Yes.' I showed the woman my passport and Dianne and Annabelle did the same.

'Could I inquire as to the nature of your business with Mr Browne, sir?' I had the feeling that this was going to be a very polite, very persistent, long and bureaucratic process.

'Unfortunately, it's of a very private nature that I will reveal only to him.' Bugger, now I was doing it.

'Yes, sir. We would be extraordinarily grateful if you would be seated and I will endeavour to have someone appropriate attend a service upon you.'

The 'someone appropriate to attend a service upon me' was intriguing. No, behave yourself, Jake

Ten minutes went by. A tall, willowy lady in her forties appeared. She smiled and said, 'Captain Robinson?' She was English, public school and middle class. Must be the selection process for the diplomatic services.

I felt the urge to do the American thing and say, 'I am he', but resisted and said, 'Yes,' and stood.

'Miss Dianne Murphy and Miss Annabelle Mabry?'

I said, 'Yes.' She ignored my answer and looked at each of them and they answered.

'Miss Murphy, Miss Mabry, please remain here. Captain Robinson, please come with me.'

It didn't seem a large embassy from the outside, but it was very large on the inside, a TARDIS-like building. I was shown into a large office to be met by a man in his thirties, dressed in expensive jeans and an open-neck shirt, over which was a lightweight jacket; his lightweight, black, Italian shoes gleamed – all very expensive. This man wanted to be noticed. He held out his right hand and on the wrist was a heavy gold chain. We shook hands.

'I've been expecting you, Captain.'

'You have?' There was some surprise in my voice.

'When the trouble occurred, we expected at some stage that you may get in touch. I expected we would have to go and rescue you from some ghastly prison somewhere.'

'Ghastly'? Here was a man pretending he had gone to public school. I just hoped he wasn't a total prat.

'Perhaps you should ring your... um, controller,' he suggested and, with that, he walked to the desk and picked up the phone. 'Put me through, please, Alicia.' He then handed me the phone and pressed a button. 'It's totally secure, Captain.'

Barrow answered.

'Barrow, it's Jake.'

'Thank goodness for that; I was wondering what had happened to you two.'

'Frances is in hospital in La Paz with dengue fever. I have Annabelle Mabry with Dianne Murphy, her woman bodyguard, with me. We are at the embassy.'

'The woman, Murphy, describe her.'

So I did.

He laughed. 'Tough little bitch; great at her job. She will probably stick to Miss Mabry like glue till you're back in the UK.'

'You know her?'

'Yes,' he paused. It was an unnecessary pause; perhaps he didn't mean to say yes. 'But not under that name. She's nearly as good as Nikki. It seems that Mabry has hired the best to protect his sister.'

I wondered what it was about this Dianne. Ignore it, Jake.

'We need to get you home and do something about Frances. Do the opposition know where you are?'

'Yes, they have been tracking us and picked us up earlier today. That's why we came to the embassy.'

'Have you had any real trouble?'

'Can I talk?'

'Is Browne with you?'

'Yes.'

'Anybody else?'

'No.'

'Okay, talk.'

'Frances was under attack at the hospital. I think we got there in time. An American guy ended up dead – it looked like a broken neck – and an American girl got shot.'

'You or Murphy?'

'Murphy.'

'See, I said she was good. Sit tight and we will get you home. Give me Cuthbert.'

I could only hear one half of the rest of the call, which

consisted of, 'Yes, sir... Tomorrow, sir... I'm sure we can do that, sir... Thank you, sir... Goodbye, sir.'

'Do you know Barrow?' I asked, but from the 'sirs', I knew that he didn't.

'No, I got a message from my boss – or rather my boss's boss – that you were loose in Bolivia and to call Mr Jones to get a brief idea of what it might be about. Your Mr Jones can exert an awful lot of clout. We will fly you out tomorrow. I'll send somebody to look after Miss Frances Portello. Meantime, we have rooms for you here and I'll have your luggage collected. Is there anything that you need?'

'Have you any information on the Reverend Mother? I think she's known as Sister Theresa.'

'No. Tell me about it.'

I briefly explained the rape and the killing of Jorge Machacamarca. I named the policemen involved and the colonel.

'Irupana, you say. He's head of a section of secret police; could be working for anybody. Not a bad guy. We have worked together and against each other. Let me give him a ring and I will update you later.'

I was not entirely happy with this, but he was the man on the spot, and he'd know what to do – I hoped.

'It sounds to me that you've everything covered.' I said. 'A coffee would be good.'

He smiled and pressed a buzzer. The tall, willowy woman came in.

'Captain, this is Amanda. She will take you to the lounge to join your companions and have a coffee, and then she will take you to your rooms. Meantime, I have some little chores to attend to.'

'Thank you, Mr Browne.'

'No, thank you, Captain. It has been and will be my pleasure. Incidentally, did you meet a man named de Lozada on your travels?'

'Isn't he the president?'

Browne smiled. 'Not anymore. This was a large man. He unfortunately met his death in a bizarre car accident in a car park.'

'Should I know him?'

'Perhaps. It's believed that he was a mafia controller here in Bolivia and, strangely enough, the security service here believe that you had something to do with his death.'

'It's very lucky then that belief is not necessarily the truth.'

'It is indeed. Thank you, Captain. I trust you will not be coming back to visit us.'

We shook hands and he left, smiling.

Amanda spoke. 'I'm afraid Miss Murphy left. She asked the receptionist to give you a message, Captain.'

I waited.

'She said it was a great ride. She said it was an excellent shower and she must try it again sometime. She knows that Annabelle will be in safe hands. Miss Murphy also said that she will return to her ecclesiastical duties until she's needed again and if you need her, give her a call.'

'Did she say how I could contact her?'

'Yes, Captain. She gave the receptionist this.' She handed me a small envelope that I slipped into my inside pocket.

'Thank you, Amanda. Oh! Miss Mabry will need some new clothes. She's a nun. Her title is Sister Veronica.'

Amanda nodded – an odd nod, forward, tilting her head slightly to the right – and pursed her lips. Her slight smile clearly indicated that she did not believe what I had just said.

'Yes, Captain, I will talk to her now about her special needs.'

'Thank you, Amanda.'

246

41

The next morning, with Annabelle restored to being Sister Veronica, a smart, black Mercedes picked us up. There was no news of the Reverend Mother or Frances and I didn't bother to ask about Dianne. I knew there wouldn't be any news and that she would be okay. All I knew was that the doctor from the embassy had visited Frances and would arrange for her to travel back to the UK when she was well enough. I had a bad feeling about this, but I'd no reason to. I knew I should go and see her, wanted to go, but at the same time I knew I shouldn't.

The drive to the airport from the city centre was not entirely unforgettable. The Zona Sur region that lies in the bowl at a lower level than the city centre was warmer, wealthier and altogether more comfortable. Not surprisingly, many expatriate families and wealthier Bolivians preferred to live there. We then drove from the comforts of Zona Sur to the city centre, where breathlessly steep cobble ways were lined with street vendors. The whole area was pulsating with seemingly endless markets and filled with a huge population of bowler-hatted Cholita women, clad in brightly coloured traditional costumes, and the chatter of Aymara: the local people of this part of the world. The whole city was set against the backdrop of Illimani: the magnificent mountain to the south of La Paz. In contrast to most cities, the poorer districts of La Paz lay higher up. The shanty adobe jumble of El Alto, the impoverished satellite district where the airport was situated, challenged the city in the bowl for size. It sprawled high above central La Paz from the edge of the crater lip across the high plain.

I was relaxed. The big Merc purred along, making easy work of the climb and poor roads. I then noticed the driver stiffen and speak to the man with him. I'd assumed he was a guard. I think I caught the words Llamar and policía. That I thought meant call the police. I suddenly felt naked as the guard began to talk on the radio; I was now sure he was talking to the police. I'd left the Springfield at the embassy. We purred on, but the driver and his companion were tense. Then, suddenly, we heard the scream of sirens. There were flashing lights coming toward us. The first police car heading toward us passed and did a bootleg turn, so it was now behind us heading in the same direction. The second police car did a similar manoeuvre and ended up in front of us. The excitement over, we continued. The driver's voice came on the intercom.

'We are sorry about that, sir. We recognized that we were likely to be subject to some form of criminal activity. The problem has now been averted.' His English was perfect and his voice was totally calm. The police reaction was so fast that they must have been waiting for something to happen.

At the airport, we booked in and were soon settled in first class. Six was definitely pulling out the stops for us. The stewardess brought round champagne in small bottles on a small tray and I decided to read what Dianne had written. The message on it was simple.

If you want to use my services, ring 020-7049-3141 and leave a voice message and a number I can call. I poll this number once every twenty-four hours. No job too small or too dangerous. Please destroy the card. On the back was written, *I will only accept payment in a shower.*

I laughed. Dianne had made contact. Would I use her services? Probably not very likely, but who knew?

I turned to my travelling companion. 'Sister Veronica?'
'Yes, Jake.'
'Do you prefer to be called Sister Veronica or Annabelle?'

'Why do you ask?'

'Why do you answer a question with a question?'

She stared at me. 'I suppose it's to protect myself.'

'From what?'

'From ridicule.'

'You think I'll ridicule you.'

'Well, no, but you'll ask me questions like, "Why did you become a nun?" And if I answer, you will give me all the reasons why I shouldn't be a nun.'

'So, some people have given you a hard time about being a nun?'

'Yes.'

'I tell you what. You ask me questions and I will answer them.'

'Okay. Why did you become a soldier?'

'Oh, I'd a lot of reasons. Let me see; I wanted to wear a smart uniform so I could attract girls. Then I thought that if I became an officer I could attract a different class of girl and then, of course, I wanted to shoot people.'

'You didn't.'

'See, you don't believe me.'

'You're laughing at me.'

'Do you really want to know why I became a soldier?'

'I do now.'

'Because I couldn't see a better thing to do. I had all these opportunities, but all of them I could do when I was older. I wanted to do something for my country and I wanted to find out about me. I'd only ever been in education and I needed to grow up.'

'You wanted to serve your country and I wanted to serve my God.'

'I think yours is a bigger ambition than mine, but all I asked was, "Do you prefer to be called Sister Veronica or Annabelle?"'

'Yes, why did you ask?'

'Because I wanted to know so I could use the form of address you prefer.'

'Sister Veronica.'

'Do you like the Reverend Mother?'

'Is that a trick question?'

'Is that a question in answer to a question?'

'Yes, I suppose it is.'

I stayed quiet.

'The Reverend Mother is special. I know I can tell her anything and she would listen and not judge me. And when I do something wrong, she tells me off. But it is all right when she tells me off because I know she loves me.'

'Do all the nuns think that?'

'I don't know. I think they all like and admire her and I think, in a Christian way, she loves us all, but she makes me feel special.'

'Do the other nuns notice?'

'I don't know. Why do you ask?'

'It seems to me that you're very close to her and I just wondered what you thought.'

'It is silly really, but she's more like my mother than my real mother. Do you think that is strange?'

'I don't know. I suppose she's called "Mother" because that is her role and I suppose that is what she does. And if she's really good at it and your real mother is not as good, it can seem like she's more of a mother.'

'Sister Teresa is also very special. I think of her as a grandmother, but that is because I never had a proper grandmother.'

'But you have two grandmothers.'

'Not really; one grandmother is American, so I've only seen her a couple of times and I don't think she likes me. My dad's mother is very old and has Alzheimer's, so, well, it's a bit difficult. Sometimes I think my dad is old enough to be my granddad.'

'Ah, well, it seems you've a complete family with the sisters anyway.' We chatted, dozed, watched the film, had lots to eat and got to know each other very well. Then, about ten minutes from landing, Annabelle said, 'My brother will meet us.'

'Yes. I think he will meet you rather than me.'

'You won't tell him, will you?'

'Tell him what?'

'You know, that we shared a room and everything.'

'And everything?'

'Well, you know, you and Sister Felicity.'

'I have absolutely no idea what you're talking about.'

She let out a sigh and relaxed into her seat.

Heathrow was as Heathrow usually was, but not quite. As we were coming in to land, the purser stopped by my seat.

'Sir, the captain would like you to remain in your seat. A VIP will be coming on-board after the other passengers have departed.'

We waited. A man, clearly a plainclothes policeman, came past us and then Randolph Mabry arrived. Annabelle's greeting was most un-nun-like. She threw her arms around her elder brother and he kissed her cheek. She then introduced me in a breathless over-the-top way. She was like a fifteen-year-old introducing her first boyfriend.

'I'm extremely pleased to meet you, Captain.' He held out his left hand. I noticed his right hand was in a bulky glove. We shook hands; it was an awkward but firm, dry handshake with total eye contact. 'I understand you're responsible for bringing my sister home safe and well.'

'Entirely my pleasure.'

'I think I owe you a favour, so I have delivered one. I think it unlikely that our paths will cross again, so I'll wish you a long and fruitful life.'

He held out his left hand and we shook again. He put his arm around Annabelle's shoulder, gave her a squeeze and placed her in front of him as they walked down the aisle. At the exit to the first-class cabin, Annabelle stopped, turned and waved. Mabry did not turn, but guided his sister out of the aircraft. I wondered what he meant by the delivery of a favour.

42

I had strict orders to have no contact with the office or any member of staff, to rest up and to put on a few pounds. I'd not even realized I'd lost weight. Apparently, it could have been caused by the dengue fever. I went home. I can't say I felt that I needed rest, but orders were orders. So, I slept, exercised, ate and watched TV and very soon it all became very boring.

Convalescence was all very well, but I was longing to return to the real world, so I was pleased when I was told I could go back to work. I was missing Frances. I didn't know where she was and I had instructions not to find out, which was a bit of a bugger really. She was the nearest person who I'd thought of settling down with, though the idea of settling down was a bit alien to me.

On my first day back, I was going back to work, and I would be able to see Frances. Strangely, I was not sure what work I was to do. When I went straight to Barrow's office and he was waiting for me. He seemed a little distracted.

'How are you, Jake?'

'Fine.'

I could hear in his voice that something was wrong.

'Give me the bad news then.'

I could see he was startled by my request.

'Look, Jake, this is not going to be easy, so I want to take one thing at a time. Let's first talk about you.'

'Okay, what do you want to know?'

'I think I have everything I need. Your reports were very clear. The other inputs I've had were very explicit and put you in a good light. Well, more than that, you come out of this as a hero. If the Reverend Mother wasn't a nun, I would say she fancied you. Oh, well, perhaps she does.'

'You've heard from or about the Reverend Mother?'

'Both. Colonel Irupana arranged that the Reverend Mother be shipped out to the States via the US Embassy and then home here. Cost a few pennies, but all's well that ends well. From the debriefing in the States, we got the feedback on you. Where she is now, I've no idea. The Roman Catholic Church moves in mysterious ways.'

'And Frances?'

'Yes, Frances... She will not recover and I don't think she would want to see you.'

'Not recover? Recover from what?' Not want to see me? I felt like shit. I just wanted to know where she was and go and see her.

'Um... Yes, you don't know. She had dengue fever.'

'Yes I know she got a second dose on the way to La Paz and I'd had it, but we recovered. It wasn't pleasant, but no big deal. The nuns nursed us and most of them had it.' I was desperately trying to keep the conversation neutral. I hid my emotions. I didn't want to let anybody see how much I was hurting.

'Yes, but she was re-infected with a haemorrhagic form of the disease, which caused a response that severely damaged some blood vessels.'

'How bad?'

'She has some heart damage and some lung damage.'

'I'll go and see her. Where is she?'

'Frances has some other problems.'

'Christ! What?'

'She picked up some sort of bug, which has affected her gut and is giving her all sorts of problems, and the medics don't quite know what it is and don't seem to be able to cure it. They think it's some sort of Chagas disease.' I'd never heard of Chagas disease, but this wasn't the time to ask.

'It would be very painful for you to go and see her.'

'Why? What else?'

'She didn't recognize me. She had a heart attack and that brought on a stroke, and that, well, you get the message.'

'So, you're saying there is no point in going to see her.'

'My advice is to remember her as she was. She's in good hands and the medics will look after her, but the prognosis is anything from a few weeks to a year. Look, I know you two became close and I can see you're hurting.'

'Shit!' And that's what I felt like. I couldn't speak and I knew my eyes were filling with tears. I could hear the wind outside and it was raining and it was a bloody Wednesday. Barrow got up and went to the window. He waited there, looking out.

I dried my eyes, took some deep breaths and asked, 'Was it the Americans?' My voice was under control.

Barrow came back to his seat.

'We think so. We now know they were freelance and specialists. The man was a biochemist and the woman was a medical doctor. This sort of attack is their specialty. From your report, you were lucky to live through your confrontation with her. She was reputed to be a crack shot. There is no record of her ever shooting anybody, but that's not surprising.'

There was silence. I had nothing to say. I wanted to ask a million questions, but none of them would bring Frances back. Barrow was watching me, reading me and then he spoke.

'When Frances knew the prognosis, she asked for your friend, the solicitor Keith Todd. He spent some time with her and he told me you have to go and see him. Apparently, it's very important.'

'Okay, I'll see him sometime.'

'No, you will go and see him this afternoon.'

'Okay.'

'Then there are your friends, Jase and Mike.'

'Okay, what have they been up to?' I was hoping for something more light-hearted.

'Jase is in prison and Mike is drinking himself to death.'

'Fuck! Shit, what happened?'

'Sergeant Jason Phillips CGC has been found guilty of the murder of Major Michael Carmichael DSC and sentenced to fourteen years.'

'But the case was thrown out.'

'Yes, but you didn't take into account the political aristocracy.'

'Antony Bray?'

'Not only Bray; your other non-friend Randolph Mabry was gunning for you, but he isn't now.'

'Christ, what is going on?

'It's about the rehabilitation of a certain soldier. The papers have been full of the heroic legend of Major Michael Carmichael DSC – a soldier's soldier, a leader destined to be a general and probably rise to chief of the general staff – taken out by a disillusioned coward who did not want to fight.'

'I'll kill the bastards.'

'Perhaps you will. Let me give you a brief of what happened. I put Nikki and Howard onto it. Apparently, there is a way of overcoming double jeopardy if it can be shown that the acquittal is tainted. There seems to have been two lines here. The first is that you cooked the books and were to be tried for that. This would lead to a retrial of the original offence, minus the spanner you threw into the works. Your two friends were put under pressure by some superintendent who was putting together the case.'

'Alex West.'

'That's the guy. Your boys called in your solicitor… um, Todd. He found himself in deep doo-doo and ended up being suspended for four years by some legal outfit that controls these things. He was fighting it and, after the court martial, it all went away. They had some other solicitor and got them another barrister.'

'Not Beresford and Bartholomew.'

'They're the guys. You know them all, don't you? Anyway, Beresford persuaded them to plead guilty. If they did, it would get you off the hook. Corporal... um, Munro would get a suspended sentence and a dishonourable discharge, which is kind of meaningless as he's unlikely to shoot another officer, and Sergeant Phillips would get a maximum of four years and probably a lot less. The bastards screwed Phillips or rather his barrister, Bartholomew, did. I don't quite understand what happened, but it's the first time I have ever seen Howard angry, and I *mean* angry. He doesn't really do emotion, but he did over this. It was all Nikki could do to stop him going out and killing Bartholomew.'

'No, Bartholomew is not the one who should die for this. He's just a slimy dogsbody. Bray holds his lead. But how did Mabry get in on the act?'

'Yes, I wondered about that, but it's all to do with The Family.'

'They're not related, are they?'

Barrow laughed. 'Yes. I asked Howard that and he came up with a neat history. Let me sort this out for you. Once upon a time, there was Albert James Carmichael, Earl of Charnforth, and he had a sister, Veronica. He got married and produced Albert Peter Carmichael, who duly became the earl. He produced Rupert Carmichael, the present earl, and a daughter, Victoria, who married Fredrick Bray. Those two marriages produced the cousins Antony Bray and Major Michael Carmichael DSC. That is a simple family chain. Let's go back to Veronica. Veronica married Paul Mabry and they produced Peter George Mabry, who produced George Peter Mabry. Now, this is an interesting bit. George married Penelope Whitehaven, the daughter of an American millionaire. Rupert Carmichael introduced her to him. The next Mabry to be produced was Randolph Mabry, just appointed home secretary, by the way, but that has not been announced yet. Then, much later, they produced Annabelle. Rumour has it that Randolph is actually Rupert Carmichael's son. Now, Randolph Mabry went to Eton paid for by – you've guessed it – Rupert Carmichael. The really interesting thing was Rupert's businesses did not take off until Randolph was born and the funding source for his businesses was a bank owned by Whitehaven.'

'Come on, Barrow! Let me get the relationships right here. Major Michael Carmichael and Randolph Mabry are half-brothers and that makes Bray a cousin to Mabry and Carmichael.'

'That is how I read it, Jake. I have a feeling you've some powerful enemies out there. Except the problems you were about to face just went away as if they had never existed.'

'Your take on that, Barrow?'

'The same as yours, I expect. You brought home little Annabelle.'

So that was the favour I was owed.

'That means that some other people could be in some trouble. What about Sir Nicolas Ross?'

'Interesting you should ask that. He has withdrawn from all military stuff. He's not on the bench now. He's back to being a barrister. Not sure if he was pushed or jumped because he was sick of the whole thing.'

I felt sick. I could feel my anger pounding in my chest and burning the back of my neck. I needed to find Mike. I decided I would kill that bastard Bray, and that shit West had better not get in my sights. And, as for Mabry, he needed to be stopped.

'I brought home Annabelle, but what happened to Mabry's wife?'

'I don't understand, Jake. Mabry isn't married.'

'So who was the other hostage in the USA covering Senator McGreevy?'

'Oh, now I understand. That was Mabry's mother. She's okay; they just shipped her back home.'

Mabry wasn't married. I'd a feeling that another piece of the jigsaw had become available. Where it fitted, I'd no idea, but it was another piece.

'Strange that, isn't it?'

'What is?'

'That Mabry isn't married.'

'I suppose it is. The press keep pairing him up with prospective wives and he always has an attractive escort for functions. There were some rumours a while ago that he had a secret love and she died. Romantic tosh, really.'

I was now getting a glimmering. Let it go for now, Jake. 'Can I have the information on the court martial thing, Barrow?'

'Here is the synopsis produced by one of the trainees, so it's not smooth, but you can see what you and your boys are up against.' He handed me a couple of A4 sheets clearly copied from an e-mail. I read it.

Sir, this is only my quick and dirty summary, but I hope it conveys the basic information. I will produce a full report by the due date.

The Court of Appeal Criminal Division reviewed the case of Sergeant Jason Phillips CGC and Corporal Mike Munro, who were charged with the murder of Major Michael Carmichael DSC and acquitted. An appeal was launched as the acquittal was considered unjust because of a serious procedural problem and other irregularities in the proceedings during the court martial.

Lord Justice Crainford, Mr Justice Small and Sir Christopher Brandston, following an extensive inquiry into the original Royal Military Police investigation and the court martial, held at military court centre at Colchester, heard the appeal against the judgment. The statement said the following, and I summarize:

'It was the conclusion of the Court of Appeal that the judgment rendered by Judge Advocate General Sir Nicolas Ross was unsatisfactory, and a recommendation for a retrial by court martial of Sergeant Jason Phillips CGC and Corporal Michael Munro was made. It follows that the judgment of Judge Advocate General Sir Nicolas Ross has been quashed.'

The Metropolitan Police and the Crown Prosecution Service carried out an investigation into the case that is considered a major miscarriage of military justice. They found serious flaws in the way the RMP compiled and presented the evidence.

Key to the confusion was the information from the autopsy and forensic deductions carried out by the US military authorities and the way that was interpreted at the court martial.

There was an error of judgment by the court in allowing Captain J Robinson to be considered as an expert witness. This obscured relevant information, creating bias and confusion.

The confusion regarding the investigation reports rendered to the Army Prosecution Authority unduly influenced Judge Advocate General Sir Nicolas Ross.

These factors have thrown such doubt on the judgment rendered by Judge Advocate Sir Nicolas Ross that the Crown is now unable to say that the dismissal of the case was a satisfactory conclusion.

Home Secretary James Bradshaw has ordered an immediate retrial of Sergeant Jason Phillips CGC and Corporal Michael Munro by court martial.

I looked up and Barrow was watching my reaction.

'If you want to do what I think you want to do, you're wasting your time. Sir Antony Newham-Taylor has had conversations with the Prime Minister to no avail. Your report on the Bolivian adventure was blocked and the Prime Minister refused to read it as you, a participant in the original court martial, wrote it. I spent time with Sir Peter Stephens, the commissioner for the Metropolitan Police. He agreed there was a problem with a couple of named senior police officers, but they were protected. I got a visit from two quietly spoken gentlemen, who belong to a similar outfit to this one that is linked to six, suggesting that I'd better not rock the boat. We can't have internecine warfare, can we?'

'What about the army?'

'Oh, yes, your army boss, Colonel Willaby-Alexander. We had lunch at his invitation. He was already in the loop and was fighting to keep you "out of the shit", was how he put it. So don't make any advances in that area.'

I seemed to be left with only two choices: surrender or kill Bray and Mabry. It might have sounded strange, but I was so angry that the latter was exactly what I wanted to do.

'Jake, I'm going to put you on leave for up to a month. Whatever problems you have with whomever you have them, I want them solved. Then, when you return, we will start you on some proper work. Am I clear?'

'Yes, Barrow, perfectly clear.' I'd one clear goal and I had one month to achieve it. 'I'd like to have a word with Nikki.'

'You can work with her for a day. See Keith, whatever his name is, today and spend tomorrow with Nikki. From then on, you will not contact her or anybody else in these offices until eleven fifteen on the –let me see – on the twenty-third of June. Is that clear?'

'Yes, Barrow.'

'Good. And if it goes wrong, don't come back.' This old bugger could read minds.

'Thank you, Barrow.'

'Oh, and you can use Frances's flat. We'll worry about accommodation for you when you return.' I was amazed that he could think of so many things at a number of levels at once.

43

I arrived at Keith's offices and had to wait about half an hour, as he had a client. Then I was invited in.

'I don't have much time, so let me press on with this. Frances sent for me and had me write a will for her. Here it is.' He held it up. 'I'm the sole executor.'

I waited. He didn't get me here to tell me Frances wrote a will.

'This is a deed of gift. He held up a folder. Frances knew she was dying, so she has transferred everything she has to you. If you sign the papers, you become legally responsible for everything given by her to you. If she dies within the next eight years, you will be subject to inheritance tax. The only way round the tax would have been for you to marry her, but that option is now eliminated, as she cannot commit in her current state.'

The sky outside was dull. It was going to rain. The office was dark and cold and Keith's voice had taken on a tinny edge. I needed a drink. He was still talking; no, he had stopped. I looked up. He was looking at me.

'I know this is tough, Jake, but she has only you and she fell in love with you in Bolivia. If she dies within the next few months, a tax bill of about four hundred and sixty thousand pounds, depending on the valuation, will hit you. The longer she lives, the less you'll have to pay the tax man.'

He pushed a paper across the desk. It had places marked for me to sign. I knew I'd money, but no idea how much. I'd never cared about such things. An investment company was looking after it for me. I knew each year they bought ISAs for me because they sent me forms to tell me, and they sent me an account of how much was in it, but I doubted it was four hundred and sixty thousand pounds. I stared at the paper.

'Look, Jake, just sign; it's a no-lose situation. If you end up in hock to the tax man, you can sell the flat.'

I signed in what seemed like a dozen places.

'This last document is an advance decision, or it's more commonly called a living will.' He was looking at me and I had no idea what he was talking about. He could see this. 'This is an odd one and it has given me some headaches. It sets out the circumstances that Frances would not want to receive life-sustaining treatment if she became seriously ill and incapable of making her own decisions. That is the situation now. She has written them out – or rather she had me write them out. It's a standard no-treatment advance decision. The only oddity is it does not become active for eight years. This is her protecting you from the tax man.'

'Christ, Keith, this is torture. Why the hell did you do this?'

'It's what she wanted, Jake. There is one stipulation, or rather there is a pledge she wants from you.' He waited to make sure I understood him.

'Go on, Keith. Surely, it can't get worse.'

'She wants you to pledge not to visit her or to seek any information about her and to accept that I will tell you when she dies. Then she wants the final instructions in her will to be fulfilled.'

'And they are?'

'I'm not allowed to tell you, Jake. Do you understand everything I've told you?'

'I doubt it, but I do know what she wants and I bet you've some stinking form for me to sign.'

Keith slipped another form across the table. I had tears in my eyes. The printing was all blurred, like the ink had run.

He pointed with his pen at two crosses where I had to sign. So, I signed.

'Now, let me take you home, Jake.'

'Thanks, Keith.'

He handed me a fistful of tissues and waited until I stopped sobbing. I suppose it was then that I made my final decision: Bray first then Mabry.

I went home. Home was empty. Home had no Frances. I had no Frances. I just wanted to kill Bray and Mabry. I found the whiskey, I found the ice and I found the armchair.

I woke and felt bloody awful. I had a mouth that I think a parrot had pooed in; my eyes were on fire, my head hurt and to crown it all I was on the floor and my ring finger was swollen and hurting like hell. I think it must be broken.

I lay there looking at the ceiling in the darkened room. I couldn't get Bray and Mabry out of my head. Because a crap officer on drugs with powerful relations who had pull and wanted to restore his name had been shot to prevent him getting a whole platoon killed we had a first rate officer with brain damage, a first rate sergeant in prison, a first rate corporal on the streets, a first rate judge removed from the bench and a black mark against a first rate solicitor and if Mabry hadn't been involved in the drug business and negotiating with the mafia then Frances wouldn't be a mental wreck in hospital. Wherein lies justice? I knew. Justice lies in a well-aimed bullet. I will kill these two rich bastards before they do any more damage.

44

As I walked in the next day, Nikki was waiting for me.

'You'll want to find Corporal Munro.' I did not ask how she knew.

'Spot on.'

'We'll go in my pool car.'

'We were heading into West London and pulled up just past the entrance to a mews. There was a fish and chip shop on the corner and the pavement was littered with containers, chips and other wastage.

'Try down there,' said Nikki. 'I'll stay here. Try the arch with the green, wooden front.'

As I left the car, she locked it. I felt alone. The mews was cobbled and ran along the back of the shops. On the other side, there were brick arches under a London Tube line. The cobbles were grey and greasy and rubbish from the shops was piled against the old, red brick wall that enclosed the yards behind the shops. Some of the arches had fronts and were used as garages and small trader workshops and some were clearly used by dossers.

As I approached the arch with a green-boarded front, suggested by Nikki, there was some movement: a woman pushing an old coach built pram. I think it was a Silver Cross but maybe not. It had once had long springs supporting a carriage, but now it was bent and lopsided.

'Piss off!' she snapped. 'Piss off, you! I ain't got none.'

I wasn't sure whether her statements were directed at me, as she did not look at me. She then hurried down the mews and turned onto the road, pushing her creaking, squeaking, dilapidated vehicle. I could hear work going on, the chatter

of men and the clinking and hammering of tools, an electric motor and the sound made by a drill operated inter-
mittently. I entered the dark and damp arch, fronted by the
crumbling, green, wooden boarding. A train rattled overhead as it may have done for a hundred years. The place was
littered with cardboard, but it soon became apparent that
these were nests: each one to house an inmate. The arch
was like a hive, alive with the dross of the capital city.

'Watcha want?' A shadow spoke to me.

'Mike Munro.'

'Never 'erd of 'im.'

'Ex-army corporal.'

'Mos' of 'em are, sonny.'

'Youngish. About my age.'

'Got any money?' A figure emerged from the shadows
into the dim light that filtered through the broken boards.

'For Corporal Mike Munro, I can find you some.'

He looked at me. His skin was yellow and streaked with
grey dust. His teeth were also yellow and so were his eyes.
He looked like an unskilled artist had painted him. His
clothes hung on his skinny frame. Perhaps they had once
fitted him.

'Ow much?' he asked.

'A fiver.'

'Ten.'

'Bollocks.'

'Fin' 'im yersel'.'

'Okay.'

'Okay what?'

'I'll find him myself.'

'A fiver, yer say?'

'Yes.'

'Wait 'ere.' He scuttled away. Five minutes passed and I'd
some concerns that I was alone in an unfamiliar situation,
but my eyes had become accustomed to the gloom. There

were a number of people in there and they were all looking at me, but not looking at me. I could smell them – the smell of unwashed bodies – but, strangely enough, there was not a strong smell of urine or faeces. They may not have been clean, but their habitat was.

'Allo, Captain.'

'Hello, Mike. Like some food?'

'I'd like a pint.'

'Let's try a bath first.'

'What abart me fiver?' The original tramp-like figure was behind Mike.

'There you are.' I held out a note. He snatched it from my hand and shot off at a pace that I would not have thought him capable of.

'Come on, Mike. Let's get you cleaned up and fed.'

I couldn't believe how much Mike had deteriorated in only a few weeks. It couldn't have been just the booze and rough living. We turned toward the road where I'd left Nikki in the car, and three men came round the corner. One was eating fish and chips from a flat plastic container. He threw it aside when he saw us (more garbage in the mews) and I knew that we were in trouble. They were obviously dangerous. They were spread out, line abreast about 6 feet apart, and were dressed the same: jeans held up by a wide belt, heavy shirts with the sleeves rolled to halfway up their forearms and heavy, rubber-soled, leather boots. Their heads were shaved and they each had an earring in their right ear. I wasn't sure whether they had weapons – maybe their aggressive persona was enough – but they had the mews blocked.

'I don't think I'm going to be a lot of use to you, Captain,' Mike slurred.

'No problem, Mike.' But there was a problem. This was three-to-one and it depended just how good they were.

'Goin' somewhere?' The one in the centre spoke. He was

the biggest of the three, complete with a scar on the left side of his face. At least we had something in common; I had a similar scar.

'Yes. For a bath and a meal. Have you any recommendations for somewhere to eat? Plain and wholesome, preferably.'

'Tell yer what. You get past us and then you can go for yer plain and 'olesome or yer can pay ta pass us.' This wasn't a robbery, the timing was wrong, too early in the day. No they had been waiting for me. Easy really, they, the ubiquitous they, would know I would come to find Mike. No, this was The Family in action and I was dead meat. Had to be Bray.

'You're going to try to stop us?'

'Yeah. Good game, ain't it?'

With that, he made his first mistake; he gave me thinking time while he clipped on a pair of knuckledusters and then walked toward me. First rule of dealing with someone with knuckledusters: don't let them hit you. I raised my hands as if in surrender. He dropped his hands by his sides and laughed.

'You wanna be a bleedin' prisoner?'

He stepped into punching range. I stabbed forward, aiming for his eyes with my fingers. My left forefinger found his right eye; it was soft and squidgy. He screamed and dropped to his knees, his hands on his face. I kicked out at his head and my shoe smashed into his hands. Blood spurted from his nose. One down and two to go. The other two were wary and adopted a fighting crouch. I moved left to face them. One seemed confident, but there was some hesitation from the other. I expected the attack to come from the smaller of the two men. He was wiry, confident and moved athletically. I was right; he took a three-step run at me and launched a karate kick to my head with his right leg. It was well aimed and if it had made contact, given the weight of his boot, it would probably have killed me. I swayed to my left, bending my knees and his boot slid over my right shoulder. I straightened my legs, driving upward under his knee, and caught his leg with my right hand. He couldn't twist away and his momentum tipped him so that his head crashed onto the cobbles, and he lay still. Thank you Li Tie, my martial arts instructor at school. I doubted my attacker would get up from that.

Two down; one to go. I shifted quickly and closed in on the hesitant one.

'Oh dear! All alone? You want to try your luck?'

'Fuck off!'

'That's exactly what we intend to do. I think you better ring for an ambulance. I think your mates need to be in hospital.'

His hand went to his pocket and came out with a knife that he flicked open, but I knew that he wasn't going to use it unless I attacked. He skipped round us and headed for the thug with the damaged head. There was a pool of blood on the cobbles.

'Let's go, Mike.'

We nipped smartly round the corner onto the street and Nikki was waiting for us. She was not enamoured by having Mike in her car, but they clearly knew each other. We drove to Frances's flat (well, technically, my flat now). Mike went into the bathroom for a shower and Nikki went off to buy a takeaway. By the time she got back, Mike was clean and dressed in a pair of my jeans, a shirt and a pair of old trainers. He stuck his own clothes in the washing machine.

'Nikki, can you nip out again and buy Mike some clothes?'

She smiled. 'Yes, master. I'll put them on expenses.'

We spent the next twenty minutes discussing clothes for Mike while we devoured the Chinese takeaway Nikki had bought. She then left on her shopping errand.

'We have a little job to do, Mike.'

'What, Captain?'

'We have an assassination job to do.'

He sat and looked at me. 'Were going to kill the bastard?'

'You know which bastard?'

'Yes, the right honourable bastard Bray.'

'You've been reading my mind.'

'No, Captain. You don't fuck about with the little fish; you would go for the shark. I'll fix it all, Captain, but I'll need some dosh.'

'How much?'

'Got a pen an' paper?'

I gave him a pad and ballpoint.

'Okay. Gun, about eight hundred; living expenses, about two hundred; then contingency.' He looked at me. 'No, not that much. Look, Captain, I'm going to need about fifteen hundred, top whack. I'll come back with a plan and every-thing we will need.'

'When?'

'Two weeks.'

'Where?'

'Here.'

'One condition: no booze.'

'Okay, Captain.'

'What do you want me to do?'

'Get out of town for a fortnight. Go to a hotel in the West Country; Cornwall should be good. Have a couple of local girls so that they remember you.'

'You've done this sort of thing before?'

'Well, I've done stuff with Jase, but we never killed nobody. Well, not until the major.'

Nikki came back with a holdall of clothes and toiletries, and left. She had also bought three mobile phones – pay as you go – one for each of us. She was a pro.

'Tomorrow, Mike, I'll see you in Paddington Station, end of platform six at two thirty, and I'll give you the money.

270

Meanwhile, find a B&B.' I gave him everything I had in my wallet.

The next day, we met as arranged. Mike was back to his old self. I watched him swagger down the station, all shoulders and roll but at least two stone lighter and he had pain lines on his face. The army needed men like him and politicians squandered them because they didn't recognize their value. The only mention they ever seemed to get from their political masters was when they were killed. We chatted briefly and prepared to part.

'I'll be seeing you, Captain, and I promise no booze. I'll only call you if I need some help.'

We shook hands. I didn't know why, but I'd absolute faith in this man. This was clearly his territory.

45

I got back to the flat just after midnight on the Tuesday. It was Wednesday morning and I decided I would just stay in bed. I didn't feel like getting up. I didn't feel like staying in bed. I was not feeling anything. I was an empty shell, a nothing, a nobody. Bollocks, I'll just stay here, I thought. The phone rang. I ignored it. It stopped. Good. Then my new mobile rang. I'd ignore it. No, I couldn't. I just wanted to kill some bastard and I didn't care who it was right now. I answered it.

'Meet me in the Pizza House near Holborn Underground on High Holborn at midday. We're in unbelievable luck.' He rang off. No intros; just the message. I knew who it was. I was feeling better. It is not right to feel good on a Wednesday.

The Pizza House was modern with low ceilings and lots of white tables with two plain Windsor chairs and slightly larger tables with four chairs: smart, clearly set up for lunches for the local businesses. I was taken to a table, so I selected a chair facing the door. It would be easy to see me. It was midday, so there was a steady but slow stream of people coming in. Then there was Mike. He saw me and took a table to the side of the dining area where he could observe me, but I would have to turn to see him. He was being very cautious. I had my American hot and coffee, asked for the bill and, when it came, I paid. I did not look round and I took my time.

I was walking away from Holborn Station when Mike caught up with me, said nothing and flagged a taxi. He gave the cabbie a road near Bond Street, there we jumped out,

272

bought two tickets, travelled two stops and left the station. We walked half a mile and got another tube to Kensington. As we left the station, Mike gave me a pair of gloves: very fine, unlined leather in black.

'Wear them until we are clear, Captain.' It was all a bit melodramatic.

Mike gave me an address, told me to come along in twenty minutes and press call button 3-0-3. This, I did. I confirmed who I was on the intercom and the door opened. I took the lift to flat 3 on the third floor. Mike opened the door to my press on the bell. He handed me a forensic suit complete with hood and overshoes.

'Put these on.'

Then he gave me a pair of fine, latex gloves to replace the leather ones that I put in my pocket for when I left.

He was dressed in a shirt, jeans and trainers. I didn't ask why; this was his shout.

The room was bare apart from a solid pine table under the window and a couple of kitchen chairs. On the floor by the table sat a Parker-Hale M85 sniper rifle that looked in pristine condition. I'd never fired one of these magnificent sniper rifles, but I knew all about their reputation. Looking at it, you might say it looked old-fashioned, mainly because it was a bolt action with a stubby magazine in front of the trigger guard and what you might call a traditional stock, except it was synthetic and not wood. This had been the British Army sniper's pride and joy up until the 1980s. It looked new. I knew Parker-Hale stopped making this rifle, so I wondered if it was an old or refurbished weapon, or a new one made by Sabre Defence Industries. It didn't matter really; what did matter was that it had the standard Schmidt & Bender scope and the M85 was mounted on an original bipod. This beautiful beast guaranteed a first-round hit capability up to 600 metres and was capable of precision fire to ranges of 900 metres. Mike certainly knew his rifles.

'Where the hell did you get this beauty?'

'Nikki gave me a phone number – don't ask. Can you use it?'

'I get to do the deed?'

'I can't, Captain, as much as I would like to.' He held out his right hand. It was shaking. 'It's Parkinson's, Captain. My dad's got it and apparently I'm one of the unlucky five per cent.'

I didn't know what the statistic referred to, but I could make a guess it was about inheritability. Now I understood his rapid deterioration. He must have had it while still in the army.

'Okay. Where and when?'

'Look out of the window.'

From the window, set high up in the block of flats, I could see the road in both directions. Mike handed me some binoculars.

'See number twenty-seven?' I adjusted the binoculars. Number 27 was to my right. From here, a clear shot could be made if aiming at the door. Timing might be difficult. A bus passed by. The top of the steps leading to the doors were still in clear view, but the lower steps were blocked. Assuming the right honourable member walked out at a normal pace, and assuming his bodyguards were not close in front of him, we stood a good chance of hitting him. That depended on the shooter's aim and his ability to pull the trigger. Now, it was up to me.

'Bodyguard?'

'No, he doesn't rate one, and he dispensed with his private one about six months ago.'

'When?'

'Six fifteen tomorrow morning.'

'Great Gordon Highlanders! I'll have to get up before I go anywhere.'

Mike smiled. 'He goes for a jog every morning. Leaves at

274

six fifteen prompt and gets back between six forty-five and seven.'

'Any pattern to the return?'

'No, I haven't found one.'

'Anything else?'

'I don't think so, Captain.'

'So, we haven't got an escape plan.'

'Ah, yes. Gun goes bang. You go downstairs and out of the back door. The back gate has a latch that can be opened from the inside but needs a key from the outside to come in. Turn left then right. You will be going along the backs of houses. At the end is a road. Turn right and keep going to the Underground. Do you have an Oyster card?'

'No.'

'Okay. Get one when you leave here. It will get you onto the train quicker. No, on second thought, take this one.'

'You've got this planned well, Mike.'

A shadow passed his eyes.

'You didn't plan it.'

Silence.

'Who planned this, Mike?'

'I can't say.'

'And I can't shoot.'

'Captain, you have to.'

'No, I don't. You tell me who set this up and I'll do the deed.' The silence dragged on. 'Okay, I'm out of here.'

'No, Captain.'

I waited.

'It was Howard.'

'Good, now I know it will work.' That was that then. I left by the back door and the alleyways so I would be familiar with them. For some reason the sea shanty, *A Life on the Ocean Waves*, kept running in my head. I suppose it was related to the last disaster I had when the bus was hijacked. I was quite calm about the whole thing. The only thing that bugged me was Mike didn't say how he was going to get out, as he hadn't mentioned coming with me. Anyway, Howard would have fixed it.

The next morning was not a good morning for an assassination. Well, I wasn't sure any morning was. It was raining and the wind was blustery: two things that detracted from accuracy. Ah, well, a life on the ocean wave! A home on the rolling deep! I was sure I wasn't singing aloud, but I wondered why that girl was looking at me. Perhaps it was the expensive raincoat over my elegant, blue suit and pink shirt with red and blue tie. Or perhaps it was my leather trilby. She would remember me. Shit! What a time to think about how I was dressed; nerves, I suppose.

At 5.45 a.m. I was in my forensic suit with all the other bits that sterilized me from the environment and I was settled. Mike was similarly clad. By 6.00 a.m. I'd checked the rifle, the sight and the position. Now all I had to do was wait.

'You know, Captain, for a Rupert, you're actually human.'

'Well, thank you, kind sir.'

'Will you come and visit me?'

'Where?'

'Oh, I don't know where. I would just like to know you will visit me.'

'Perhaps you'll be visiting me.'

'No, I don't think so, sir.'

How odd, and now he used 'sir'.

The sight was clear and the crosshairs centred on the brass, lion-headed doorknocker. It moved as the door opened and the right honourable bastard Bray was in my sights. He half-turned, probably saying goodbye. The crosshairs were on his chest and I'd taken first pressure on the trigger with the butt firmly buried into my shoulder. Then the rifle cracked. I don't really remember pulling the trigger; I had pressed it so gently.

The right honourable bastard Bray staggered back against

the door. It opened and he tipped over backwards into the house and his body disappeared. Only his lower legs to his trainers were visible over the doorstep.

'Got im!' cried Mike. I could hear joy in his voice like the supporter at a football match when his team scores.

I'd operated the bolt. There was another round in the breech and the safety catch was on. Drill. It all came down to drill: actions without thought carried out on command, although there had been no command. I shared Mike's joy. It glowed and burned within me. Yes – justice lies in a bullet.

'Away you go, sir. I know you'll visit me.' Action agreed and obeyed.

I went down the stairs, slipped out of the white forensic suit and overshoes and put them in my briefcase. I really don't remember anything until I reached the road at the end of the alleyways. It was then that I heard the crack of a rifle. I now understood. Mike wasn't going to get old and I would visit him. His planning was immaculate. I bet Howard didn't plan that bit.

I was free and clear and if I were the policeman in charge, I would believe the assassin was still in the building.

The Standard that night had a big splash on the front page:

High-Flying MP Murdered.

I read the report. Mainly drivel. Yes, Mike was dead: shot by a brave policeman storming the eyrie. Eyrie? What rubbish they write. No injuries to anyone but Antony Bray, the personal private secretary to the Home Secretary James Bradshaw. Why anyone should kill such a man was a mystery. I thought the mystery would unravel when the journalist found out the identity of the dead man, Mike Munro.

277

46

I phoned Barrow and asked to come back to work. He agreed and the next morning I went to work – back from holiday.

Nikki smiled at me. 'Barrow wants to see you. He has a visitor.'

'Oh! Who?'

She smiled, shrugged and said, 'Enemies.'

'As I walked in, I saw Superintendent Alex West and Inspector Richard Alleyne of the Metropolitan Police.'

'Good morning, gentlemen. Sorry to disturb you; I'll come back later.' I was trying to sound surprised, but I wasn't sure I succeeded.

'Come in and sit down, Jake.' Barrow was being urbane. He smiled. 'I think you know these gentlemen.'

'Good morning, Alex. Good morning, Richard.'

I sat down as they both mumbled greetings. This was not how they wanted things.

Barrow spoke again. 'Alex and Richard would like to ask you a few questions. Apparently Antony Bray was shot yesterday.'

'So I read. Couldn't have happened to a nicer person.'

'Do you know who killed him?'

'Well, it wasn't me. How on earth would I know?'

'Have you seen Munro recently?'

'Ex-Corporal Mike Munro? How recently?'

'When did you last see him?'

'Did he bump off the right honourable?' Silence and sour faces. 'Good for him.'

'You didn't answer my question.'

'Very true. I don't intend to answer any questions asked by you on the grounds that you'll use my answers to pervert the course of justice.'

Barrow intervened. 'Come on, Jake. We're on the same side.'

'Same side? Is ex-Sergeant Jason Phillips, Conspicuous Gallantry Cross, in prison for a crime he didn't commit, sentenced by evidence that had been tampered with?'

West stood. 'I'll not stay here and listen to this.'

'Oh, goody, you're leaving.'

West stormed out followed by his inspector.

'Barrow, if I'd the opportunity, I would have shot Bray.'

'And there was me thinking that you did.' He put his head on one side and pursed his lips. 'It was a good plan and you both could have got away. Why did Mike stay? It's okay; it will go no further.'

'He has Parkinson's.'

'Surely not. He's not old enough.'

'No, but he has it and it was a way out for him while doing a good deed.'

'So, he needed you to pull the trigger?'

'I think it will rain again today.'

'I don't think Alex West likes you.'

'If he comes anywhere near me, he will join his friend, the right honourable bastard Bray.'

'Um, I'd better make sure he doesn't then. There is only one small problem; they need someone to identify Mike and he has no next of kin.'

'Where is he?'

'Kensington Mortuary. Here's a phone number for the police. Inspector Halloway is the man who got dumped with this and, by the way, don't wear that hat and raincoat.' I was really glad Barrow was on my side. 'Oh one other thing, Jake.' I was about to leave and stopped. 'About Mabry.'

'Aha.'

'I would like you to drop any plans that you might have for him.'

'Why?'

'When walking close to the edge of a cliff it is often sensible to watch where you are stepping.'

'One day then, Barrow, when I'm not near the edge of a cliff.'

'Good. Focus on getting Jase Phillips out of prison, but first you'd best identify Mike.'

I made the call and it turned out that Inspector Hallo-way was female, not a man, and was the leader of the murder squad. We arranged to meet at 2.30 p.m. at the factory.

I must admit that when I arrived, I was treated with some suspicion. Inspector Halloway met me and asked if I would answer some questions before I identified the body. She was small, about 5tf 6in, about thirty with dark hair, cut in a bob, light-brown eyes and a small nose. I followed her to the interview room. I liked her trim figure. She was dres-sed smartly as a businesswoman; the cut of her skirt emphasized her neat, firm bum, which indicated that she kept fit.

We sat at the table and she had a pad and pen. She put on reading glasses. That was a bad move. They were very large and she disappeared behind them. She had no rings on her fingers.

Sergeant Gaygan Gupta joined her in the interview room. This was set up as a formal interview, which, given the cir-cumstances, was, in my opinion, odd. Her attitude was that I was something from under a stone.

'Mr Robinson,' she began, 'why did you come forward to identify the body?' The question was posed in a tone that suggested I'd some despicable reason.

'My boss suggested that I should and he gave me your number.'

'Your boss?' Her tone was one of contempt. The 'your' was drawn out.

'Yes.'

'Who is your boss who takes such an interest in ensuring you do your civil duty?' The contempt continued. It seemed to me that in her mind I was now some underling that kowtowed to my boss.

'Mr Barrow Jones.'

'Could you be more explicit?'

'Yes.'

'Are you being deliberately obtuse?'

'Yes.'

'Why?'

'Because you're being an arsehole.'

I could best describe her reaction as gob-smacked. Her mouth just hung open.

'Have you any identification?'

'Yes.'

She looked at me and I could see she was now thinking about how to phrase her next question.

'Please show me your identification, Mr Robinson.'

I handed her my MI5 identification. The gob-smacked expression appeared again.

'You're MI5.'

'Wow, you must be a detective.'

'Why the hell didn't you tell me? No, don't answer that. I made all sorts of assumptions and I didn't ask.'

'A good analysis, well summarized.'

'Look, I'm sorry, okay. Can I ask you some questions?'

'Sure.'

'How do you know Munro?'

'I arrested him for the murder of Major Michael Carmichael DSC.'

'Please tell me about it.' She gave the impression of someone paddling out of her depth.

'Okay, short version, Sergeant Jason Phillips and Corporal Mike Munro shot Major Michael Carmichael. I arrested them for murder. So yes, I knew him well. They were tried and the case thrown out.'

'Why would this Mike Munro shoot Antony Bray?'

'Bray, with the connivance of some other people, had the court martial findings overturned and Jason Phillips got life for murder.'

'With the connivance of some other people?'

'Unfortunately, yes.'

'Have you any evidence for what you're saying?'

'Only the discrepancy between my finding as the investigating officer and the evidence presented in court.'

She sat and thought for a good minute.

'So you're suggesting a complicity between a police officer and a member of parliament. Why would Bray even bother with this?'

'Carmichael was Bray's cousin; they were brought up together. It was a family thing.'

'Even so. No, forget it. Bray gets Phillips banged up in revenge for his cousin's death and Munro kills Bray in revenge for his mate.'

I liked the way she said 'death' and not 'murder'. She was listening to me.

'That's my view, but the men in white coats may be coming to get me.'

'So, why weren't you at the retrial?'

'Because I was abroad.'

'On holiday?'

'No comment.'

'An assignment then?'

'No comment.'

'And you can't talk about it?'

'No comment.'

'When did you last see Mike Munro?'

'Um, that would be the day before the killing.'
'Where was that?'
'Pizza House near Holborn Underground on High Holborn.'
'Why?'
'Why did I see him?'
'Yes.'
'It was funny really. He rang, asked me to see him and named the place, so I did. When I got there, we chatted and then he asked me to come visit him. I asked him where and he again asked would I just come and visit him. He just wanted me to say "yes", so I did and he was happy with that.'
'To come and visit him? What do you think he meant?'
'I know what he meant now.'
'You're implying he was going to commit suicide.'
'That's what I think now, but I didn't think that at the time. It just seemed an odd thing to say.'
'Was he all right?'
'No, he wasn't. He had the shakes. He said he had been on the booze, but he was off it now.'
'Did you believe him?'
'Yes, I'd no reason not to.'
'I suppose not.'
'So, let me run something past you. A man with the shakes using a high-powered rifle shoots a man. Can you explain that?'
'What was the range?'
'Hundred to a hundred and fifty metres.'
'The rifle?'
'Parker-Hale M85.'
'That's a sniper rifle. Telescopic sight?'
'Yes.'
'Tripod?'
'No, a bipod.'

'No problem. A soldier as experienced as Munro could take a man's eye out with a weapon like that at that range.'

She was looking at me. Inspector Halloway was an experienced officer. She knew there was something wrong with my answers to her questions, but she did not know what it was.

'Even with the shakes?' This question was delivered in an 'I know you're conning me' type of way.

'Not sure. If his shoulder was solid, his head was solid and he had a bipod, a hand shake would make little difference.'

'But if he couldn't close his hand?'

Wrong question, Inspector. You needed to get me talking, not direct my answers.

'Then he couldn't shoot the rifle, but he did. As we know, he shot at the armed response unit, according to the newspaper report. The odd thing is that he didn't hit any of them, yet they killed him.'

'It doesn't say that in the newspapers.'

'Come on. One policeman gets hit and that hypes up the story. No policemen hit, no story.'

'I suppose so. Did MI5 have an investigation going into Antony Bray?'

'Not to my knowledge, but I just find this whole thing odd.' I was laying a doubt trail.

'What do you find odd?'

Gotcha! 'Well, assuming that Mike Munro did shoot Antony Bray, and that seems likely, and then he takes pot-shots at the armed response team – I assume that was the case, but none of the shots kill or injure anyone – why did they shoot him?'

'What are you getting at?'

'How many bullets hit Mike?'

'Six.'

'Right, as I thought: overkill for an elite hit squad, don't you think?'

'What are you suggesting?' She was now on the trail and that was where I wanted her.

'Who put pressure on the Armed Response Unit? Because to me, I would think it was murder. I bet those six bullets came from at least four rifles.'

'Now look here, Captain–'

There was anger in her voice, but I interrupted. 'Wow, Inspector! This is your case, not mine, but if I were you, I would guard my arse.'

She was looking at me. She was wondering. She was balanced. 'I've a feeling you know more than you're letting on and, in your own way, you're giving me a heads-up, but I won't press you because it wouldn't get me anywhere. Let's go and identify the body.'

So we did.

Mike was laid out neatly under a sheet. Inspector Kitty Halloway was nervous. She had an elastic band and she was winding it and unwinding it in her fingers. When they pulled back the sheet, it was clear that they had already done a post-mortem, but they had covered up the wounds that had been inflicted on his body. The pathologist was there.

'Did you know him well?' he asked.

'Yes.'

'Best he went this way.'

'Why?'

'Because he had Parkinson's disease and a stomach tumour that would have given him agony before killing him.'

'He was a good guy, Doctor. I was proud to have known him.'

I felt emotion welling up in me. I liked Mike Munro and I was going to do something for Sergeant Jason Phillips.

There was nothing more I could do for Mike except visit his grave. I was finished there, so I went home.

47

I was back with my civil servants. At least it wasn't in Liverpool but they were part of the same bunch. I expected it would be more going round in circles or wading through deep, soft, slimy mud – hard work going nowhere. I got into the ministry establishment near Farnham at about 8.30 a.m. We had a number of people to interview about – well, that did not matter – when the phone on the desk I'd been allocated rang. It was the operator asking if I could take a call from an Inspector Halloway. I said yes and it clicked over, so I said, 'Good morning. Jake Robinson.'

'Good morning, Jake. It's Kitty Halloway.'

'What can I do you for, Kitty?'

'I've a small problem and I don't want to make a big deal out of it if I can avoid it.'

'Okay. How can I help?'

'We pulled all the tapes from all the streets around the murder zone.'

'And?'

'We found a picture that looks extremely like you going into the Underground about eight minutes after Bray was shot. I had Gaygan walk to the station from the back of the house. It took about five minutes. So, if you were in the room and went down the back stairs, got dressed and then walked to the station, the timing is about right.'

'My word, you're a smart detective. Have you found any evidence at all that a person answering the description of the person in your photograph was actually in the room where the rifle was fired?'

'No.'

'Would you like the clothes I was wearing that day for forensic examination?'

'Would there be any point?'

'No, but you can have them anyway, providing there is total security and no senior police officer from any other branch has any access to them.'

'Jake, you sound paranoid.'

'Kitty, if you can have a photo of me at that station at that time, then any of my clothes can be contaminated by an external – shall we call it – special... um, branch.'

'Odd you should say that. We had a visit from the special branch yesterday. Legit of course, as a politician was shot.'

'Let me guess: Superintendent Alex West and Inspector Richard Alleyne. I said to guard your arse, Kitty, and I meant it. Don't give him anything, even copies of anything or access to anything.'

There was a pregnant silence on the phone.

'You bloody have, haven't you? Christ Almighty! We could all be in the shit: you for a failure to do your job, me for being an accomplice or conspirator or some other charge.'

'You can't be serious, Jake.'

'Tell that to Jason Phillips; you can find him in Peamarsh.'

'Peamarsh, isn't that the new prison up north miles from nowhere; I thought he was a Londoner.'

'You're getting the message, Kitty.' I thought I'd blown enough smoke to get me off the hook. I would just have to wait now to see what else turned up.

Kitty paused and then said, 'I think I've just lost a tape, Jake.'

'I think you've just earned an orange for Christmas.'

'But, Jake, have you seen the *Standard* or listened to the news today?'

'No.'

'You were recently in Bolivia.'

'Tell me more.'

'We did a simple check on why you were not at the trial. You used your own passport and travelled with a woman, Frances Portillo, to Bolivia.'

'Yes. I was in Bolivia.'

'Did you come across a nun called Sister Felicity?'

'Um... no, why?' I kept my voice steady.

'She's dead: killed on a bus by a bomb.'

'I'm struggling with the connection.' I was fighting to breathe normally. So, did the bastards think she had killed Bray? But then I realized that it could have been any assassination that she had carried out.

'So am I. We checked one thing, find you were in Bolivia, and then in the newspaper is a story of the murder of somebody who was in Bolivia at the same time as you. It was just the coincidence.'

'No, I never met her.'

We said our goodbyes and rang off. I only hoped her phone was not bugged. I rushed out and bought a *Standard*. On the bottom of the front page was a heading, *Nuns Bombed*. The snippet read:

Five nuns died in the blast on the M26 today when an explosion ripped through a bus. The police are looking into every possibility. They believe the nuns were targeted but, as yet, have no indication why or who the perpetrators of this appalling crime are.

The police have stated that the bomb, probably consisting of 5 kg of high explosive, was in a bag in the luggage rack at the rear of the bus. It was a sophisticated device, probably triggered by a mobile phone. The bus belonged to Saint Joseph's Roman Catholic School. It was normally garaged in a secure area that was fitted with a CCTV system. The police are reviewing hours of footage.

Sister Felicity, whose given name was Dianne Murphy, one of the nuns, had recently returned from a visit to Bolivia and was going to give a talk on the relationship work that the Church is doing there, linked with the acceptance of the growing Muslim population.

289

I wondered why she was the only nun named.

The funeral of the Right Honourable Antony Bray was on the same page. That was the thing about front pages; they were for newsworthy events and supposedly important people. It was smaller than the funeral of Major Michael Carmichael, but that was because it was not stuffed with generals, fellow officers and soldiers doing soldierly duties. But there were more important people as well as the expected suspects: the Prime Minister and members of the cabinet, with some senior civil servants and a couple of mayors and council leaders reflected his history in politics. In attendance were family members such as Rupert Carmichael, Earl of Charnforth, Randolph Mabry, Sister Veronica, Harvey Cannon Duke of Bartonshire and Doggie Cannon, all complete with wives and children, and minor members of The family and one or two celebs. The surprises were Superintendent Alex West and Inspector Richard Alleyne, Major Nigel Reynolds QC, Mr Peter Bartholomew QC and one or two other people from influential areas, such as the press. Ah, if only the devil were to cast his net. Stupid me: he had done that already.

The rest of the day was boring, but I did believe that I was getting the feel of these civil servants.

48

I was walking toward the flat that evening when I was, what I think they call, door-stepped. A man in a raincoat stuck a microphone in front of my face, a flash went off and he asked me, 'What do you. . .?' There was a burble as he went down under the punch that hit his solar plexus. The guy with the camera went to run, but I caught his collar and he hit a wall as I swung him round. The man on the ground went to get up, so I stamped on his fingers. There was an agitated woman on the other side of the road. I called out to her to phone the police and I restrained my muggers by threatening them with a kicking if they moved from the prone position they had now adopted. The police arrived in a car. One, a female police officer, went to talk to the woman, who had done her civil duty, and the other spoke to me. My explanation was simple. One of the muggers let off a flash to blind me and the other attacked me with a short truncheon. I pretended I was angry and scared. The police had a short confab and it seemed the woman thought I'd been attacked. The downed men showed their press cards and the whole thing was settled amicably with us all getting a telling off for inappropriate behaviour. I was pleased that they never asked me for any identification. I had no idea what the reporters wanted so I needed to find out. I apologized to the two press guys and suggested I buy them a stiff drink.

We retired to the pub at the end of the road, and I bought them a couple of double scotches. They were interested in a story that they had come across that Antony Bray had been murdered because he had a guy named

Jason Phillips banged up and that I was a friend of Munro and Phillips. I told them I would talk to them if they left me out of the story. They already had the transcripts of both court martials.

I explained the first court martial simply – with the apparent tampering with the evidence and the release of Jase and Mike, then the overriding of double jeopardy – and then the second court martial. I told them where to get the information they needed from a solicitor, but not to door-step him and to have the questions well-honed so that he could answer without dropping in the clag.

That Sunday the *Sunday People* ran an exclusive. It named names but no sources. There were the good guys and the bad guys, and the good guys included Mr Todd, a solicitor, and the two soldiers, who were tried and a defence witness called Captain Robinson; the bad guys included a Major Carmichael and, unfairly, the prosecution barrister who had accepted corrupt information from an unnamed police superintendent, who was working for a very evil man named Bray, who Munro justifiably murdered for his evil deed. They must have had good advice on the report, because the only things they were specific about were the details that could be proved; the implications were sitting in the piece without moving into defamation or anything illegal.

On Monday morning, Barrow asked me if I'd seen the *People*. I confirmed that I had. He just smiled and I knew he knew who was behind it, and I knew nobody would ever be able to prove it.

Almost immediately, questions were asked of the Home Secretary in The House and a review into the case was implemented. I was amazed at the power of the press. I was even more amazed at the skill of Barrow.

'I was sad to hear about the death of Murphy,' said Barrow. 'She was good, bloody good. I'm still surprised that anybody found her.'

'I'm surprised she went back to her old cover.'

'Yes, that didn't make sense to me.' Barrow wasn't telling me the truth again. 'Mabry knew, so it was probably him that ordered the hit, but she was his soldier. They must think she hit Bray; but why such a high-profile hit? Knowing she was undercover as a nun, it would be easy to make her quietly disappear. Funny that. It was very strange that she chose being a nun as her cover.'

'Why?'

'She was Jewish. Or at least her family was Jewish. Her real name was Averill Cohen and she married a guy named Murphy. He was a Roman Catholic. They worked together for a while and then she killed him.'

'Barrow, are you–'

'Definitely not. It's what happened.'

'Why?'

'Old, old story; he had a relationship he shouldn't have had. So, she became a nun – sort of. No more men for her. Anyway, you better hop off; we have a job to do.'

None of this made any sense at all to me. How could you be a nun and go round killing people? And as for no men! Perhaps I'd chat to Barrow sometime about what sort of psychosis she had.

49

I wanted Jase out of prison, so I went to see Keith Todd to find out what could be done. He was now reinstated and the experience of the hearing and his suspension had left him wary. His opening remark when I was shown into his office was, 'I know why you're here, Jake, and, to be frank, I don't want to tangle again with the people who pull the strings. Perhaps the inquiry will get somewhere, but there are too many vested interests.'

His negativity knocked me back.

'So you're prepared to let Jase rot in prison?'

'Christ, Jake! The last time they really screwed me.'

'Who was it that screwed you, Keith?'

'I think it must have been Bray.'

'Bray is dead.'

'But The Family isn't.'

'Look, I'm going to see Sir Nicolas.' I had to show Keith my determination.

He thought for a moment. 'Okay, I'm in if Sir Nicolas is on board supporting us.'

'I think I have a call to make.'

'No, let me handle it,' he said, so I let him.

Later, I received a message on my mobile from Sir Nicolas's PA, informing me of a meeting with him at 3.00 p.m. the following day in his chambers with Keith Todd and Roland Parsley, who had been the solicitor and defence advocate at Jase's original trial. I'd no sooner noted that in my diary when I got another message to be at HQ at 10.00 a.m. the following day. It was coded urgent and compulsory. It had one or two other instructions, such as cancel all meetings for the day. I immediately made a call to the chambers of Sir Nicolas Ross.

The receptionist answered. I asked for Sir Nicolas and was put through to the clerk. I explained that it was unlikely that I could be at the meeting and I was just flagging it now as an issue. The clerk asked me to hold and Sir Nicolas came on the phone. I explained that I was in a no-option situation and Sir Nicolas understood. He suggested I get to see him as soon as I could. He added that he was determined to overturn this verdict of fourteen years.

I'd some interrogation tapes to filter, so I spent the afternoon and evening working on them but concentration was difficult as I kept thinking about Jase and the trials

Morning came. No rush. I didn't have to be in the office until 10.00 a.m., so I browsed through the *Telegraph*. On page 2, under 'News Bulletin', was a snippet:

In view of the rising e-crime linked to terrorism, a new security unit will be set up. This will lead to some restructuring within the security services and Mr Barrow Jones is to be appointed the head of a new unit reporting to the director general. This is an anomaly, as this unit would be expected to report to the deputy director general. Fears of duplication have been dismissed, as the new unit will operate on a project basis and draw resources from the other units. It's believed that this is a first element of the restructuring of the security services into a matrix organization to cope with the increasing complexity of the security threats to the United Kingdom.

So, that's what the meeting would be all about, but I wondered why this had been leaked. Security services just didn't leak stuff, particularly to the press.

When I arrived at the offices, the chatter indicated that the message had got around. At 10.00 a.m., we were gathered in the briefing room. It really wasn't big enough for the twenty-odd people gathered, some of which I'd never seen before. I parked myself on a windowsill so I had a clear view across the room. Then Barrow came in and applause greeted him. I joined in. A skinny woman, whom I knew was Clarissa Downs, the head of human resources, and an obese man, whom I'd never seen before, accompanied him.

'Who is he?' I asked Nikki, who was now perched next to me.

'That's fatso: Mr Cyril Fattore, head of administration.'

'You *are* joking.'

'No, it's one of those natural jokes that nobody could possibly make up.'

Barrow held up his hand and there was silence. 'I expect you've guessed why you're here. The note in the *Daily Telegraph* is true. I wanted to be the person to tell you before others knew, but common decency and common sense do not appear to be priorities anymore, let alone the security considerations. You'll be wondering what will happen to you. Mr Fattore, Miss Downs and I will see each of you individually. I apologize that I'm not dealing with all of you. I beg your understanding and tolerance. I will be in my office; Mr Fattore will be in interview room one and Miss Downs in here. We expect all the individual briefings will be done fairly quickly, as some teams will move together.'

While he had been talking, Barrow's secretary had been handing out sheets. I was seeing Barrow on my own. From the sheet, Nikki and Howard were seeing Barrow together. Perhaps he was seeing the unemployable and those that didn't belong. Nikki and Howard were a team and nobody knew exactly what they did. Well, I did, but I would not say.

Nikki and Howard came out of Barrow's office. I could not read their faces, as they looked the way they always did.

'Okay?' I asked.

'Yes,' said Nikki. I expected her to answer. 'We are going into private practice.'

'You have an agent to advise you and manage your affairs?'

'Jake, you always ask such bloody good questions. We are

assured we will get contracts from agencies and that will give us time to set up a business model. Will you have dinner with us tonight?'

'I'd love to. Time?'

'Say seven thirty at my place.'

'You're on.' I answered and then it was my turn to see Barrow.

He stood and shook my hand. 'It has been a pleasure to work with you, Jake. Now comes the parting of the ways.'

'So, what is it all about?'

'Politics and The Family. The Family has won another round. We were getting too close. We have the who and the what. We had moved a long way on organization and structure, so they counterattacked.' He smiled. 'But it has created an exposure and we are already one step on our recovery, and I think that they think we are down and out.

'Let's talk about you. I spoke to Willaby-Alexander yesterday and he will make all the arrangements for your transfer back into wherever the army wants you. There may be an opportunity in MI5, but not yet, and it would be with one of the other units. Guessing, I think you might prefer the army, but I will be needing you again, Jake.'

I hosted in the information. 'Good. Thank you, Barrow. When do I see the colonel?'

'He said to drop in to see him tomorrow.'

'Thanks, Barrow. It's been an adventure. I've seen things that I didn't expect to see.'

He laughed, 'No, thank you Jake, for what you've done. I've learned a lot from you.'

We shook hands and I left. Oh, well, Jake, that's another adventure over. At least I could now go to see Sir Nicolas Ross in his chamber, so I gave him a ring and told his clerk that I would be there.

50

Just before the appointed time, I arrived at Holborn Station and walked down to the Strand, where Sir Nicolas has his chambers. I supposed you could call them ostentatious, but only after you've entered. You move from a busy, main thoroughfare, through a wide, black, shiny door with some discrete, brass plaques on the wall to the left-hand side, and you entered wonderland: quiet, modern, with exquisite paintings hanging on the walls over superb oak and leather furniture and deep, deep-pile carpets.

The receptionist was freestanding. By that, I mean she was not hidden behind some barrier, isolated from the visitor. She walked to me, holding out her hand and, as I took her firm, cool grip, she said, 'Good morning, sir. How can we help you?'

'My name is Robinson and I'm here to see Sir Nicolas Ross.'

'Yes, Captain Robinson, please come this way.'

Her smile lit up my day, banishing the bad news from the morning. No computers, no paper, no telephones, just a smooth service and she knew my title, so I was more than just expected. How the other half lived.

I was taken to a small lift and whistled up to the top floor, fast and smooth. Here I was announced and handed over to a secretary. She had a desk, but was not behind it. I suppose she heard the lift and moved to meet it. No handshake this time.

'Please come this way, sir,' she said, and we moved towards an oak door. She knocked lightly, opened it and said, 'Captain Robinson to see you, Sir Nicolas.' I was definitely in wonderland.

Sir Nicolas stood up and came over to shake hands. The others, Roland Parsley and Keith Todd, greeted me similarly, but they were not a happy bunch.

'We have a problem?' My question was met with an uncomfortable silence. 'It can't be that bad.'

Sir Nicolas responded, 'Sergeant Jason Phillips CGC is dead.'

I was stunned and sat down in the nearest chair.

'Are you all right, Captain? Here, have some water.' He poured me a glass from a jug and handed it to me. What water was supposed to do I had no idea, but it showed me my hand was shaking.

'The bastard! The fucking bastard!'

'What are you saying, Captain?'

'This is that bastard, Mabry. Let me guess: Jase was stabbed, probably in the shower; nobody saw anything; nobody heard anything; no weapon; no prints; whole area washed down. Could have been one of a hundred people. He was found by a prison officer.'

'Actually it was a lavatory, but the rest is as you describe it.'

They were staring at me.

'What?'

Keith Todd broke the silence. 'You named the person behind this killing and the method. Can you explain, please, Jake?'

'Simple. Carmichael had been restored to glory with Jase going to prison for his murder. With the killing of Antony Bray, a small pebble hit the smooth pond, creating a ripple, but that was spun to smooth the pond, making Carmichael a hero again and his killer the epitome of evil – a cowardly sergeant. Now the *People* threw another bigger pebble in the pond. There was a splash and waves. The government started an inquiry. We could just win, so that meant Carmichael might again be a baddy. How could you stop this once and for all? Easy: kill Jase.'

'But why do you blame Mabry?' It was Roland who asked.

'Because Mabry and Carmichael were half-brothers.'

The silence stretched on. They had not known.

'Explain,' said Sir Nicolas.

'George Mabry married Penelope Whitehaven; she had been introduced to him by Rupert Carmichael. Randolph Mabry was supposedly their offspring, but the evidence and rumour indicate he was actually Rupert Carmichael's son.'

'Evidence?'

'Yes, sir, it's all circumstantial but very compelling.'

'Unfortunately, gentlemen, I think this is the end of the road. Our primary goal was to have Sergeant Phillips released and rehabilitated. Our secondary goal was to uncover the root of the injustice. With the death of Sergeant Phillips, the first goal is not possible. As the government inquiry is within the Home Office, and the home secretary could be implicated, it will die. As I said, this is the end of the road. Does anybody have anything to add?'

Nobody spoke. You could feel the disappointment in the air.

Sir Nicolas finally broke the silence by saying good-bye to Roland and Keith. When they had left, he asked to have a word with me.

'What is your situation now that Barrow Jones has been elevated?'

'I have no idea really. I'm out of the security service, but I'm still in the army of course, so I can just return to the RMP.'

'Do you want to?'

'Strangely, I don't.'

'Would you consider working for me?'

'You, sir? Doing what?'

'By using your interrogation skills; using your investigation skills as my own private police force. I'll pay you what you get now plus ten per cent and a car.'

'Pension and health care?'

'Yes, of course, you get that now.'

This was a non-decision situation. 'Yes, sir. I'll let you know when I can start.'

All I had to do was resign. Well, that sounds simple and it was, except it could get a bit bureaucratic. I wrote the letter, filled in the forms and Lieutenant Colonel Willaby-Alexander wanted to see me. He did not beat about the bush.

'Captain, Jake, we want you to stay in the army. We need good officers and you've proved that you're a good and brave officer. I've spoken to the powers in the MOD; should you withdraw your resignation, you will be promoted to major and there are one or two very good jobs on offer.'

It really wasn't the way to handle me.

'Let me be clear, sir. The only reason that I'm being offered promotion and the opportunity of a plum job is because I'm resigning.'

'I wouldn't look at it like that, Captain. The probability is that this is what would have been offered you on completion of this MI5 assignment.'

'Probability?'

'Well, I'm pretty sure it is. Look, you have an excellent record. You have demonstrated the capability that could take you to a very senior rank and I think you should stay in the army.'

'Sir, I thank you for your words. I've been proud to serve my country, but I've decided to move on.'

'So you're going to work for Sir Nicholas. It should be interesting. Have you any particular goal?'

'Yes, sir. I intend to watch and study those who I think had something or anything to do with the death of Jase Phillips and, when the time is right, avenge him.'

'Good Lord, Captain, I hope you mean bring them to justice.'

'We'll see, sir.'

'Let me wish you the best of luck in that venture and in whatever you do. I'm certain you won't need luck with your capability.'

He shook my hand and I knew he meant what he said. So that was me, gone. 'I'm on the road again. I ain't got no woman just to call my special friend.' Funny how songs sprang into my head. I wondered if this happened to other people.

51

I'd missed Jase's funeral, but was able to be there a week later. The cemetery was silent. I was alone. It was an old cemetery and I passed many gravestones that were toppled and at odd angles. It was a homely graveyard because of its very unkemptness. I felt cold and lonely. I *was* cold and lonely, but I wasn't there for me. I was there for Jase, and I was there for Mike. There was a light spattering of rain and little gusts of cold wind. I drifted along until I found Jase's grave. It was neat. On the white stone, cut in black letters, were the words, *Sergeant Jason Phillips CGC, Loved by many, a leader of men. Peter and Mary.* I expected they were his children.

I stood in the freezing cold at the foot of the grave, facing away from the old church. In front of me was a scraggy hedge and a flint wall that was the boundary of the cemetery. Beyond that sat a row of dilapidated houses built at the time of the First World War. The sky was grey and the sun was weak; as it descended, the poor street lamps came on. The twilight's miserable gloom was giving way to darkness. There was no joy in this place. There was no joy in me; just loss, loss of a good man killed before his time in a prison where he was falsely incarcerated.

That was that then. Goodbye, my brave friend. You never had justice at the end of your life, but you're going to get it in death. It was getting darker and the weak, yellow street lamps were no help.

It was time for another adventure. I remembered what I'd said to Lieutenant Colonel Willaby-Alexander: 'I intend to watch and study those who I think had something or anything to do with the death of Jase Phillips and, when the time is right, avenge him.'

Yes, Jase, Mike and me, we know wherein lies justice.

Look out for the sequel to *Wherein Lies Justice?* coming soon.

Hunt The Killer
By Barry Johnson

Follow Jake as he hunts the killer of Jase Phillips and fights to stay alive during his time in the highest security prison in the UK with some of the toughest prisoners in the country controlled by The Family.

The leads from the prison reveal the real reason that Jase killed Major Michael Carmichael and Jake teams up with Inspector Kitty Halloway to hunt for a horrendous serial killer. At the same time, there is a contract out on Jake.

The story wheels and rolls in a helter-skelter of excitement and suspense as Jake and Kitty feel their way through the shadowy world controlled by The Family. But who in The Family is Jake's 'friend'?